PRAISE FOR THE NOVELS
OF DANIEL PYNE

Fifty Mice

"Exceedingly clever, expertly timed, and dripping with paranoia, the nightmarish scenario at the center of this thrilling story turns on a kick-ass dime."

—Karin Slaughter, *New York Times* bestselling author of *Cop Town*

"[A] wonderfully paranoid jaunt through competing realities. . . . Pyne's confident hand guides readers to a surprising, popcorn-dropping final twist." —*Publishers Weekly*

"Drawing on the noir tradition . . . a serious consideration of memory and how it functions, or doesn't." —*Booklist*

"Pyne weaves a smart, exceedingly clever, and unusual tale with a horrible secret at its center, which is as much a late coming-of-age story as it is a thriller. Fans of brainy noir will find much to love in this highly satisfying, big-screen-ready book." —*Library Journal*

"A unique thrill ride . . . a real cat-and-mouse story. . . . This plot is both gripping and suspenseful, as the author offers up a secret that will make all us 'normal' people out there think long and hard about the people powerful enough to change lives in an instant. Pyne is an extremely clever writer." —*Suspense Magazine*

continued . . .

"[Pyne] knows how to control a thriller, but in *Fifty Mice* he intentionally removes any notion of control. There is no telling what will happen from one page to the next because he creates a flawed, vulnerable character with no sway over his own memory. *Fifty Mice* illustrates the obscurity of life, how easy it is to erase a life not lived, and how difficult it can be to tell the difference between a mouse and a man." —*Boston Herald*

"*Fifty Mice* is loaded with surprises, twists, and turns that kept this reader guessing until the very end." —Bookreporter

A Hole in the Ground Owned by a Liar

"Daniel Pyne's *A Hole in the Ground Owned by a Liar* will put to rest any idle fantasies the reader may have of setting out prospecting for gold. A harrowingly funny story of brotherly strife, amorous misconduct, and small dreams blown disastrously out of proportion. I loved it." —Scott Phillips, author of *Hop Alley*

"Smart, sexy, funny, and a brilliant storyteller. And that's just me. Wait till you read Dan." —Eric Idle

Twentynine Palms

"Character is key in this deliciously edgy thriller, screenwriter Pyne's first novel. . . . With dialogue that sings and action that sizzles, this is a prime candidate for the big screen." —*Kirkus Reviews* (starred review)

"Pyne sure-footedly blazes a fresh trail through Chandler country in this taut, expertly wrought desert noir. *Twentynine Palms* will leave you buzzing like a heat-dazed cricket." —Jonathan Evison, author of *The Revised Fundamentals of Caregiving*

FiFTY MiCE

DANIEL PYNE

 NEW AMERICAN LIBRARY

NEW AMERICAN LIBRARY
Published by New American Library,
an imprint of Penguin Random House LLC
375 Hudson Street, New York, New York 10014

This book is a publication of New American Library. Previously published in a Blue
Rider Press edition.

First New American Library Printing, December 2015

NEW AMERICAN LIBRARY TRADE PAPERBACK ISBN: 978-0-451-47395-0

THE LIBRARY OF CONGRESS HAS CATALOGED THE HARDCOVER EDITION OF
THIS TITLE AS FOLLOWS:
Pyne, Daniel
Fifty mice: a novel/Daniel Pyne.
    p.   cm.
ISBN 978-0-399-17164-2 (hardcover)
1. Witnesses—Protection—Fiction.   2. California, Southern—Fiction.   I. Title
PS3616.Y56F54   2014   2014027135
813'.6—dc23

Printed in the United States of America
10 9 8 7 6 5 4 3 2 1

Designed by Amanda Dewey

Penguin
Random
House

To those who brought me along

We are able to find everything in our memory, which is like a dispensary or chemical laboratory in which chance steers our hand sometimes to a soothing drug and sometimes to a dangerous poison.

—MARCEL PROUST

Where you come from is gone, where you thought you were going to never was there, and where you are is no good unless you can get away from it.

—FLANNERY O'CONNOR

FiFTY MiCE

| 1 |

The cool ripple of stale oily electric onrushing air.

The thrum of the tracks.

The wan headlight slurring over the tunnel tiles.

The flickering windows of the Red Line train, a filmstrip of fleeting images, like thoughts crossing consciousness, the expectant faces of arriving passengers overlaid with the spectral reflection of travelers anxiously waiting to get started, and none of it sticking, none of it mattering. The raw unspooling of life, unexamined.

And everything about to change.

Slurring, slowing, slowing, brakes sighing. The slack clatter of the cars coming to rest at the Hollywood/Western Metro platform.

He remembers waiting, listening to Wilco on earbuds, his tie loose, his gym bag at his feet. A text message hums in from Stacy: l <3 u. And a slightly creepy emoticon he has trouble interpreting. Is it smiling, or crying? He chooses not to reply.

The Metro Rail warning tone sounds, doors hiss and split; Jay sidesteps departing passengers, bikes, backpacks, and a gelatinous man on a Hoveround, and queues with the boarding riders, making room for a tiny old woman with too many plastic grocery bags, one of which gets snarled on the handlebars of a messenger's bike as it wheels past her. The bag rips. Canned vegetables and Jell-O boxes and mangos spill out across the floor of the car and onto the platform.

The old woman sighs. "Oh Lordy. Crap. Crap."

Jay stoops to help her collect her scatter before the train takes off. Fruit, dry goods, a bottle of Metamucil. He's half in and half out of the car, stretching for a can of low-sodium soup, when the warning tone bleats, A-sharp, but the doors can't close because Jay's in the way.

"Clear the doors," bargles the driver over the intercom.

"All my tapioca."

"Hold the doors," Jay yells. "Will somebody hold the doors?"

Rider eyes are on him, but, of course, nobody moves. The voice of the driver rumbles again gruff, inarticulate, some other kind of warning, the A-sharp bleats again. But now another rider, a woman, is helping them, and they're going to be all right, her dark hair brushing across Jay's face, something hard and angular under her coat thumping his hip; she collects the last of the loose groceries and hops onto the train. The doors start to close on the befuddled old lady, still just reacting to her bag breaking, and Jay has to pull her inside.

"You okay?"

The old lady just goggles at him, world rushing past her. Jay, somehow, has all her bags. He looks for the woman rider who helped him, but can't find her in the car; he settles the old lady into the handicapped courtesy seat, putting the bags in her lap and her hands through her bag handles, securely, Mr. Chivalry, before he steps back, and realizes—

"Oh, man."

His gym bag.

Jay has left it on the platform during the crazy rush to collect groceries.

Shit. "Dammit." Jay stares out the window back into the tunnel

darkness as if he can still see his bag back there. *Get off, go back.*
"Dammit."

Someone asks him if he's okay.

He turns, suddenly self-conscious, to a brunette standing next to
him, and starts to explain: "My bag . . ."—he gestures, pointlessly,
with his shoulders, fists shoved in his pockets, resigned— ". . . my
keys and everything," he says.

She offers no reaction.

The brunette's got earbuds too, and thump-happy rap music leaks
from them loudly enough for Jay to understand she can't even hear
him. He smiles. Her eyes cut through him, not at him: he's not even
there. He sidesteps, giving her more room, reaching for the overhead
handrail to steady himself as the train picks up speed.

Looks away. Closes a shoulder. No play here.

When he glances back at her, though, indifferently, with a dull-
dawning sense of recognition, wondering if she's the one who helped
him—she's grinning right at him.

Weird.

Jay's eyes drop to his shoes, then drift up, casually assessing the
whole package: pointy black pumps promising long legs and narrow
hips, pale hands hooked in her jeans pockets, no rings or jewelry,
chewed-down nails, the swerve of her waist, the slight sideways swell
of her breasts . . . and the glimmer of a handgun tucked under the
lapel of her soot-black blazer.

What?

She's still staring at him.

So Jay looks nervously away again, to his own slightly puzzled reflection in the subway car window. This is exactly what he was trying
to explain to Stacy, earlier: the inescapability, for Jay, of the promising, the new, the next.

Packing heat.

Said brunette is behind him, swaying with the movement of the car, her eyes finding his in reflection, now. And holding his gaze. Still grinning.

She's older than he thought. Thirty-five, forty?

But she's not flirting with him, it's something else.

And the train is slowing. And his gym bag is waiting, back at Hollywood and Western.

Sudden leak of fluorescent light from the Vermont/Sunset platform, rush-hour riders outside crowd toward the arriving train. A-flat warning signal, and the doors gape. Jay is jostled by an impatient passenger, starts his move to the door, but gets shoved hard—in truth spun around so he's backpedaling—by unseen hands, and the brunette with the legs and the gun and the tailored black suit is right in front of him, smiling, and then somehow Jay's out of the car, onto the platform, off-balance, spinning like a capstan, caught in a casual crush of commuters coming and going as the two (or are there three?) men with their hands on him steer him out of the crowd.

He says something, he's not sure what it is, a kind of half-angry, half-panicked protest, and the brunette says, "Shhhhh."

Jay's jacket is yanked up over his head.

"Hey. HEY!" Now he's shouting. He lashes out, but his arms are pinned back.

He thinks: *This isn't happening.* He thinks: *Am I being mugged?* Nobody hits him, they just hold him. *What do they want?* His heart skips and he's sure that he's calling out for help, but he can't hear his own voice from the thump of his pulse in his ears, so maybe not, and the coat tightens over his head and his arms are rendered useless by the handlers, their grip unshakable, his feet stumbling under him, and his breath coming too quickly, which doesn't help.

He's dizzy.

His stomach in his throat.

This can't be happening.

What Jay sees: darkness, splinters of light, then weirdly the thousands of empty film canisters tiling the vaulted subway station ceiling as he dances beneath them, the painted pillars, the scuffed concrete platform, and scattered fragments of faces, hands, shoes, pointy black pumps.

A small syringe.

This can't be happening.

A needle bites into his shoulder, and his arm floods warm.

A new fear grips him. He floats up, hollowed, out-of-body: on the Vermont/Sunset Metro station platform during rush hour on an otherwise unremarkable Tuesday, mid-autumn, there is a moment of thrashing confusion as worried commuters dart out of the way of three unremarkable men and one unremarkable but pleasant-looking, dark-haired woman, wrestling with a fourth man who appears to have his coat upside down and tangled around his head. The man cries out, muffled, "WHAT the—wait—you—" but several people will swear, when they go home and tell their husbands or brothers or children about it, that it was just he was having some kind of seizure, and luckily there were people trying to help him who knew what to do and—

Jay's knees buckle and blue darkness blooms inside his head and his thoughts tangle. He hears the train depart, senses the emptying of the platform from the echo of footsteps and bodies moving. If only he could run. He makes one last violent effort to get free and then the three men take his full weight as his body sags into them, and the coat comes halfway open and the pretty brunette is flashing at what remains of the worried or just curious commuters entering and leaving the platform something bronze and badgelike from the leather folding wallet that she holds high in her hand and she says something pleasant Jay can't hear—

and then—

| 2 |

SKIP BACK.

Two days. Sunday night, or early Monday.

His eyes blinking open to a bedroom he knew and yet sensed with dull dread was not the bedroom he fell asleep in, because something had been added.

This is what he remembers:

Fear.

Darkness.

Baroque patterns dusting the walls, thrown upward by streetlights through the beveled diamond windowpanes. The heavy night air and an uneasy stillness. Stacy shifting under the covers beside him, dreaming, fitful. Her pink bare body threw off a dozy heat.

Slender hand, upturned.

The engagement ring with its cold hard little diamond.

Heart beating, mouth cotton, he debated waking her, but first tried to convince himself it was just trace echoes of the past, fear he'd felt before and still hadn't, couldn't, after all this time, contrive to forget. So he lay quietly and listened, willing his heartbeat to slow, measuring his breathing, listening until the quiet turned itself inside out and he was all but certain that, yes, somebody was in the apartment with them.

And his pulse started pounding all over again.

He reached down and groped under the bed for the aluminum softball bat he kept there, just in case.

Shadow among shadows, he slid from his bed and drifted, bat gripped two-handed, into the hallway. He heard the rustle of bougainvillea, felt a breeze on his neck. He smelled lantana out in the courtyard, wet, sickly-sweet. And mildew, from the entry stairwell, where the plaster was ruined by January's rains.

The front door to the apartment was open, halfway, light from the outside corridor spilling in.

He froze. Brought the bat to half-mast and re-gripped it, and re-gripped it, wondering what he'd do if the intruder stepped out of the darkness now. More than anything, Jay wanted to get back in the bed, back under the covers, the way he would when he was eight and afraid of the darkness, convinced that if any part of him was exposed to the night whatever was lurking in it would take him. Safe, under the covers, until the rescue of daylight, and his mom waking him, smiling, everything good.

He peered back down the hallway, where he could see the sheer curtains rippling because the French doors to the tiny balcony were open.

Doors that had been closed when they fell asleep.

He waited, listened for the intruder.

Nothing.

The common corridor was empty when he walked out of his apartment to the stairwell banister and looked down.

Two floors below: a hand on the railing: someone descending: the faintest complaint from the loose riser near the bottom.

Then gone.

. . .

Y ou call the cops?"

"And tell them what? Somebody took a shortcut through my place?"

"Well . . . yeah."

"I didn't, no. Call them."

Manchurian Global, lunchtime, Vaughn's lab. Not quite *The Island of Dr. Moreau*, but pretty freaky. The chemical smells. The shivery racket of caged rodents, hard drives, refrigerators, and floor fans.

"Maybe you imagined it."

"No."

Jay didn't tell Stacy what he thought had happened until morning. He just closed all the doors and locked them and sat for a while in the darkened living room, thinking about his brother, Carl, and what he might be doing if he were still alive. Then he booted up *Call of Duty* and played with the sound turned off, abandoning strategy for maximum firepower and discovering what he already knew: it doesn't work. Toward dawn, Jay slipped back into bed and did the trick he'd learned about forgetting, turning reality into a dream, because dreams could be dismissed and forgotten, lost in the veiled awakening to a new day.

"Freaked me out, I'll tell you that."

He watched a white mouse smear through a luminous white world of white dead ends and white disappointment; it stopped, sniffing, determined, the droll pink eyes staring, spooked. Distorted and washed out and his nose a fleshy insult, Vaughn's green eyes peered intently back at the mouse through Plexiglas etched by countless tiny laboratory mouse scratches, watching the helter-skelter progress of today's furry volunteer.

Or victim, Jay thought.

"Nothing missing?"

"No."

"What'd Stacy say?"

"She thinks I imagined it."

Vaughn let his silence make its point.

"She's wrong, Vaughn."

The mouse scampered bumbly down the white pathways, making one sharp right turn after another, sure of itself now, remembering the way, hurrying toward the expectation of a reward and oblivious to the possibility of a punishment—*like us,* Jay thought. A white plastic dreamscape with the voice of God moving behind it, monitoring his geometric paradise, if God was a lanky post-doc named Vaughn: "Maybe it was that guy."

Jay frowned. "What guy?"

"Stacy's, you know—her old boyfriend. The boxer."

The boxer. "Juan Pablo?" *No.* Jay said, "He moved to Houston. And he wasn't a boxer—or a cage fighter or whatever—that was just you telling stories that one night, after a couple of French 75s."

Vaughn's face rose and loomed over the Milky White Maze, with proto-geek safety glasses and a tentative, beardlike facial growth, his hair gelled up all porcupine, finger-in-socket, over the chalky labyrinthian passageways, a brooding Magog. "We're so vulnerable when we're asleep," Vaughn mused darkly.

Jay shrugged. "Asleep, awake, it's not that different."

"Oh." Vaughn waited for Jay to expand on this observation, then looked disappointed when he understood that Jay wouldn't.

The mouse was momentarily still. Listening to them.

"What do you know about experimental neurosis, Jaybird?"

"A little," Jay lied. "Remind me."

"Mice," Vaughn explained, "whose genetic makeup is more similar to that of human beings than most of us care to admit, are submitted to a maze at the end of which are two doors, one with a

circle that rewards them with food, and one with an ellipse that pun-
ishes them with an electric shock."

"Sounds fairly unremarkable, so far. Junior-high science fair stuff
from, I dunno, 1954?"

"Don't snark." Vaughn's gaze was hard on his test mouse as it
scampered toward what Jay guessed would be a dreamy white failure,
since that was usually the experimental goal. "Over time," Vaughn
continued, "we change out the ellipse on the shock door, slowly re-
placing it with a less and less ovoid shape. Or, in other words, the symbol
becoming more and more similar to the one on the safe door, more
and more circular with each successive iteration."

"Bet that pisses off the mice."

"Mice don't have feelings."

"Everything's got feelings, Vaughn."

Vaughn just stared.

"Right. Okay. Please continue. Becoming more circular with each
iteration," Jay prompted.

"At that critical point where the synapses in the mouse mind can
no longer grok the difference between circle and ellipse, the mice go
crazy and eat themselves."

"*Eat* themselves?" This was why Jay no longer worked at Manchurian Global.

"'*Timeo Danaos et dona ferentes.*'"

"Uh-huh. Cue the Latin, Mr. Wizard, which you know I don't
understand."

"Look, if I thought somebody broke into my apartment in the
middle of the night, I would have called the cops, Jay."

"How is that in any way related to mice going all autocannibal?"

"I'm just saying."

Vaughn's current victim was slip-sliding down a stainless-steel incline, frantic to stop itself, as if it knew what was coming, careening

toward a pair of hinged doors designed to open to a short drop into an aquarium of ice water. But not this mouse, skittering, shrieking, stubbornly stopping itself just short of the plunge.

"Shit." Vaughn made some marks on a clipboard and plucked the mouse out of the maze. "That's not supposed to happen."

Jay sighed. No sense in drawing it out. "So, it's the stress, right?"

"We're not completely sure," Vaughn said. He disappeared into the rows of cages. "We can't be certain."

"And you're thinking my midnight intruder, that's just—"

"I don't think anything. I'm a scientist. I observe and record."

Jay played the straight man: "Well, what else could it be?"

"That's what we're asking ourselves."

"And this, the eating thing, happens to every mouse?"

"Yes." Jay watched his friend's head of quills shark deeper into the lab. "With the exception of these fifty mice they cloned in Utah." Jay heard the sound of a soda can hissing open.

"Apparently, they don't give a shit."

Jay was twelve minutes late back to Buckham & Buckham from Vaughn's lab, a mortal sin duly noted by Buddy DeLuca from his open floor supervisor's office, "Again."

He remembers the acrid afterburn of overcooked coffee: somebody'd forgotten to switch off the Krups.

"Today," Jay announced to the cube farm of murmuring fellow phone drones, a labyrinth of workspaces not so different, he thought drily, from Vaughn's milky white one, "today is the first day of the rest of your pointless lives."

"Bite me," from the nearest desk.

"You all weighed down with the ball and chain, or are you playing hoops with us tonight, J.B.?"

When Jay worked at Manchurian Global, in the sprawling rat maze of animal cages, test stations, and analytic hardware that Vaughn whimsically calls his office in the sprawling rat maze of think-tank and research facilities that Manchurian Global whimsically calls its campus, slacker Jay carried animals to and from experiments, keyed in data, cleaned, fed, watered, cremated the obdurate or unlucky, and still squandered a good part of his 346 days there inert, slouched in a chair, lab coat and wrinkled khakis, legs splayed, flip-flops, iPod wired into his ears, squeezing a rubber stress ball and fiddling with his phone and successfully ignoring the endless stream of data that chattered across multiple workstation screens like so many Chinese billboards among the rats and mice who scampered, paranoid, back and forth, back and forth, across their cages, searching for a way out, in vain.

Now a crisply starched J. B. (Jay) Johnson—an all-new gung-ho Jay 2.0 (beta), nearly six months in the making, and hoping to stick: scrappy, young, feckless, cyan eyes and a puzzle of black hair, rocking some dove-gray wool slacks, white cotton button-down, and a club tie—slowed his perp walk, and called across the partitions, good-natured, "Stacy's got some kind of yoga spin-lati thing at Curves, so I'm good to go."

"Downward dog."

"Whatever."

"Okay. Yo. Seven o'clock. Need a ride?"

"No. Catching the Red Line."

"You're awesome green, bro."

Purling plainsong of the free market. Everyone rigged with Bluetooth phone headsets and false bravado, low-watt smiles, scared shitless that today won't be the day, their brittle sales conversations overlapping in a din, and Jay remembered how mice are highly social animals who speak at frequencies humans can't hear; play, wrestle, love, sleep curled up together, because without companionship they get lonely and depressed, anxious, lost.

Or eat themselves. Fuck Vaughn. Now he couldn't get the mice out of his head.

"Herself, Jay. Line five."

"Thank you."

Jay's cubicle: ergonomic, monochromatic and soulless, the requisite Herman Miller knockoff chair squeaking as he swiveled into it, adjusted his headset, and: "Hey Stace, what up?"

There were no personal effects save a Chris Paul bobblehead and a thumbtacked photograph of the prepossessing-but-underfed Stacy, thigh gap, petulant plumped lips and salon-blond hair, a soft electric kind of girl who elicits from bros in bars the inevitable waggish: I'd hit it. Which Jay found sadly comforting.

He can't remember what she said on the call.

When subjected to painful stimulus, mice make humanlike facial expressions of displeasure, and before Jay quit his lab job, Manchurian Global had developed a mouse grimace scale (MGS) for measuring rodent pain based on five distinct "pain faces."

He can't remember which face he made while Stacy talked. Maybe all of them.

The relevant truth is that what Jay remembers from her call is not listening and choosing instead to rerun in the theater of his head an unreliably enhanced highlight reel from some stay-at-home Saturday, his ball and chain huffing like a corgi in heat, clothes peeled, curlers popping from her hair, tipped backward on and gripping the edges of her dining table, one bare pink ankle crooked around Jay's neck, poleaxed with pleasure while Jay crimped up buttery between the clamp of her thighs, inelegant because of the positional physics at play: jeans jammed down around his knees, holding her other foot out like a tiller—

(Nothing wrong with Jay and Stacy's sex life, was what Jay was always trying to convince himself. Vigorous and creative. All good.)

—and by the time his head cleared, Stacy and her no doubt valid worries about the trajectory of their relationship, its purpose, its potential, was off the line and Jay was in the middle of a cold call with a potential customer in Minneapolis. The rote pitch, memorized:

"What we are, sir, basically, is an e-commerce shopping mall where you can set up for and be exposed to and monetize hundreds of thousands of potential click-throughs."

Does he love her? He wants to. He hopes so. He doesn't want to hurt her, so there's that. But he knows it's not enough. During the courtship phase, male mice make simple, plaintive whistles or modulated calls. After mounting the female, however, male mice make chirping sounds that are strikingly similar to human laughter.

"Scalability? No, sir. Not a problem. We've got a bunch of Caltech web-weenies shackled down in the basement working on this thing twenty-four/seven/three-sixty-five—just kidding—ha ha ha ha ha but—"

And so on, and so on, and so on.

In his twenty-seven weeks, three days, six hours, forty-nine minutes at Buckham & Buckham, Jay has twice been named Salesman of Merit, but more often called in and warned that his shift yield has sagged and put him in danger of missing his quota, which is grounds for dismissal, which is its own kind of death. He earns to a base pay scale of just under forty-four thousand dollars a year after taxes, carries almost sixty thousand dollars owed in student loans; has a horizontal game that's better than his vertical, and a decent mid-range fallaway jump shot; his vintage 325i is in the shop because he can't afford to have the transmission rebuilt.

"The robustness of this site is key to us," Jay had promised his

Minneapolis prospect the way he always did, "and that's why we're approaching only the most attractive vendors."

Stacy's climax: usually less a scream than a choked-back, fragile, high-pitched hiss. After sex: male mice often sing in triumph, at around 20 to 22 kHz. He remembers how Stacy's eyes would close and her lips curl back, and her whole body gone rigid—he can recall her hands fluttering and searching for his hips—and her heart beating so hard he could feel it against his chest—and remembers how sometimes he could imagine being married to her, but more often he couldn't.

Jay never sings.

He remembers looking at the clock, five to six, and thinking, *Forty minutes home, grab my Nikes and my bag, Silver Line to the 7th Street station, Red Line to Hollywood and the Y.*

There was the crossover dribble he'd perfected and was dying to use on that jamook from North Hollywood with the hairy shoulders and too much Axe. He can't remember the guy's name though.

Or maybe it's just that he never knew it.

There was the train change at Hollywood and Western.

His bag on the platform.

Old lady. Groceries. Cougar with a gun—

| 3 |

A splitting headache.

The mazelike grid of cracks and fissures in a white plaster ceiling as his unconsciousness falls away simply bewilders: a latticework of gypsum crazing.

Where is this? Where am I?

Stale air, a spookish quiet.

Dull moan of an ancient heat-pump air conditioner rising, white noise kicking on. The stiff mattress crinkles plastic underneath him, there's a scrape of cold sandpaper pillow against his skin.

Scared: *This is not a memory or a dream.*

Skimcoat of daylight blushes through translucent institutional windows, there are no wall decorations, just this hospital bed, containing Jay, a sideboard, and two metal chairs. His fingertips tingle; he smells floor polish and a trace of disinfectant.

One of the chairs beside the bed is occupied, by a fit-looking man in his mid-thirties, unevenly sunburned, open face, sad eyes. Plastered to the lapel of his sport coat, this man's got a "HELLO My Name Is" sticker on which he's scrawled the name PUBLIC, cursive, with a Sharpie.

"Hey. How're you feeling, Mr. Johnson?"

Jay blinks, lost, doped, the dull panic swirling, and still emerging from the fog. His tongue feels thick. He wants to say *I feel like shit* or *Who are you?* but nothing comes out.

Public nods. "Sometimes the tranquilizer really kicks your ass. I'm sorry about it."

Jay finds a word. "What?"

"Tranquilizer. Do you remember what happened in the subway station?"

"Yes." Then: "No. Maybe."

"Good. Okay. We acquired you there. I apologize for the artlessness of it, but sometimes . . ." His voice trails off. He shrugs. "The short of it is, you're in a safe facility, Jay. No one knows you're here, nobody can get to you."

"Get to me?" He tries to push himself up, but his wrist rattles a handcuff that binds him to the bedrail. *Jesus.* A wave of panic breaks over him, and he has to close his eyes for a moment to let it pass.

"Oh, that, it's . . . for your own protection," Public explains. "I don't have the key on me, or I'd . . ." Again the trailing off, the shrug. It all feels too practiced. A voice in Jay's head is whispering: *You have to get out of here. You have to get out of here.* He glances to the open door, and the empty corridor beyond it. Feels the cut of the handcuff against bone. Public says something else, but Jay's mind can't process it. He blinks and says, "What?"

"You're in the program, now."

"Program."

"Witness protection."

Jay hears himself say it once more: "What?"

"Safe. Nobody can get to you because you're in the Federal Witness Protection Program."

"I'm in witness protection."

"Yes."

Shaking his head slowly, Jay, genuinely trying to wrap his mind around it: "Why?"

Public laughs. And the freshet of fear it engenders chills Jay like an ice bath.

Does time pass? Did his eyes close?

"Jay?"

He feels a gap, empty of sense or sensation, but resurfaces to the man labeled Public still beside his bed, a subtle shift of light, a distant lonely keening of siren, or alarm, outside this building where he's being held.

"Jay. Hey." Public stands over the bed, a tracing of worry in his expression. "I think I lost you there for a sec."

"I think," Jay says, voice raw, "there's been some kind of mistake here."

"Say again?"

"Mistake."

"How so?"

"In every way," Jay says, and it doesn't sound like him, but his thoughts are at least gathering with more purpose.

Public laughs again. And says, "I know, right?"

"Seriously, I'm—"

"—It's okay, it's okay," Public says kindly. "It's normal to feel completely weirded out at this point. Even paranoid. Take your time."

Jay asks if he's in custody.

"Protective custody. Yeah, I guess."

Jay rattles the handcuff again, pointedly. "Under arrest?"

"No."

Jay makes another attempt at sitting up, and manages to get his torso roughly vertical, shaking off a swim of vertigo, and discovering that his fingertips are bandaged with gauze and tape, and extremely tender because:

"Oh, yeah, hey, we did some acid abrasion, there," Public is saying, "just in case. That weird paresthesia tingling deal you're feeling should be way better by tomorrow."

"In case of what?"

"Also your hair," Public confesses, ignoring the bigger question. Jay reaches up and feels the stubble of a brand-new buzz cut with the palm of his free hand. *What do they want from me?*

"We restyled it a bit. Do you feel any different? IQ-wise, I mean," Public jokes, "now that you're a blond?"

Jay just stares back blankly. This has got to be like one of those government screwups: families evicted for mortgage default from properties they own, SWAT teams storming the wrong apartment, people showing up to vote and getting told they've died.

"Somebody broke into my apartment. Couple of nights ago."

"Oh."

"Or at least I think someone did. Is that what this is about?"

Public is expressionless. "I don't know. Is it?" He uses a remote to motor up the back of the bed and make Jay more comfortable. For a long time neither one of them speaks.

"Here's where I am with this," Jay says finally. "I have no idea why you would think I need to be in witness protection. I'm completely confused. And a little scared, if you want to know the truth." He's still hoping that if he stays calm and cooperative, and explains himself, this crazy error they've made will become self-evident, there will be embarrassed faces, waivers of culpability to sign, sincere apologies, and he'll go home to deal with the bad haircut and the acid burns.

"I know, right?" Public says.

"So, I mean. How about this: if you could just tell me what it is you think I've seen, or witnessed . . ."

Public shakes his head. "Better that you tell me. What you think it is."

"But I just explained—"

"—No, see, you have to tell me," is what Public says, firmly, like a parent to a child. "That's where we are with this. That's why we're here."

Jay closes his eyes. Frustration has shoved his headache down to the base of his skull, where it pulses, almost cold. "I'm here," he says, as levelly as he can, "handcuffed to a bed. Like a prisoner."

Public opens his mouth, then closes it, reconsidering what he was going to say. Out in the hallway, old-school linoleum shines like it's been recently waxed. There doesn't seem to be anyone standing guard on the room. If it's a hospital, Jay decides, it's not a new one, possibly not even a functioning one. And for the first time he wonders if Public is who he says he is.

"I'm supposed to have a key," Public says apologetically, sitting down again and crossing his legs. "Okay, look. A lot of people feel the way you do right now, at first. Upside down. Don't know if we can be trusted, or even are who we say we are, which is completely understandable. But over time—"

"Am I under arrest?"

"No, of course not"—but continuing his prior explanation, Public—"what I'm saying, over time it's just the overwhelming feeling of helplessness—of having to rely on total strangers—"

"I'm the wrong guy," Jay tells him. "I'm nobody: work in a telemarketing office, play a little basketball. My girlfriend thinks I'm afraid to commit, my friends—"

Public interrupts, "Jay—"

"I don't have anything to tell you. I didn't do anything, I didn't *see* anything," Jay pleads.

The briefest cloud of doubt crosses Public's features, then clears. He shrugs. "That contradicts our information."

"Then somebody gave you bad information," Jay reasons. "You know. Or transposed a Social Security number. It happens."

Public nods his inexpressive nod. "Jay, I'm a deputy U.S. Marshal and not inexperienced at the acquisition, securing, and unwrapping of confidential informants. We're very, very careful and we don't make those kinds of mistakes, but sure—I totally get where you might be coming from. Your fears, your distrust. And you don't have to say anything at all to us until you're ready."

"No, I'm ready. Ask away."

Again, clouds, this time of impatience. "There'll be plenty of time for that, once we get you somewhere more secure."

"What if . . . I don't want to go?"

Public just shrugs.

"But I'm not under arrest."

"No."

"Can I call somebody? I should call my fiancée so she doesn't worry. How long has it been since you took me off the train?"

Public ignores the last part, and says that calling Stacy probably is not a good idea; what the girlfriend doesn't know, the girlfriend can't tell anybody.

Who would she tell? Jay wonders.

"And you have no family," Public adds.

"No," Jay agrees, which is the lie he always embraces, but now he's curious about just how much Public knows, and where the U.S. Marshals, if that's who they are, are getting their information.

"So," Public adds, in case Jay didn't pick up on the significance of the statement, implying: Jay won't be missed.

"What will you tell Stacy?"

"It's all been taken care of."

"What does that mean?"

"No worries. We're very thorough."

"And what if I want to talk to an attorney?"

"Jay, you're not under arrest. You're in protective custody."

"Abducted and held against my will," Jay tries to say, in the most matter-of-fact way, but knows it comes out brittle. And he no longer cares. All the stories he's heard about people convicted of crimes they didn't commit, who spend nearly a lifetime in prison before somebody proves them innocent. He's Alice, down the rabbit hole, and the drug they gave him has made him pretty fucking small.

Public shrugs. "It may be that you simply don't fully comprehend the potential fragility of your situation outside of our aegis. We have to be careful during this transition. We would be callous if we let you go."

Jay stares at him. The man is grandstanding, smug. Jay takes a deep breath, exhales. It doesn't help. "Aegis. I don't even know what that means," Jay says bleakly.

"My point being, you could be in danger, from the people who would be most impacted by what you know. Or saw."

A current of fresh air brushes Jay's skin, from an open window or door somewhere in the building. Again, a vague urge to just run away from this rises. *But how?* He asks: "What if you aren't what you say you are? Or what if you are, but you're lying about what you want? I mean . . . what if *you're* the danger, *you're* the people most impacted by what I know?"

"I'll concede that point," Public says. "How can you trust people who grab you off a Metro train and jack you with tranquilizers and tie you to a bed?"

"I don't know what you want me to tell you," Jay says, the broken record. "I don't know what you want."

Public is patiently agreeable. "If I were you, I would take that position. Under the circumstances. So, like I said, go slow. I would." His calm is absolute, and Jay can see that there's no shaking it. "But here." Lifting a battered briefcase from under the chair to his lap, Public pops it open and removes two dossiers with blown-up photographs clipped to them. On the first: what look like crime scene photos of a young woman's body, naked, murdered, twisted across a wet tile bathroom floor.

"We want to know what happened to her," Public says.

Jay's mind reels over the stark, disturbing images of the girl. He feels sick. Thoughts tumble too fast for words. The cold fear crawls through him, his breathing shallow, his voice a thousand miles away.

"You don't know her?"

"No." He doesn't. He didn't.

"Never seen her?"

That's a trickier question, one that freezes Jay, and one that Public lets slide, or answers for him, resigned to Jay's intransigence: "No. Sure. Okay." Tucking the crime photos away, Public looks up and openly studies Jay for a moment. Trying to read him? The second folder has a sheaf of documents, reports of some kind, with snapshots clipped to them, hastily taken images of a sulky, angular young woman with black eyes and a crooked smile, and of a grim little girl who looks nothing like her.

This file Public doesn't explain, or share.

"In a couple of days," Public, conversational, "we'll be moving you to an interim temporary-permanent situation"—he waves at the folders—"where you'll be sequestered for a few weeks of debriefing while we grow you an acceptably secure, permanent location. And help you adjust to your new life."

Jay wants to say so many things he can't speak. The relentless impulsion of what is happening roils him. A corkscrew of college philosophy class surfaces out of his imbroglio, namely Nietzsche: the irrationality of something isn't an argument against its existence, but actually a condition of it. He shifts his weight, and unintentionally his trembling wrist rattles the handcuff, and he wonders how fast, after being drugged silly, he would be able to run, if the opportunity presented itself. Public tosses a sheaf of legal boilerplate onto the aluminum bedside tray and swings the tray across Jay's lap.

"Power of attorney. If you'll just"—he proffers a pen—"put your Sam I Am here and here, after you've read the fine print, we'll need to secure your personal effects and resources yadda yadda ASAP since, for all practical purposes—you no longer exist." He shuts the briefcase and stands up.

"I don't want a new life," Jay says emptily. *No longer exist.* He wonders if that will be such a change.

Public smiles, avuncular. "Everybody wants a new life."

"Oh," is all Jay says. He can't keep the panic down. The room spins. "I really need to use the bathroom."

Public, chagrined: "Right. Sorry. I'll have to . . . get somebody." Public hesitates, then takes his briefcase and starts walking out.

"What if I refuse. What if I say no?" Jay calls after him. It's his last stab at resistance. He doesn't expect it to work, but it feels right to say it out loud.

Public turns around but continues backpedaling toward the door, Fred Astaire. "We'd have to kill you," he says, and allows the requisite deadpan, then cracks the requisite smile, and admits, "Just kidding," making a gun with his thumb and finger, pointing it at Jay, pulling the trigger, and slipping into the hallway.

Shoes squeak on the industrial tile, trailing faint echoes as Public goes away.

Jay closes his eyes and tries to breathe.

| 4 |

VAUGHN?

Or Manchurian Global, the shadowy government contractor, some covert study that's gone off the rails, a secret experiment Jay doesn't even remember he walked in on, and—

—no. He's pretty sure he knows what it can't be, but not what it is.

He doesn't like to look backward; Jay has never really cared where he's been. He prides himself as always forward-moving: here, in the moment: unbeholden to an immutable and, by the way, completely irrelevant past. Gone. Done. How to remember what he did six months ago, six weeks ago, six days ago, at a specific time in a specific place—it seems impracticable. Time flows, life passes, memories are compromised by distance and the distortion of perspective, mood, focus. You look in the mirror and you see not your face as it is, but your face approximated by the millions of times you've seen it before, tired, hungover, happy, broken, sick, young, younger, the baby, the boy, the survivor, the man, staring back at you, reversed, reflected, ever since you first were aware it was your face, the sum total of your-self, not even close to what another person looking at you would see.

Not to mention the hard fact that you might not want to remember that person you were before.

For a long time after Public retreats, Jay's motionless on his hospital bed, eyes closed but wide awake, struggling to determine what he could possibly know, or have seen in the past year, that would be of value to federal law enforcement. So, yeah, a good guess might be Manchurian G., something to do with his old job, or the behavioral research Vaughn does; something perilous that Jay has seen without knowing he's seen it.

There is, however, the dead girl in the photographs. And Jay's conviction that there is no Venn intersect between that girl and Vaughn.

He wonders: What was Vaughn's point about those fifty cloned mice?

How many images do we process, in a single day? How many people do we encounter?

How many times waking in the night to the touch of breeze across his face and the soft darkness and the fear and indecision and the certainty of an interlocutor; that reflexive spike of terror tethered to another time, a different breach. Was that important? Was that part of this?

The more he tries to remember, the more jumbled the memories get. Last year's birthday. Christmas. March Madness, he lost fifty bucks on his office pool bracket. The faint impression Stacy leaves in the covers of the bed, the tendrils of her perfumes. Her closet packed with clothes and shoes she never wears. The sound of January rain on the French doors, the leak down the wall.

His father's face, alive, asleep, dead.

His sister's empty bed that next morning when they took him back to get some clothes.

His mother's vacant stare.

There was that night he saw the motorcade, leaving Westwood, when was that? May? Every intersection blocked on the west side. Getting out of there was a nightmare. The pooling streetlights, the spectral gauze of marine layer off the Pacific, and the brittle gleam of motionless traffic. It might have been a shutdown for the President. The blacked-out windows of all those long limousines. And the homeless man with the megaphone and the red tinfoil cape who brought it all to a standstill, screaming gibberish, until LAPD and Secret Service swarmed him and carried him to a waiting van, thrashing and spitting.

Was there something that night he missed?

His mouth is dry. His fingertips itch like crazy. He rubs them against the clammy palms of his hands, and tugs against the handcuff, and then sinks into himself, frustrated, almost resigned. Everything seems out of his control, and control, for Jay, has always been everything.

Public's boilerplate documents wait on the steel tray angled across the bed, and Jay is deciding that he needs to have an attorney look at them when a woman's voice startles and observes: "You could have someone review those, but the trouble with lawyers is that they are the most-likely-to-squeal-like-a-squirrel component in all our studies of why witness protection programs get compromised and people we're trying to save die."

The brunette from the subway has breezed in, brisk, lively, self-possessed, jeans and a hooded sweatshirt. Empty hip holster for the weapon she's left somewhere (for safety?), but she's jangling a fistful of keys and has her own "HELLO My Name Is" sticker on which she's scrawled in purple Sharpie: DOE.

Unlocking his handcuff, she continues, "It's just, once lawyers get to talking it's hard to shut them up. Plus they're abject cowards, which makes them particularly susceptible to torture." She adds, "Hi," and takes a ballpoint pen from her pocket to put on top of Public's waiver documents.

"Hi." Jay slides upright, again, queasy with discomfort, light-headed but starting to shake off the muddle, deadened legs swinging out and dangling over the side of his bed, blood rushing back to his tingling feet, determined to stand up until he feels the air-conditioned air on his ass and realizes he's in one of those backless hospital gowns that nobody has bothered to tie. He rubs his wrist and looks up to meet Doe's implacable gaze.

"Fortunately, under the U.S. Patriot Act and its amendments and revisions," she tells him, "we are empowered, if we want, to simply dispense with that potential risk factor. Lawyers, I mean. Not that we will," Doe admits, "some of us still believe in the rule of law, that it's your right as a citizen to have counsel, although the Supreme Court may have a different opinion soon, and, I know it's been said before by my colleague, but: you aren't being accused of anything." She finishes her speech there. And waits. Not as pretty as he remembers. Maybe it's the cold gray light.

"You can keep me in limbo forever, is what you're saying."

"Forever," Doe muses, still friendly, "is a long time. So. On a scale of one to ten, how freaked out are you?"

Jay doesn't want to answer this. Instead he gestures to her name tag. "Doe?"

"Jane. Yeah." She reads Jay's doubt. "Deputy U.S. Marshal. Do you need to see my badge?"

"That's not really your name."

"Don't hurt my feelings," she says playfully.

"And Public? Stab in the dark: John Q.?"

Doe smiles, big. She's got one molar capped gold in back. Weirdly blue-collar and endearing. "*Exactamente.* Good guess."

Jay is not amused. "I might feel better talking to you with an attorney present," Jay says, reaching back and struggling to make a knot in his gown tie. It won't take.

"Yeah? Why? What have you done?"

"You sound like your partner."

"Oh, we're not partners," she says categorically. "But I am sorry. For messing with you. We're just attempting to keep it, you know, light. I can only imagine how incredibly strange all this must be."

Jay breathes out, tight. "Just a bit, yeah."

"Although, what's interesting to me is how you're not nearly as freaked out as I would think you'd be," she says purposefully, twisting her mouth, wry, and cutting him a curious look that seems to suggest, if he's not diligent, she'll get right into his head. Jay's pulse skips. She doesn't wait for a response from him, doesn't seem to expect one. All friendly again: "You want some help with that gown?"

"No, I think I'm good." Jay lowers himself from the bed unsteadily to the floor, feeling the icy tile on the soles of his already cold feet, and holding his gown shut behind him with one hand.

"Okay."

The bathroom door is in the far corner, twenty feet of open floor, and Jay just focuses on getting there and keeping his backside to the wall.

"You can put your clothes on," Doe tells him. "They're hanging on a hook in there."

"Great." He meets her steady gaze reluctantly. Doe worries Jay more than Public; the amiable good nature, the genuine concern, it's seductive, and winning, and he doesn't believe it. This woman orchestrated and conducted his forceable abduction only a few hours—or is it days?—ago. "Oh, wait." Jay stops, slide-steps back to the bed, reaches, takes the legal papers one-handed from the bedside table, and flips the pen up off them and catches it in his mouth.

Doe, impressed: "Whoa. He does tricks."

"Boarding school. You learn . . . all kinds of useless stuff." Reversing again, and the same weird sideways shuffle takes him to the bathroom, with Doe, arms akimbo, watching.

"Show me something else."

Jay smiles reflexively as he backs into the bathroom, and thinks: *Watch me disappear.*

Safely inside, Jay locks the door, leans against it and takes a few deep, ragged breaths. The notion of escape has been dancing in and out of his thoughts for a while now, but he has no plan, no skill set that would suggest he could pull it off. It's a small space: toilet, sink, and a rust-streaked, cobwebbed shower nobody has used in a long time. His eyes slide to his reflection in the mirror over the sink. He sees a pale, stubbled face under bleached, chopped hair and, for a moment, doesn't even recognize himself.

"Everything okay in there?"

Jay stares. *Oh, man.*

"Did you say something?" The soft slap of her hand on the door. "Jay. Everything okay?"

"Yeah. My hair especially."

"Touch of the dramatic," she says, still trending to cheerful. "It'll grow out."

The glare of the single bulb.

The grating hum of the air-conditioning.

What happens next unfolds in loose fragments that will later defy any rational explanation. The rasping noise brings his eyes to the ceiling above the toilet, and any number of bad action movies where the hero escapes through the ducting.

Gray slacks hurriedly taken from the hook on the back of the door and pulled on; the toilet flushed, seat cover dropped, and Jay stepping up onto it, barefoot, buttoning his pants, hospital gown billowing open in the air currents from the big latticed ceiling grille for the central air. Jay's gauze-clumsy fingertips claw at it, hoping it's one of those spring-secured grilles, but, no—*shit, shit*—hex nuts hold the vent in place.

He flushes the toilet again.

From outside: "Jay?"

"Nothing, all good," Jay blurts incoherently. Then improvises, "Can I take a shower? I'm, like, pretty funky."

A slight hesitation. "Sure. Whatever you need."

"Thanks."

"Towel?"

"Right. Yes. Thank you."

He steps down, cranks the handles in the shower stall to send a loud splatter of tepid water into the splash trough, and thinks he hears Doe's footsteps trail out into the hallway.

Public's ballpoint pen, unscrewed, disassembled, pieces spilling out across the dusty white vanity counter, will serve as a crude tool. In boarding school, Jay had breached any number of off-limits spaces using only his pens, scissors, and paper clips. Moments later he's up on the toilet again, using the husk of the pen like a socket wrench to jimmy the hex nuts from the grille. They pop and yield; the vent cover goes gently to the floor. Jay throws shoes and socks up into the darkness, then reaches into the steel ducting, to find leverage and pulling himself up awkwardly into the opening, skin scraping against sharp metal. Two of his fingers are cut and bleeding through the gauze. Steam is billowing up, condensing on the steel. His hips stick. By the width of the waistband of his pants he can't fit. It's so stupid he almost laughs, but his fingers are bleeding, and the hot, damp air is blinding him, his arms are shaking, and some elemental part of him doesn't want to give up to them. He makes one last, desperate pull, twists, and his pants slide off, dangle for a moment from his calves, and then fall to the floor beside the toilet as his pale legs fold up into the duct.

And now he understands just how stupid this was.

It's pitch black in front of him; the ductwork is filthy, the palms of his hands already grimed. Up ahead he can only faintly make out a ghosting of light that spills sideways from a blunt angle of darkness at some indefinite distance (five feet? five hundred?) that must be a bend in the passageway, and, beyond it, the next possible means of egress. He's already exhausted from pulling himself in. Shower steam floods the vent and slicks him. He can't get fully to his hands and knees. Legs scraped raw, no pants, just his sweaty boxers and the flimsy, backless hospital gown, Jay has no way to put his shoes on, so he pushes them ahead of him and starts to slither-crawl away.

The thin metal flexes, of course, and thunders like a kettledrum. So much for the element of surprise. Or any real hope of success. What keeps Jay going at first is just the certainty of the consequences of getting caught, now that he's made his intention to run known. He keeps crawling, mouse in a maze, Vaughn be damned, hoping for that impossible resolution to an experiment with a foregone conclusion.

Mice, Jay muses ruefully. *Whose genetic makeup is surprisingly like ours.*

At the first intersection he veers right into a slightly bigger, and filthier, ducting, curtained with sheets of lint and cobwebs, praying that this one may lead somewhere promising, but having no confidence that it does.

Hands and knees, now, faster, he keeps crawling. The squeak and thrum of his knees and skin. Somewhere far behind him there is the sound of the bathroom door burst open and he hears Public saying: "How lame is this?" And then: "He is not helping himself here." And, shouting, louder, presumably with his head up in the vent: "Jay?" bent and amplified by unforgiving air duct acoustics. "Goddamn it."

Doe is also talking, but not to Public, and not behind him, but below him. On a walkie-talkie or cell phone. Coordinating his containment from the room or hallway across which the ducting is taking him.

But now there's no light at all. His eyes try to adjust, he can feel them straining to see anything. Jay is moving as fast as he can, oblivious to any obstruction in front of him, throwing out one hand after another so that at least he'll touch it before he crashes into a dead end, arriving abruptly at an intersection of three different, smaller ducts, each snaking off into its own dark oblivion. Each too small, as he touches the sharp edges of the openings and makes the quick calculation, for him to continue.

He hears movement and footsteps below him. Doe and Public, strolling, taking their time. He imagines them listening for him: eyes tilted up to the ceiling tiles of a big empty ward. He holds his breath.

"See, a woman would never do this," Doe is saying.

"What—escape from safety?"

Their voices keep moving under and away from him.

"No. It's this: a man crawls back down the umbilical, expecting the womb . . ."

Jay's eyes track fits of spark and color that first he thinks are some kind of entoptical floater, but when he moves his head they reflect hard off the galvanized steel and betray a vertical shaft directly above him, with vents leaking daylight in dreamy stripes. *Maybe*, he thinks carelessly. *Hope is for suckers*, Nietzsche responds—well, more or less. Jay contorts to a standing position as quietly as he can, and starts to wriggle upward in the vertical shaft, pressing his elbows and his knees against the opposing planes of steel, like a rock climber in a chimney. The ducting groans and shudders on its mounts.

". . . but a woman, a woman confronted with this cold, dark, narrow passageway to God only knows where . . ."

Doe and Public, walking back.

"How's that divorce going?" Public ribs.

A burst of static from a walkie-talkie, high above; a huge grille has been pulled and the purplish-pale and square-haired head of a uniformed cop appears, leaning half inside, with a flashlight, sending an optimistic flutter of beams down the sides of the air shaft, but never quite reaching Jay.

". . . a woman sees it for what it is. She knows it's hopeless, because it's exactly like her last four relationships. Dark, narrow, and humiliating dead ends."

Public laughs.

The flashlight retreats and the cop disappears and Jay is left slipping, groaning, his greasy sweat-streaked skin burning as he tries to hold himself up with only the friction of his limbs against the sheet metal. He's about ten feet up; falling down is not an option. He has those queasy gym-class butterflies he'd get rope-climbing when he was finally able to go all the way to touch the ceiling. But a frantic twist and shimmy brings him up to the next junction, where he can find purchase on the horizontal shaft there and slowly pull himself to relative safety. But now what? This duct is smaller than the lower ones, and he can only wiggle forward, on his belly, arms flippering to propel him, his lower legs barely clearing the angle of the up shaft. Thump thump thump-thump thump-thump. He struggles over a series of interchanges, scraping across seams. All the fight is out of him, a weird aimless momentum keeps him moving forward: escape imitates life. The duct snakes left, snakes right, and executes a sharp L-turn, each new passageway growing narrower and tighter than the last.

He feels a zephyr on his face, and smells fresh air. The tunnel ahead slopes away dramatically, curving down and twisting. Jay stops and contemplates the drop. It's not viable. No way can he control the descent, and he doesn't know what lies ahead. It could be another vertical, down which he would plunge headfirst. And probably die.

Shit. He has to go back. Backward. No turning around. An access panel pops open behind Jay's feet, and the flush-faced cop jabs his crew cut into the ducting, jack-in-the-box, flashlight beam aimed right at and blinding Jay as he looks back into it.

"Yo."

Jay, spooked, reflexively pulls himself away from the pop-up cop, forgetting the steep drop ahead in the ducting, and then as gravity wraps its heavy arms around him he tries to catch himself, but the sweat-oily palms of his hands find no purchase on the air duct steel, and his weight passes the tipping point and Jay plummets down the duct, a fleshy toboggan, helpless, into utter darkness. It happens so fast he barely registers the abject terror that, later, he will always feel when he remembers the fall. There's just the vague, disembodied feeling that this probably won't end well. His nerves and senses are seared by the dull shriek and agony of his skin skidding on metal. A square of light hurtles toward him, breakneck, hardly the glow at the end of the tunnel that near-death stories always go on about, but maybe death comes at you in an angry rush, or maybe it's just daylight through the metal screen crosshatching of a rodent guard affixed inside an exterior vent.

Bigger and bigger and bigger as he plummets toward it, holding in its tracery sky, clouds, and that bright flare of sun into which Jay literally explodes, hashing his face and shoulder as the grille tears loose, and he tumbles out and drops, mostly naked, scared, heart pounding, hips and shins raw in the fresh air, legs and arms whirling without purpose. Later he'll be told he fell thirty feet into a dumpster filled with trash bags that saved his life, the cardboard and loose garbage erupting as it swallowed and cushioned him.

He doesn't remember it.

He remembers the narrowing air shaft, the impossible decline, the cop-in-a-box discovering him, a howling tornado of pain, an odd limbo of float, and suddenly not being able to breathe.

The wind is knocked out of him. His lungs heave and spasm, emptied by the impact of the fall. He isn't sure if he's been paralyzed or if it's just the dead weight on his limbs that's making it so hard to move.

"Breathe, Jay. Come on."

Someone claws away the collapse and gently lifts him at the waist, easing air back into his empty chest. John Q. Public has clambered up and over and into the bin, dug through for Jay, and found him, stunned, blue-lipped, eyes wide, and: "Alive. Thank God."

Thank God? For a moment, Jay wonders if he's misjudged them. Or is it just another indication of how desperately they need what he can't give them? He gasps, gulps air. His arms fold into his chest, weak. Blood beads and runs down his neck from the crosshatch wound that stretches from his right eye and temple to his ear.

"Jay."

"Yes."

"Don't move."

"I'm all right."

"Sure, but don't move. Let us—let us—"

Mulish, Jay rolls over, getting his knees underneath him, and another pair of hands helps him rise out of the garbage, the smell of it suddenly overwhelming him, his senses returning, aligning, and the worried looks of Public and the purple-faced cop who have taken him into custody for something he didn't see, and the bright sun and the glare of the whitewashed concrete side of the hospital or whatever it is, and one tall, lean laughing lunatic palm tree looming over him and shaking its unhinged head.

"I'm okay," Jay says, and nods for some reason, though he most assuredly is anything but.

| 5 |

HE TRIES TO MAKE IT A GAME.

All the unrelenting stress has sharpened his senses to a kind of jittering hyperlucidity that feels almost like a superpower.

Or just too much coffee.

His fall has taken the fight out of him. He's a stick in the gutter after a storm, caught in the current of runoff, hurtling helplessly toward a drain.

They're on their way to what Public has called a transfer point; a black cloth bag is loosely draped over Jay's head, his hands are free. Where daylight bleeds into the darkness at his neck and shoulders, a bright clutter of what Jay guesses is landscape passes outside. And what else? The press against his shoulders of two fleshy U.S. Marshals in the backseat of a vehicle that smells of vanilla air freshener and cigarettes and french fries. He could take the hood off, but they've asked him not to in a way that precludes arguing about it. The mewling hum of the car means it can't, he decides, be more than four cylinders, and a murmur of low front-seat voices, and the wheezy muffled shoop shoop shoop of traffic passing in the opposite direction suggests they're still on city streets, windows up: muffled talk radio bleats for a moment from an adjacent car, then bus brakes wheeze, a distant siren tails away and the tires click and pop across rents and seams in the roadway. Must be the 101. A turn indicator ticks. Now they're taking an exit ramp. Stale frozen air blows back from the air conditioner; it's been unseasonably hot.

One of the marshals wears an unfortunate cologne. Everything goes dark as they pass through a tunnel, or freeway underpass. A greenish flicker belies a canopy of trees, and the car slows to residential speeds, slows, stops. Hot, sweet fresh air floods the backseat as both doors gape, and the marshals on either side of him slide away, one of them pulling Jay with him, and helping him find his feet on a sidewalk.

His arm, shoulder, and hip are really starting to ache from the hard landing in the garbage bin.

They're walking, and he's trying not to stumble.

Leaves shiver around his feet in light breeze, the midwinter sun reflects up at him from flagstone pavers, brown shoes beneath khaki chinos on one side of him, sneakers and new jeans on the other.

"Step up."

More flagstone.

"Step up."

Sun, shade, some kind of porch; he's at the mercy of their lead. Someone knocking on wood. The wheeze of a screen door, the hands on his upper arms urge him over the threshold and inside.

Someone's house? Wall-to-wall carpet, a suggestion of sectional sofa, the legs of a table. Sound of a television, more voices from another room, overlapping, and the *Scooby-Doo* theme song. Jay knows all the words.

"We ran into gridlock again on the four-level, got off at Silver Lake," Public is explaining to whoever is immediately in the room with them, "took Beverly to Highland, then cut down to Olympic, which was, I don't know, so messed up. They're putting in storm drains, it's backed up from Hauser. Pack a snack."

"You should have dropped down to Pico," someone says.

"Yeah, but Pico sucks when you hit Robertson. That whole Cheviot Hills run? Brutal."

Jay's hood is pulled up and off.

He stands in a modest, sparsely furnished living room filled with strangers bathed in soft light. Jay's focus whipsawing as Public makes introductions: "Jay, this is Gavin Patterson . . . that's Julia Del Valle. Mark Meyers from the Justice Department—" There are hands to shake, and the faces, one after the other. Jay can't possibly keep them all straight. "—Ms. Doe you're acquainted with; the marshals, Rodriguez and Kelly, who escorted you here and who are only temporarily assigned to this location, so say hello and good-bye, you won't be seeing them again—"

Amid the mixing, shuffling cast of characters a small television screen in the far corner glows with Cartoon Network. A very small girl sits cross-legged in front of it, shoulders hunched, with her back to Jay, and on the sofa sits a tired and sulkier-looking version of the young woman with the crooked smile Jay recognizes from Public's file snapshots, back in the hospital, in another life.

"—and over there, that's Ginger. Say hi, Ginger. And her little one's Helen . . ."

Ginger raises frank black eyes to Jay and doesn't say anything, expressionless: no makeup, angry ink-black hair that could use some brushing out, an oversize pale green cardigan sweater pulled over her knees, as if she's freezing in all this empty Santa Ana heat. The little girl, Helen, doesn't turn, stays lost in her cartoons.

Under Ginger's steady gaze, Jay self-consciously touches the crosshatched scab on the side of his face, and Meyers puts a hand on his shoulder and slides into Jay's line of sight, blocking mother and child.

"So, hey. Listen, Jim. On behalf—"

"It's Jay."

"—*Jimmy*, on behalf of the entire U.S. Justice Department, I just want to say—"

Jimmy?

Public interjects, "—um, Mark, he's not—"

"—say that anything you need, you know, just holler, because we're here for you on this one thousand percent—"

"—not fully on board yet," Public cautions.

He means I'm uncooperative, Jay thinks. *Not quite down with the program.*

Meyers fronts a frown. "What?" Jay watches the man's eyes drift to Public, clouded with doubt. Public just shrugs.

"I want to talk to a lawyer," Jay says simply. He's trying to be cool, cooperative, still holding out some thin Panglossian hope that they will come to their senses and realize their mistake. The room goes quiet, except for Helen's cartoon show.

Jay feels the woman named Ginger's dark eyes shift to him again. He looks at her. She pushes the hair off her face, like she's just now noticing he's there.

It occurs to him that she's not beautiful, not like Stacy. But there's something about her that makes it hard for him to look away. And when he does, she stays with him, indelible.

"Please?" Jay adds, more subdued, and probably, he understands, unnecessarily.

For a while, they leave him alone in a bedroom with crinkled Jay-Z posters taped to the wall and a NASCAR bedspread and high-school textbooks stacked haphazardly on an IKEA bookshelf. The desk is messy, but the carpet is new; there's a faint smell of fresh latex paint; it's hard to say whether this is supposed to be a boy's or a girl's room, or, Jay thinks, maybe it's neither, maybe it's all for show. His reality turned inside out, Jay is no longer confident that he knows where the centerline is.

Shadows crawl into the room and settle. The comings and goings and muted conversations in the house disarrange and offer him no answers to his increasingly anguished preoccupation with what the Feds could possibly want from him.

His mind is sodden, his memory scrambled by disquiet. His recent past, as he thinks back on it, the weeks and the months, lurch and stall, rock forward, backward, an inconsequential blur, details pinwheeling into foreground and just as quickly spinning away: a breakfast at Platters in Glendale's Frogtown (who was that with?), a few random lines from *The Breakfast Club*, the big storm that knocked the tree down across Franklin, Vaughn sick from mescal shooters (or was it Aaron Olson? Or that strange guy Vaughn calls Trey?), the White Stripes at the Wiltern playing an uninspired short set, Stacy's loser Kappa sisters with the beach house at Dana Point (he can never remember their names), the six-hundred-pound drag queen in a tennis dress at WeHo Halloween. But then other years leak in and cause chaos, scraps of nothing: fourth grade, a trip to Mammoth, his dad sacked out on the sofa during March Madness, the unfortunate collagen lip treatment that his mom didn't need, the controller attack patterns in Nintendo Super Smash Bros. Melee, his first girlfriend Lisa's lopsided breasts, the virginal Emma's peculiar preoccupation with feet that creeped him out, and what was that bar on New Year's '06, in New York, the Village, with the grapefruit martinis?, and one particularly sweet reverse layup on a driveway backboard, among the desperate farrago of television, the scatter of Internet signal and noise, texting, posting, friending, gaming, taggings and selfies, the disconnection and loneliness, the information overload, the tedium and repetition: day, after day, after day, after day, immutable, unremitting, unremarkable.

What of this could they possibly want?

Eventually one of the escort marshals, still trailing his miasma of aftershave (Rodriguez? Jay guesses) comes to get him, and leads him out into the narrow hallway and down to a kitchen where Public and Doe wait at a Formica breakfast table with a scary-thin lady lawyer who introduces herself as Arden Richter, and smokes a Marlboro Red with abandon.

"Constitutionally speaking, you're here voluntarily," she says.

Jay shakes his head. "But I'm not."

"Right, well, and your government is claiming they've brought you into custody for your own protection. So." Arden grips the edge of the table like a schoolgirl waiting to get her test back, and expecting an A.

"They can do that?"

Richter takes the cigarette from her lips and stares at it. "They can do whatever they want, and you can take them to court for it, later, and—"

"Like unlawful detention, or something."

"You've been watching your *Law and Order*," Richter observes. "Yes. Or something."

"But meanwhile?"

Richter's hands flutter up in what Jay assumes is a shrug of helplessness.

Jay looks to Public. "I guess I just want to know, protection from what?" He looks at Richter. "Or whom? Can you get them to tell me that?"

Doe tells Richter that Jay has already asked it, but she, they, the

Federal Authorities, this group of marshals, can't answer that question without completely compromising the investigation in which Jay has been deemed a materially significant player.

"That doesn't really make sense," Jay observes aloud, "but, okay. So where does that leave me?"

Again, a fluttery shrug.

Public shows his teeth, not really grinning, unamused, but apparently interested for the first time. "You really have no clue why we brought you in?"

"I don't. No." He looks to Richter again. "This is what I've been trying to get through to them."

Doe starts to interrupt, but Public holds up his hand, so Jay can finish.

"I didn't see anything," Jay tells everyone in the room, as calmly as he can. He still wants to believe that these are rational people who have made an honest but aggravating mistake and if he's just convincing enough, and lays it out for them, right here, right now, they'll let him go. "I don't know . . . anything. I have nothing to offer you. And because you won't give me a clue as to what it might be—"

"We can't. Don't you understand? We need it to come from you, unsolicited—it's essential that you tell us without our asking for it—"

"Why?"

This causes another awkward hiccup in the conversation. Evidently, they can't tell him that, either. "This is either a case of mistaken identity or some bad information you got on your end," Jay says. "I'm nothing. I'm just a regular, normal, boring guy. I lead a regular, normal, boring life, a telemarketer who sells virtual real estate on his way to a Thursday-night three-on-three roundball with some other guys, friends, when you, I dunno, accosted me, and pulled my coat over my head and drugged me and took me away and dropped me into this . . . well, yeah, I'm sorry, but for me it's a nightmare. Okay? You can see that, right?"

Richter looks at the marshals. "My client says he didn't see anything."

"How can he be so sure that this is about something he saw?" Doe asks simply.

Richter looks at Jay.

The room spins. Jay crimps his eyes. He doesn't know how to respond. The discussion keeps circling on itself, an endless loop of flawed logic, and each time the argument comes back around, he feels a little less sure that what he knows is true is true.

It's Vaughn's crazy experiment with the doors and the suicidal mice.

"Jay. The civil rights of the individual," Richter begins, as if composing a brief, "can on occasion be subsumed by the rights of the community to"—someone sneezing in the hallway distracts her into a thought-stutter—"to certain, to certain, to certain information that the individual may possess, which could prevent," she pauses, eyebrows furrowed, starting to lose her way, "a larger . . ." And then she's completely lost, and looking for shore. ". . . well . . . harm . . ." She takes a long drag on the last of her Marlboro, eyes apologetic, and then shakes out and lights up another cigarette, end to end.

Doe, to Jay: "If you don't know anything, if you are—not in a legal sense, but generally—innocent, why did you try to run away from us?"

"I was scared. I feel like nobody is listening to me."

Public, to Jay, cold hard fact: "Because you aren't saying anything."

Jay looks at his lawyer. "And they can just keep me like this? Hold me indefinitely?"

"No. But yes. I mean—the law is, legally, well, clear—but, as I said before, in practice, vague. In this area." Arden Richter does a French inhale of cigarette smoke, lips pursed.

"Vague?"

Richter nods, rounds her lips, puffs out a smoke ring and taps the ash into her coffee cup. "For example, they could argue that what you know is dangerous, or in the public interest to protect—or acquire—and until you tell them—"

"You don't *exist* anymore," an impatient Public says sharply, the veneer peeling. "We've *erased* you, my friend. So technically we're not keeping you at all."

Erased. Jay feels like he's floating up, off his chair. Out of body: where reality becomes a dream, and dreams are something you wake up from.

Doe sighs, leans back, visibly upset with her colleague. Evidently, this is more than she wanted Jay to know.

Erased. Jay has known weightlessness before. "Wake up," he says. Bang. His head hits the table. "Wake up." Bang. "Wake up."

"Jay." Doe is watching him, kindly, worried.

Public pushes away from the table, walks to the wall, and comes back, hands on hips. Drone of the television bleeds through from the front room. Sitcom laugh track. Jay leaves his forehead on the tabletop, frustrated, tired.

"I'm sorry," he says. "Don't mind me."

The others stare at him, confused. "He doesn't trust us," Doe tells Public. "Which is perfectly understandable." The way she says it makes it sound like Public's fault.

Public nods, blows out air. "Okay."

Richter raises her hand. "Perhaps if my client and I could have a moment alone?"

Head on the table, drained, defeated, Jay murmurs that that won't be necessary. Ms. Richter is just a prop in this play.

"Okay. Well." Public is moving to the door, lively, energized. "I guess we're good, then? Ready to rock and roll?"

"I can try to get an injunction," Richter says to Jay without confidence, and she stays seated. "A writ of habeas corpus. I could try."

Jay says nothing.

Public: "Comeoncomeoncomeon—" He opens the door, and marshals flood the room, grasping Jay under the arms and lifting him from the chair to his feet, out the back door, which opens to bright sunshine and long shadows and the sullen, settling day's heat. Down two steps, hurrying under the canopy of a grapefruit tree and over manicured fescue to a wooden gate, and, in the alleyway behind the house, an idling white twelve-person van with ebony-tinted windows; everybody piling inside, the van moving forward even before the side door finishes sliding shut.

Jay, wedged again in the middle seat between Public and another marshal whose name he's already forgotten (Kelly?), cranes around to locate the little girl named Helen, sitting small in the backseat, holding hands with her mother. The girl's eyes are wide, her face expressionless.

"You ready for this?"

She says nothing. Eyes straight ahead. Jay looks to her mother, the woman named Ginger, who has brushed her hair and applied a skim of pale lipstick and who shakes her head ever so slightly, gaze steady, right into him, almost a challenge.

Jay nods. "Jay," he says, in case she's forgotten. "I'm Jay."

"Are you," the woman says drily, and it's not really a question.

Mental states of every kind,—sensations, feelings, ideas,— which were at one time present in consciousness and then have disappeared from it, have not with their disappearance absolutely ceased to exist. Although the inwardly-turned look may no longer be able to find them, nevertheless they have not been utterly destroyed and annulled, but in a certain manner they continue to exist, stored up, so to speak, in the memory. We cannot, of course, directly observe their present existence, but it is revealed by the effects which come to our knowledge with a certainty like that with which we infer the existence of the stars below the horizon.

—HERMANN EBBINGHAUS (1885)
Memory: A Contribution to Experimental Psychology

| 6 |

AND WHAT ABOUT ALL THOSE THINGS he would rather not have to remember?

The drunken stupors, the petty betrayals, the missteps, the blown layups, the bad sex, the wasted hours, days, weeks, the lies, the secrets, the shame and the regret.

Why wake the dead?

A cheap numbing percussive roar like ten thousand vuvuzelas cores the smear of blue that is a glassy sea, Pacific Ocean, traveling close and fast beneath the low-flying silver belly of the charter helicopter they boarded in San Pedro. Having never been in a helicopter, Jay is surprised that such an expensive piece of aircraft would make such a low-rent racket.

The eight-seater banks sharply and a scorched blunt of island slides into view through the cockpit window: fat, brown, treeless mountains taper off into the sea, and, behind it, no horizon, just a subtle shift in hues of gray where sea meets sky. Jay, wedged in a back cockpit corner seat, stares dully out the windshield at his future—earmuffed, hip-to-hip with the little girl, Helen, who sits low, cratered between Jay and her mother.

He feels nothing. He has no expectations. Skills he perfected at eight years old in a hurricane of grief have come back to temper the storm of his current dislocation. The life he had falls away from him, lived: lightly, indefatigably, a shedding of skin.

Can he wait them out? He has done it before.

Jay nudges Helen. "First time in a helicopter?"

The little girl looks right at him, as if startled. Her eyes are as deep as the water below them.

"Yes." Ginger answers for her. Helen's mom smells faintly of some fruity perfume, and, in the San Pedro charter office bathroom she put on some regrettably dark eye shadow that lends her a weird, suburban vampiress feel. She's younger than she wants to be. But older than Jay.

"For me, too," Jay says to Helen, then tries again: "So what do you think?"

"She's afraid of heights," Ginger says. Helen's hand grips Ginger's tightly, knuckles pink white from pressure.

"Same with me," Jay says, to Helen, and then he looks up at Ginger, trying to smile, wry, but not sure that he manages it: "Does your mom charge you a monthly fee for the answering service?"

Ginger's expression is neutral. "She doesn't talk."

Jay nods, backing off. "That's cool. Okay."

"No, she doesn't talk. To anyone. Not even me. She's . . ." Ginger loses her momentum. Looks out the side window, then back. Eyes overcast, momentarily vulnerable.

"Oh," Jay says.

They study each other for a moment longer, then Ginger looks out the window again, dismissing him. A crescent, box-canyon harbor, dimpled off-center on the fat southern end of the long, rocky, submerged peanut of terra-cotta island has revealed itself: trees and roads and docks and quays and white yachts and trawlers and sandy beach and seawall, and a mad clutter of geometric shapes: houses, apartments, hotels, crisscrossed by the grids of narrow, blacktop streets that make up the town of Avalon on the island of Santa Catalina.

It pinwheels below them, long cerulean shadows spilling out into the bay as the helicopter descends to the Pebbly Beach heliport and disgorges Jay and Ginger and the girl and his federal escort into chilly Catalina dusk. The sky is cloudless, gauzy with marine inversion and the westward drift of mainland smog. The harbor is empty, the town quiet save the slip-slap of moored boats and soft lap of surf on sand, some tourists on Segways, a leaf blower deep up-canyon, the seasonal shops shuttered.

Jay has been to this island before, with a couple of friends, just after college: a lovely, disheveled resort twenty-some miles from the mainland—California's Capri—bastard spawn of left-coast Deco, Arts and Crafts, and Mediterranean Revival. He sorts the splintered fragments of that long weekend on Descanso Beach, baked and broiling, suffering the fat black biting sand flies and hoovering beach bar piña coladas from plastic cups and staggering along Crescent Street and throwing up onto the tumble of bleached rock breakers off the Cabrillo Mole, near the desalination plant. Evan and Jessica. Later, they broke up, and both went to law schools back east. Two of what then he would have called his closest friends. Jay doesn't even know where they're living now.

There are even fewer people out on the backstreets, and none give a second glance when a caravan of golf carts shuttling the new arrivals hangs a right on Vieudelou Avenue and labors up a steep-sloping street lined with clapboard summer homes arranged like steps up the hillside, nosing in, finally, in front of a weathered-brown quasi-Craftsman bungalow: new butter-yellow shutters yawn for shaded windows, there's a porch swing, hummingbird feeder, and a SOLD sticker on the real-estate sign out front.

Inside it's small and neat. Fully furnished. Surprisingly welcoming.

"It's nice," Ginger says, flat. She looks at the little girl. "Isn't it?"

Jay watches Helen ignore her mother and beeline to some moving boxes on the floor, to open them, one after another, determined bordering on frantic, looking for something. A clutter quickly accumulating in her wake.

"We brought what clothes we could," Public says to Jay and Ginger, "did some shopping for essentials, basic food." His smile is efficient, and without warmth. "We all chipped in and got some toys and things for the little one."

He walks through to the dining room, bangs his briefcase down on the table, opens it, and empties the contents of a fat, long envelope, providing inventory:

"Credit cards, checking account, driver's licenses . . ."

Jay angles past him, into the kitchen. Tiny, warm. Old appliances; the stove smells faintly of gas.

". . . Helen is all signed up in the local grade school. It's probably a little smaller than she's used to, but . . ." He drones on: weekly stipend, cover jobs in town, act normal, basic rules and restrictions of witness protection, which will, he assures them, be a largely forgiving trial-and-error kind of thing until they get settled. "Just use your heads. Be smart . . ."

A double-hung window looks out across a narrow gap and straight into the kitchen of the adjacent house, where Jay can see a beefy man, his close-cropped, faux-hawk haircut sharked up with product, washing dishes or something. The man looks up and sees Jay and grins happily for some reason. Opens his window and motions for Jay to do the same:

"Jimmy! You made it! When'd you get in?"

Jay doesn't know this guy. And Jay is not Jimmy.

"When'd you get in?" the neighbor asks again.

Jay has a sinking feeling that this is part of his new fiction. "I'm Jay," Jay says. "I don't think we've met," he adds.

"What are you talking about? Barry Stone. We went to college together."

"No, we didn't."

"You went out with my sister. Lee."

"No."

"In New York. When you were working for Morgan Stanley."

Jay starts to close the window. It's as if he's walked onto the stage of a play already in progress. He doesn't know the players, he doesn't know his lines.

"Sandy'll be back in half an hour. We'll pop over. Make the official—"

Jay snaps the window shut, locked. Barry's mouth is still moving, slow to react.

The panicky presentiment that drove him into the air ducts overtakes him again. Jay backs away, numb, and returns to the dining room, calling to Public: "You know what? This is just creepy now. I mean, I understand why the island, I get the desire for isolation—but is it really necessary to have . . ." His voice trails off.

Ginger sits at the table, her head in her hands. Does not look up. Public and Doe are gone.

In the front room, Helen, tears streaming down her face, rummages through a box of decidedly masculine whatnot, and it dawns on Jay that this is *his* whatnot, from his dresser drawers and bathroom vanity: socks, briefs, toiletries, vitamins, electric shaver and other personal grooming items, a broken roll of quarters (for parking meters), an American flag pin, a tarnished roach clip (he'd forgotten he

owned), safety pins, loofah sponge (whose is that?), several condom
packets, and a watch he never wears.

"Hey. That's my stuff."

He says it automatically, and much more sharply than he intends.
Helen looks up at him and freezes; all the nightmare of disorientation
he's been experiencing since the old lady fumbled her groceries on the
Red Line is manifest in the little girl's face, and Jay grieves suddenly
not for his own lost freedom, but for hers. Ginger gets defiantly between Jay and her daughter, eyes flashing, like some feral animal
protecting her young. A gesture of surrender: Jay's hands are out,
open: he's sorry, he's really sorry, and understands something he
didn't before, something he can't articulate, so he looks away from
them, chastened, down to the table blankly and at all the credentials
that Public has left behind:

A credit card in the name of EDWARD JAMES WARNER.

A driver's license: Jay's awkward photograph, but the name beside
it is Edward James Warren, and the address is unfamiliar.

A second license with Ginger's photograph, and the name
GINGER WARNER.

A joint checking account.

A birth certificate for HELEN WARNER with both Edward
James's and Ginger's names on it.

More erasure. Jay's head jerks up, cold sweat. Walls closing in.
Cuts anxious eyes at Ginger, whose expression is unreadable, and
Helen, who hasn't moved.

He darts past them both, to the front door, throws it open and
goes lurching out across the porch.

"PUBLIC!"

Down the front steps, into the street, he can just make out the
parade of golf carts disappearing back around the corner at the

bottom of the hill, vanishing into the quaint clapboard backside of Avalon's business district.

He catches his breath.

Avalon Bay: a sheet of imperfect, handmade glass.

The sky: teal blue.

The sun: fully disappeared over the rocky island's western summit, casting its gentle twilight up into the narrow back reaches of the valley that cradles the town.

This really is happening. And yet, in a sense, what is happening isn't real.

"Jimmy?"

Jay turns to the voice of his neighbor. Barry Stone is a vague shape in the doorway of his house next door, framed by the beams of his short porch and shrouded by the darkness falling.

Splintered ghosts of Ginger and Helen watch, from behind the front window, overlaid by Jay's reflection as he comes back up onto his own porch. Seeing them, feeling the dull weight of neighbor Barry's vigil in the shadows, everything gone spectral, illusive, his ability to parse this world confounded by legerdemain, scrims and props, constructs and consensual lies—Jay thinks: *Oh, fuck.*

Cantonese opera, with all the face paint and swordplay and caterwauling, but without the happy ending.

Or any ending.

We're all making it up as we go along.

Helen clutches a pale stuffed animal Jay hasn't seen before, and was, no doubt, the subject of her dogged search through all the boxes.

Is Helen real?

Clearly Ginger is a construct, captive just like him; she troubles and intrigues him, and despite her physical similarities with the girl, Jay begins to wonder if Ginger and Helen are in fact even related.

Does it matter?

Barry barks something from his porch, with an earnest tone of concern. Jay doesn't know what it is, doesn't care. He pretends he didn't hear, and rolls his shoulders gently, testing the ache from his fall.

Night's curtain drops on Avalon.

End of scene. No applause.

Jay goes inside, where his new family waits for him in the warm embrace of artificial light.

| 7 |

"TWO O'CLOCK TOMORROW AFTERNOON, upstairs, Zane Grey Building, suite number 204. Dr. Magonis. Put the BE BACK AT sign in the window, the clock hands are broken, don't worry about it. Nobody really cares. You want me to write this down?"

No, he doesn't.

"Why tomorrow?"

"Take a day to settle in."

A tiny space crammed with archaic entertainment product.

Island Video.

This is Jay's new avocation: DVD impresario. An anachronistic business model left over from the last century. Public has carted him down here from the bungalow after Helen and Ginger left for school, and now the Fed loiters behind the glass display case that doubles as a counter, absently punching the old-fashioned cash register, watching the empty drawer roll out, and pushing it back in with his stomach.

There's a vintage landline wall telephone with a knotted, extra-long cord, but Jay holds little hope that it's any different from the one in the house, which he already tried, as soon as he woke up, and discovered will connect with other phones on Catalina, but not the mainland. Not the world.

"What's Ginger in for?" Jay appears from a narrow side aisle with a couple of old videocassettes in plastic protective box sleeves. "Or am *I* supposed to tell *you*?"

Public gives a pointedly delayed reaction. "Ha ha. That's witty." He shuts the drawer again with his gut. Sometimes Jay can sense something slightly off about Public; compared to the other marshals, less cop and more flimflam artist, making it up as he goes along, as if all this was just snake oil spilling off some crazy medicine wagon. But then he'll gather and settle, clipped and officious, Eliot Ness: "Um. No. Ginger—"

"Is that her real name?" Jay interrupts.

Public ignores him, continuing, "—sort of helped her boyfriend kill a guy. So."

The way the Fed says it, *kill a guy*, makes it sound like nothing. Like it was a household chore, folding some laundry. Jay stays between the high shelves crammed with alphabetized jewel cases, studying Public for any sign of sarcasm or fallaciousness, wondering whether he should believe this or not.

"But now she's flipped on him for immunity, it's all good."

All good. Jay wonders what it means to "help." In light of Public's dispassionate attitude toward killing. He's found he can't shake a picture of the silent little girl, Helen, fragile in her new school clothes, lunchbox and backpack, holding tightly on to Ginger's hand as they went down the hill, warped unexpectedly by a flaw in the glass pane of the bay window in the bungalow's front room, strange and beautiful, through which Jay, earlier this morning, watched them walk away from the house.

And now he has to add this noise—that Ginger helped kill

somebody—to the signal, and try to reassemble a clear picture from it. He can't.

"We're hiding her until we can find the boyfriend." Public continues talking. Deadpan: "He's understandably upset about it. And worried that she might help, you know, convict him."

Jay wants to know who they killed. Public just stares back at him, blankly. "You can tell me why she's here, but not why I'm here."

"Entirely different protocols," Public says. "We need you to remember. I imagine Ginger would like to forget."

Jay holds up the VHS cassettes. "People still rent these?"

Public shrugs. "People scarcely rent DVDs, do they?" Pops the cash drawer out, shuts it.

Jay asks about the store policy on movies, can he just take them home and watch whatever he wants or does he have to actually sign them out and debit some account?

Public shrugs again. "It's your place, Jimmy."

"Jay."

Public sighs.

"Jay," Jay says again.

The front door jingles and opens for a sun-browned, weather-beaten beach boy pushing forty: bleached hair, bowling shirt, flip-flops, and Oakleys. Jay thinks he saw him yesterday, on the back of a chubby old fishing scow moored along the main dock, sleeveless T-shirt and a crushed high-crown Padres cap, watching them caravan in to town from the heliport.

"French films *suck*." He slams two DVD jewel cases down on the counter. "And don't even talk to me about pan and scan or the subtitles which live and die at the bottom of the screen where you can't barely read 'em." Noticing: "Where's Gabe?"

"New owner," Public says, gesturing to the aisle.

Beach boy squints at Jay. "Hi. Sam Dunn."

Jay glances at Public, knows which name Public wants Jay to use with this customer, and can't bring himself to say it. "—Hi."

"What'd Gabe—?"

"Skate Park in Fresno," Public says. "Straight swap."

"Yowza. Really? Whoa." His mouth droops, dubious. "Really." Curious about Public: "Who are you?"

"I'm the facilitator." Public inclines his head toward Jay. "He's the new Gabe."

Sam looks from Jay to Public, back again. It all seems to track for him. "Okay. Good enough. Okay. Well. Welcome to the rock, man. I don't think I owe any late charges on these bastard children of frogs, so there you go. Nice to meet you."

"I'm here to serve."

"Where you living?"

"Vieudelou," Public tells the man.

Sweet, is Sam Dunn's opinion about that. "Some bitchin' little Arts and Crafts gems up that way, right?" Then, almost wistful: "Gabe was a big-time Roberto Rodriguez fan. *Grindhouse. Machete.*"

"*El Mariachi,*" Public says.

"Yeah, but the original one."

"Don't get me started."

Dunn's quick laugh is a foghorn. Jay wonders if this is all more Kabuki theater for his benefit. Maybe everyone in Avalon is working with Public, part of the program, a performance-art piece in which Jay is the organizing principle.

"Yo." Dunn points to the jewel cases he's left on the counter, slaps a big hand on Jay's shoulder as he hurries past, door jangling behind him.

"You didn't tell him your name," Public says, after a moment.

"What?"

"Your name."

"You mean, Jay?"

Public waits, unfazed.

"Jay," Jay says again.

Public shakes his head. "You're a willful man."

"Who chose 'Jimmy'?" Jay asks.

"James? I dunno," Public replies, stubborn. "Probably your mom. Is it a family name? And why don't you use the 'Edward,' I wonder?"

"My mom is dead. Mom, dad, sister, brother—"

"Stop." Testy: "I'm sorry. We've gone to a lot of trouble to create a safe situation for you here. And that includes using a name that no one can—"

"Who? Who's after me?" Jay snaps. "Maybe if I understood at least that part of it . . ."

Public looks away, out the front window, at the harbor.

"Unless you don't know who it is," Jay says.

Nothing from Public.

"That's part of it, isn't it? You don't even know who you're dealing with?" Maybe he's misread Public completely, mistaken uncertainty for calculation. Jay smiles; he can't help it. It's just possible that they're as lost as he is. "What do you know?"

Public shakes his head, again, sardonic. "No. You first."

A standoff.

The two men trade empty gazes.

Cotton-ball clouds race low across the crest of the rocky island mass only to dissipate over a whitecapped open sea. The mainland, Long Beach, San Pedro, is a smoggy mass, like mold on bread. A slatternly, once-modern, teal-and-ivory hydrofoil ferry idles at the concrete landing, waiting impatiently for the last few passengers to hurry aboard, then breaks free of its moorings, drifts sideways, engines rumbling, and slides away, into the bay dotted with sails and boats.

Jay watches the boat from the small, deserted plaza at the south end of Crescent Street, where in the summer portable kiosks offer island tours, snorkling, kayaks, bicycle rentals, and shave ice. An old man with a stand-up easel is painting watercolors of the casino on the point. A day-trip couple sits at a steel table under a faded, flapping awning, with takeaway coffee and colorful caps.

A silver-helmet tour group on Segways whirs past upright, its weary guide droning a Chamber of Commerce wiki: "When Spanish explorer Juan Rodríguez Cabrillo found shore here in 1542, indigenous people had been occupying the island for over eight thousand years; they called this place Pimu and called themselves the Pimuvit."

At the edge of the bay the bow of the hydrofoil lifts and it guns away, dull thunder, leaving a contrail wake.

"November twenty-fourth, 1602, on the eve of Saint Catherine's Day, the galleon of a second Spanish adventurer, Sebastián Vizcaíno, sighted the island and named it Santa Catalina in honor of the princess and martyred patron saint of knife sharpeners, hatmakers, apologists, and unmarried girls." And as the rolling tourists curl around a corner and disappear, "The Pimuvit were wiped out by syphilis gifted from the Spaniards, and were succeeded over the years by otter hunters, smugglers, prospectors, soldiers, film crews, adulterers, and William Wrigley Jr.'s Chicago Cubs for spring training . . ."

A salt-pitted pay phone still offers service near the entrance to the main marine dock, the Green Pleasure Pier; Jay lifts the receiver, punches in numbers, listens to a phone ring on the other end of the line, and an operator answers:

"What number are you calling?"

"It's a credit-card call to Los Angeles," Jay says. "Can I give you—?"

"I'm sorry, Mr. Warren," the operator says, "but you can't make that connection."

Jay toggles the cradle hook. Dials again, different number.

"I'm sorry, but this call cannot be completed as dialed."

Same operator, not even trying to disguise her voice. Jay racks the receiver hard. Thinks. The phone starts to ring. And ring. And ring. He backs away from the booth. Sea gulls circle and scree.

Crescent Street is empty. Faded flags snap and furl from shopfront eaves. An outboard motor pops, races, dies.

A security guard stands hands on hips, akimbo, outside the ticketing booth on the ferry landing, sleeves shoved up and smiling, eyes behind dark aviators aimed directly at Jay. It's Patterson, one of the federal denizens from Public's L.A. safe house.

He waves amiably at Jay.

Jay turns away.

There is an impressive selection of Catalina Island maps and trail guides at the tiny grocery store where Floria, the wizened Latina behind the counter, extends him—James Warren, of 333 Vieudelou Avenue, she knows he just moved onto the island with the *esposa melancólica* and the *niña reservada*—a kind of informal store credit when he realizes and tells her that he left Jimmy's wallet back at the house.

Because it isn't his.

"*No se preocupe de el,*" she tells him, friendly. "You can pay next time you come in."

He spreads the Franko's Guide Map he settled on across the flat of the seawall, and has to hold it with both hands to keep it from blowing away in the wind.

All the private charter boats are off-limits, according to Hondo,

the effervescent aspiring gigolo in the booking shack at the entrance
to the Green Pleasure Pier. Hondo has teardrop tattoos under his eye
that Jay has always assumed represented prison terms, but which
Hondo cheerfully explains can mean number of years you did, yes,
but also the number of people you whacked or the number of times
you got done up the ass. Depending. But, prison, yeah, and, yes, he's
"in the program," too, which is how he can say without qualification
that there is no fucking way Jay would ever get access to a boat, not to
mention they put a tracking device in their heads, did he know that?
Hondo indicates a spot just under his ear that looks like a skin tag or a
mole, and offers to palpate Jay's neck skin to prove that something's
there, but Jay says he'll take Hondo at his word, which Hondo much
appreciates. "The bitch of it is," Hondo says, his mood shifting, darkening, "you don't know, you're talking to some guy on the street, or in
the Parrot, is he legit? or is he a Fed? or is he just another poor jerkoff
like you and me? You don't know. And after a while, man, that gets to
you, I gotta say."

Now, a kayak, Hondo explains, you could steal, and will get Jay
away from Avalon, sure, but Hondo doubts even he can paddle back
to the mainland with the current and such, and Hondo's been bulking
up and taking supplements. And trying to find a hiding place in the
rocky grottoes on the southern tip of the island is pointless, given the
resources of the Feds.

Not to mention the secret GPS tracking device implant in our
heads, Jay points out.

"To a T, man," Hondo says gravely. "To a T."

Catalina is mostly uninhabited, and almost all of its permanent
population lives in Avalon, a jumble of small houses and two- and
three-story buildings with no cohesive architectural aesthetic. Nothing plumb, avenues coiling back on themselves, the perplexing street
grid of the city is a pauper's bowl of half-cooked spaghetti, a few stray

noodles snaking up the hillsides and away to the highlands, north and south, providing access to the unpopulated interior of the island and an "airport in the sky" midway to Two Harbors, where rugged iconoclasts share with Boy Scouts and church camps and a marine science compound on the narrow isthmus of lowland that divides a deep and narrow rocky windward dent on the Pacific, from the more gracefully curved, leeward bay facing the Catalina Strait; hence: two harbors. According to Franko, there is ferry service from the mainland direct to this northern, unincorporated part of the island, and it occurs to Jay that perhaps he could find a way back to the city simply by hiking there.

Of course, it subsequently occurs to him that this is so obvious as to be pointless in practice. Running to Two Harbors is the first contingency to which Public and the Feds would attend while securing the island, the first place they'd look when they found Jay had disappeared.

But he's convinced himself that this is what he should be thinking about, getting out.

His reasoning: the shock of the abduction gave way to panicked delusions of escape by air shaft, too soon and too hastily improvised. Then the helpless interlude fueled by Kafkaesque conundrums fostered by strange marshals and blindfolds and legal limbo, followed by dislocation, followed by fear, but here, now, settled, feet on the ground, the reasonable course of action is to find a way out.

After all, he got away once before, and it saved his life.

Saved his life. Or lost it—as Hondo would say, depending.

Fish smells bliss in the cold wind from the bay.

The water shimmers like foil, and the casino on the point provides bleak punctuation to the arc of seawall.

Dozens of full-color property listings are pasted on the Beacon Realty window on Metropole, blocking any view of Jay as he unplugs the Beacon Realty golf cart parked just off the sidewalk, backs away, and takes off in it.

If anyone asks, he's just borrowing it.

He humps southish, inland, past the summer rentals and small hotels, looking back over his shoulder to make sure nobody's following him, rising up into the canyon until a switchback takes him on Tremont, then Country Club, the steady complaint of the electric motor worrying him a little; the golf cart tops out at maybe 20 mph, so if anybody has seen him go and wants to catch him, it won't be hard.

It doesn't worry him, though. This is a reconnaissance.

The road zags and hairpins, and for a moment he thinks he's going to wind up where he started, but by stubbornly taking a left at every intersection, and aiming uphill, Jay finally breaks out of the jumble of hillside bungalows onto Old Stage Road, passes through a grove of disheveled eucalyptus, and crests a rise that spits him onto a plateau tangled with scrub oak, manzanita, and wildflowers; the empty windswept wilds of Catalina are sprawled before him, quaint Avalon tumbles down into the sea behind him. A furl of ashen fog breaks over the Pacific-side hills like floodwater, sending ghostly fingers down the arroyos, weird, because the sun above the marine inversion is so bright, the sky so blue. Jay takes his foot off the accelerator and the golf cart coasts. Serpentine blacktop transitions to asphalt slurry and disappears into the incoming fog, but Jay glides forward into it, sunlight refracted by the brume into blinding scattershot dreamstuff. Jay feels the cool glaze of moisture on his face and hands, his shirt goes damply limp, he loses all sense of direction. Visibility drops to maybe two feet, and he stays on the road only by extrapolating its direction from the edges he can see on either side of his cart.

It's a metaphor for his present situation and his state of mind: no-where, directionless, blind.

But for the moment he's free.

There was heavy fog the night Jay's family came apart. A heavy, lightless, mourning fog; he had to run through it, to get to the warm blush of the neighbor's house, on the higher ground; run through the black vertical insults of leafless cottonwood on the steeply sloping hillside, run barefoot on the frost-flattened grass and leaves, blind with fear and tears and horror.

The angry cold of that night was like a series of thick curtains pil-ing up as he ran through them. Swirling smoke from a fireplace up-wind. The crazy jack-o'-lantern windows of the Bruces' house. So much that he can't, won't, shouldn't, doesn't want to remember, as he runs, ran, eight years, two months, six days old, uphill, feet slipping on rotted leaves, running, ran, forward to the light, thinking then only about the light and the futureless safety it promised to a little boy with nothing left behind him but a void.

Jay jams on his brakes. The cart slides, drifts. A huge dark shape looms directly in front of him. And another. And another. Floating in with the fog. He can hear a heavy rasp of a kind of primordial breath-ing, smells the buffalo before they resolve from the mist, tragic eyes, grim muzzles, fur glistening with droplets of water that drip drip drip as they shuffle past him, snuffling and unimpressed. There are at least twenty shaggy black-brown creatures, maybe more beyond the white veil of the fog. He waits for them to pass, then realizes they're not passing, they've slowed, stopped, several bulls blocking his forward progress on the road.

The fog eases unexpectedly: blue sky, sun, Jay shades his eyes, looks back the way he came. Now Avalon is gone, carpeted by the gray-white cloud, but he can back through the motionless herd; switches the lever on the cart and it bleats an irritating meeeeeeeeeeeeeeeep that causes the buffalo to grunt and shift and he weaves reversing through them, tires slipping on the soft gravel that shoulder the road, finally finding traction on the blacktop where he's swallowed again by the mist.

Jay stops here to get his bearings. The wind picks up and the fog dissipates again for fifty yards in every direction and the bleary sun settles into the rimy southwestern sky and bleeds away, and the buffalo are gone.

Somewhere a prop plane engine whines as it hurries away from the island.

From his vantage point on this plateau, Jay can look east to the mainland, the curve of Long Beach and San Pedro and Portuguese Bend; Palos Verdes lumps darkish up out of the grayblue wind-chopped sea but melts into the grayblue blur of city that, save the sprinkling of early lights, melts into the grayblue eastern sky as if there are no borders between heaven and earth, now or then. Jay tries to remember what the city looks like when it's clear. He can't. He's not surprised by this.

More shrill beeping as he turns the cart around, slots the lever back to forward, and begins his retreat back into an Avalon now nested deep in the Pacific winter's four-o'clock shadow.

| 8 |

GINGER'S VOICE, SWEET, DISTANT, SINGS:

Pack up all my care and woe—
—here I go
singing low.
Bye, bye, blackbird.

Jay is stretched out on the lumpen tweed sofa, with a leopard-print Snuggie as a comforter; he stares into the darkness and listens:

Where somebody waits for me
sugar's sweet
so is she
bye, bye, blackbird.

She sings every night. The mental picture Jay has of Helen and Ginger in the high poster bed is borne of the glimpse he got into the bedroom as he shuffled down the hallway from the bathroom to his sofa: Helen clutching a well-worn, plush white stuffed mouse, curled small against the pillows, Ginger in an oversize blood-red Cal State Northridge T-shirt with socks still on her feet. Her face slick with tears.

No one here can love or understand me.

Her voice falters.

Oh what hard luck . . . stories . . .

She stops. The house is quiet for a while. Jay can hear his pulse in his ears, steady. Then, so softly her voice is a mere tracing on the darkness:

. . . light the light
I'll arrive . . . late tonight . . .

Helen must be asleep. Jay pictures Ginger, motionless, afraid that if she moves she might wake the girl up. Her gaze is like nothing he's ever seen in a woman, what he and Vaughn call quarterback eyes—in the zone: dead calm, scary focused, stripped of emotion despite the frequent unexplained spill of tears. Calculating and distant and confident and cold.

Is she crying now? Is she watching the up and down of her daughter's breathing? Does she ever worry it will stop?

What does she not want to remember?

The light cast into the hallway from the bedroom snaps off.

The hush of night. Crickets. Distant roll of the ocean surf on the stoney beach.

. . .

Then, a child's screaming.

He's dreaming. His sister.

Cara?

No.

The lamplight behind the sofa flicks on, and Jay, squinting painfully, wonders how long he's been asleep, or if he's been asleep at all. A child's screaming, not a dream. He stares stupidly at the luminous face of his watch, coiled on the coffee table. Little hand on the two. The screams are coming from the bedroom, staccato, hysterical. Jay gets up, his leg still asleep, and thumps down the hallway to the bedroom doorway, past which he can make out, in the ambient light from behind him, Helen, thrashing, screaming, still asleep but eyes wide open, mouth gaping, wild with a discarnate hysteria, and Ginger freaking out, trying to hold her and calm her with words:

"Babygirl, it's okay, what's wrong, I'm here, it's okay, shhh, okay, I'm here, come on, it's—"

Jay in the doorway, awkward, tentative, says something barely articulate that he means to be a question.

"Night terrors," Ginger says.

Helen struggles and kicks: "No no no no—"

Jay's head buzzes, anxious; he hasn't felt this useless in a long time.

"Can you—" Ginger asks, her arms struggling to contain all Helen's bad dreams, "can—"

"—What?"

"—hold her—just—while I—" Ginger looks up at him plaintively. Jay inadvertently takes a worried step back.

"You know, um, look, I'm not . . . really—"

Ginger barks. "I'm not asking you to fucking adopt her—"

"—kids aren't my—" Cara had nightmares.

"—I just need some goddamn help for five fucking seconds so I can get a cold washcloth and—"

Helen shouts, kicks Ginger hard in the face, breaks away from her mother and darts for the doorway. And Jay is in it. He has no choice but to catch her up in his arms, grabs her, awkwardly, pulls her against his chest and holds her and she screams and her legs flail and her tiny hands slap against his shoulders with a torpid, half-hearted fury, and he's never felt anything like it before, all that life in his arms.

"Okay," Jay says, astonished, worried, "I got her. Here. Here—"

But Ginger powers past, veers around him, out of the bedroom and into the bathroom directly across the hallway.

"I got her," Jay promises, although he's not completely sure.

"It's okay, honey, Helen"—Ginger calls back out at them, high-pitched, stressed, but as if sweetly—"it's okay, it's okay—"

Water running. Splashing in the basin. The rattle of a towel rack, the snap of fabric.

Helen screams.

Jay's starting to lose his grip on her. "Um—"

A soft pink random kicking heel finally catches Jay in the groin and sinks him with a dull moan. But he holds on to the delirious little girl. It's a test, he tells himself. He's not going to fail it. And then Ginger is back with a cold, dripping washcloth that she gently draws across both sides of Helen's face, and water runs down his arms, and he feels the static charge of Ginger next to him, impassioned, intense, and the little girl mumbles and squirms and winds down. Looming over them both, fragrant with perfume and soap, Ginger's bare skin is cool when it brushes his, her eyes all in shadow, her cheek fiery where Helen smacked her. She helps Jay find his feet, and guides him, still holding on tightly to the little girl, back to the bed, where he eases Helen down in the soft rat's nest of bedclothing and Ginger presses the washcloth to her forehead.

"It's a dream, Helen," she says softly. "Just a bad bad dream, baby-girl, it's okay," and then, like a mantra: "Mommy's here Mommy's here Mommy's here . . ."

Helen uncoils, limp. Still sleeping.

Ginger: ". . . shhhhhhhhhhh."

Jay steps off, retreats to the doorway, looks once back over his shoulder, and leaves them alone.

Ginger finds him in the kitchen, hunched over the tiny breakfast table, steam from an Herbalife promotional coffee mug swirling like tiny ghosts, and two tea bags leaking puddles onto the Formica.

"Thank you."

Jay looks up at her as if he's seeing her for the first time: bare legs, wrinkled T-shirt, the gentle, awkward slope of her breasts, the nasty swelling on her face and ragged-weary cast of those eyes. Her fingers twist together with a kind of contrition.

"Look. I'm sorry, I . . . You know. What I said," she adds.

Jay nods, noncommittal. "I made you some tea."

"Thanks."

But she doesn't come into the kitchen, and Jay doesn't make any move to hand her the other mug.

They allow the quiet that ensues. In the half a week they've been together, there's been a lot of quiet, they've rarely talked, and Helen's strange, fierce silence hasn't required any pretense of token conversation.

"She's not usually—"

Jay says it's okay and they lapse into a second silence. He thinks about what Public told him was her crime—*accessory to murder*—and tries to reconcile it with the woman he's been living with for the past three days. He's not afraid of her. Should he be?

"There are buffalo here."

Ginger nods. "From the movies. I read about it in a guidebook," she says, "or supposedly. They brought fourteen here for a film shoot, and, typical, never bothered to take them back. Too expensive. Beefalo, actually. Part cow. Once there were as many as six hundred, but—" She fusses with her hair, abruptly self-conscious. Evidently she's said way more than she intended, but wraps it up, anyway, subdued: "They had to put them on birth control."

"What is going on, Ginger? Can you tell me what's going on?"

"I don't know if I understand what you mean."

"All this," Jay says.

She's frowning. "Okay."

"This is weird. What we're doing."

"Witness program?"

"Yeah."

"Weird." Ginger hesitates, as if she suspects it's a trick question. "Yes it is." Careful: "But, seriously, what about the witness protection program is a surprise? You gotta sign about a million documents to get a new life."

"What if I don't want a new life?"

"Your old one was that good?"

This stops Jay short. He shakes his head, stares at the reflection of light in his tea mug. "I never thought it would be subject to comparison," Jay says. "It was what it was."

"Yeah, that was cheap. I'm sorry," Ginger says, sad suddenly, then offers, gently, "Thanks for helping me with Helen. You've got a knack with kids."

Jay looks up at her. "No, I don't."

Ginger nods. "Maybe not." She takes a moment to try and find another compliment, can't, so resorts to a hopeful: "But." Then a sadder: "Well."

"What was your old life like?" Jay asks her.

Ginger doesn't have to think about it. "Hard," she says quickly, and with an inflection that tells him she doesn't want to be asked a follow-up.

But Jay can't stop himself: "Public says you helped kill somebody." If it's outrage he wants to hear from her, he doesn't get it.

She looks incredibly sad, then her eyes flash something savage that she veils quickly, countering curtly with, "Public says your name is James," in a way that makes it clear she knows it's not.

Point taken.

A third lapse of silence. It swells, fills the house, overcomes them. "So." A soft exhale of breath and Ginger steps back from the doorway, slipping into darkness.

Jay calls after her, "I'm here by mistake."

No response.

Her footsteps, the rustling of blankets, the sigh of the mattress.

Jay gets up and turns out the light, but returns to the table and stays in the kitchen for quite a while longer, to finish his tea.

9

IT'S AN UNGAINLY, mid-sixties, skillion-roofed building. Tan and white.

Who was Zane Grey?

The entrance is propped open with a brick.

A cool, unlit hallway, redolent with discouragement.

A stairwell with a stack of small square windows framing post-card views of the Avalon hills.

After a long morning of tepid coffee from Big E's Café, no customers, and several failed attempts to access the Internet in any useful way on the Island Video desktop computer (he can browse, but he can't post; can't access his e-mail; can't find his Facebook page), Jay took his two-o'clock lunch as instructed, turned the BE BACK AT sign to face the street, killed the lights, and came through the translucent door into a muggy marine midday, locking up behind him.

The Zane Grey was at the dead end of a walkway street, no sign of its other occupants as he walked in, but he could hear faint strains of an opera, hissing low on cheap speakers somewhere on the first floor.

Upstairs is no different, a low, cottage-cheese ceiling and a series of closed doors along a zigzag corridor, at the end of which number 204 is ajar, wan daylight streaming through the gap between door and doorjamb, and angled across the thread-worn, piquant corridor carpet.

Jay enters the office, cagey. Given Public's track record so far, nothing would surprise Jay, but he's anxious anyway. Takes in the modest desk, bookshelves crammed with psychology and counseling textbooks, a few fuzzy toys spilling off the lowest shelf, two comfortable club chairs with a hook rug between them. Diplomas tastefully tucked in among generic seascape paintings.

"Sit. Get comfortable."

Jay whirls. A small, wide, round man with a bad hairpiece comes in from the hallway, leaning heavily on a walker, hands dripping wet, a lit cigarette dangling from his chapped red lips. Sheepish: "No towels in the toilet again." He straightens, shakes his big hands out, finally wipes them on his linen pants, regrips the walker and rolls through favoring one hip to settle heavily in the chair by the window. Backlit by this day's bright gray fog gloom, his face darkens, softens, features suddenly made wooly with shadows.

Smoke curls around him.

"I haven't witnessed anything," Jay says.

"Ho! Forget the pleasantries, right to the point. Good." The man shifts the cigarette from one hand to the other so he can adjust himself in the chair. "My name is Magonis. I'll be your headshrinker for the foreseeable future."

"Are you a doctor?"

Magonis says he is.

"Psychologist? Or a medical doctor?"

Magonis lets this go, because either it should be obvious that he is or he doesn't care that he isn't. And all of a sudden, emotions roil up from where Jay has held them in check, he's dizzy, his head pounds from caffeine and frustration, he worries that he might just explode.

"Mr. Warren—"

"—Johnson," Jay corrects him brusquely, letting his bridled thoughts spill out, "and can I just say that, for the record, changing my name, cutting my hair, without asking my permission, while it may be legal and everything, it doesn't much make me want to co-operate with you, or Public, or Jane Doe, or whoever. It's lame. It's actually stupid, because now I don't trust you—and you change my name—and you give me a fake family, and you think—what? That's going to make me feel more comfortable spilling my guts?"

Magonis just listens, and smokes.

"Did you do any background on me at all? I mean, Jesus Christ, this is some kind of crazy mistake, anybody who spent half a second on due diligence would realize I am not of any value to anyone, not even my fiancée, really, since I can't even commit to her," but now Jay's lost his way: "I'm tired, I'm confused, nobody will tell me what this is sup-posed to be about, just a lot of cryptic double-talk and knowing winks and fuck me sideways if you don't have the wrong guy."

Magonis nods, contemplative, eyes at half-mast. Jay catches his breath and wonders, irritated, if the shrink is falling asleep. And why the cigarette smoke doesn't smell.

"Sit down."

"I'll stand, thanks," Jay says.

Magonis leans, stretches to his desk, his fingers waggle, find, and remove a fat, worn old-fashioned day scheduler from atop a pregnant manila file folder and bring it back so Magonis can hold it up for Jay's inspection.

"I believe this . . ."—he Frisbees it crisply across the room to Jay, who manages to catch it before it hits him—". . . is your day planner."

"Yeah, okay."

"Very retro."

"Okay." *Where's this going?*

"We liberated it," Magonis says. "Because, you see, what we're gonna do, *James*, since you can't, or won't, or shouldn't, remember—"

For Jay, the response is almost automatic now: "—remember what?"

Magonis smiles crookedly, revealing tiled yellow teeth. "Hey, make sure that your name is in there." There's something weird going on with his eyes. Only one of them is looking at Jay.

Jay flips the cover. Front page dog-eared and scribbled with notes and odd phone numbers and the name JAMES WARREN printed in pen, as if by Jay, in Jay's handwriting.

Of course it is.

"It's yours?"

"This isn't my name."

"Well, neither is Jay, really, is it?"

He keeps forgetting that they may know more about him than he cares to ever admit. But this is word games, really, and Jay's more than willing to play. "Yeah. It is, yeah."

"But—"

"It's mine. Jay. I chose it." He wonders if that information is in one of Public's files.

Magonis balks. "Okay. But on your birth certificate."

"Which one?" Jay asks sharply.

Magonis nods, shakes his head, retreats into his professional avuncularity, and waits.

Jay recognizes the entries in the day planner, yes. Hurriedly scrawled in his cramped half-cursive, cryptic, incomplete, sometimes lacking even sense. Words and phrases that remind him of nothing, but, yes, his writing, his days, his journal.

With Jimmy Warren's name.

"I'm not ever going to be okay with this."

Magonis ignores him, pressing fat hands together. "So. What we're gonna do, James—James or Jimmy? Or do you prefer Jim?" He's enjoying this. "What we'll do is go through the last year or so of your life, day by day, but not necessarily chronologically, and just, well . . . talk about what you've written in there about certain days. What happened, what you *say* happened, what *really* happened . . . what you *remember* happening . . . because together we're going to try to color between the lines, if you will, fill in the missing details of each day of your lived life over the past three hundred and sixty-five days, or so, since what we have there, in your datebook, is, you have to admit, fairly sketchy."

Jay just stares at him. The cigarette, despite Magonis's hard work on it, has remained the same size because, Jay realizes, it's a smokeless, electric one.

"How come you don't use a computer calendar program?" Magonis muses aloud. "Or a phone app?"

"What if I can't remember details," Jay asks, instead of answering.

"Or don't want to?"

Jay doesn't feel the need to respond to this, either.

"Mmm. Sorry. Or. Or. Or. The variations are endless, this rumination can go on and on, Jim." The shrink shifts in his chair with discomfort. Crosses his legs at the ankles. "For example, what if you have lacunar amnesia and simply blocked the memories?"

"Oh, snap," Jay says, momentarily abandoning himself to pure snark. He can't help it. "I dunno. Gee. Maybe you can coax 'em out? Hypnotize me?"

"Down, boy. This isn't a test," Magonis responds, subdued, but with just the slightest edge. "There are no right or wrong answers."

"Evidently, there are. Or I wouldn't be here."

The hairpiece has slipped slightly. Rakish and silly, Jay thinks. Magonis's left eye is lively and penetrating, the right eye fixed defiantly over Jay's shoulder. "I want to help you. Can we call a truce and—"

"—I want you to call me by my name," Jay says.

"What?"

"Jay. That's my name, Jay Johnson, and I'm asking, please, that in here we use my name, okay? Because that's who I am."

He Frisbees the day planner back fluttering at Magonis, who makes no attempt to catch it, so it just misses the older man's head and slaps against the high back of the armchair, dropping straight down behind him, where he struggles to twist and reach and get it out from between the cushions.

"And if your own name may put you at risk?" Magonis asks.

"I'll take that chance. It's mine. I don't want another one."

"Fair enough," Magonis says, as if he really understands. He balances the cigarette on the arm of the chair, twists the other way, and finally retrieves the day planner. "Fine. Okay. Jay, then. Jay. Please. Have a seat." Smiles sadly, and means it.

"No."

". . . Or not." Magonis takes up the cigarette. The LED at the end glows blue when he sucks on it. Maybe it's running out of batteries. Coils of vapor skew sideways. He splits the planner open to FEBRUARY 12. His face angles up; right eye dead-aimed at Jay while the left one studies Jay's scrawled entry.

"Let's start . . . here—"

He thumbs Jay's familiar chicken-scratch and haplessly abbreviated notations: a couple of phone numbers, a halfhearted stab at sketching a popular comic strip character, and a lopsided Valentine's heart that's been distractedly shaded in.

And Jay thinks: *Of all days, this day.*

"On the morning of February twelfth, you went to a flower shop on Melrose to order a dozen roses for—"

And Jay remembers:

Long, lissome fingers, black pearlescent fingernails, filling out a delivery order form with the name:

"—S-T-A-C-Y." *Jay spelled it out.* "Stacy."

The flower salesgirl, probably about nineteen, a kind of proto-goth mascara, low-cut black T-shirt spilling swells of pale blue-veined décolletage but half hiding the curving red-and-black tattoo of a snake; her black-set liquid amber eyes tilted up, tentatively, flirting. Or nearsighted. "Girlfriend?"

Busted. "—Um, what? Oh, no, she's, uh—"

Magonis looks from the day planner to Jay. His eyes cast with unsettling indifference. "Your girlfriend was away?"

"Fiancée. On business, yeah," Jay says, his face burning. He sits down in the chair facing Magonis.

"Fiancée. Stacy."

"Yeah."

Jay smiled at the salesgirl. Casual: "—She's my sister. Yeah. Stacy. She, um, just broke up with her boyfriend and I . . . wanted to, you know."

Flower salesgirl (genuine): "For your sister. Ohmygod, that is so sweet."

Magonis touches his toupee lightly, checking its position, and, apparently satisfied, reads the rest of the February 12 page, quiet. Jay waits. "The phone numbers here," Magonis muses. "Cold calls, we checked them. This doodle? Dilbert?"

"Yeah."

Magonis flips the page over, glances at the blank backside, then returns to the scribbles Jay made on the day, then up at Jay again. Eyes hooded, off-kilter, unnerving.

"I don't keep a very . . . my notes, they're, you know, to myself, so they're not exactly . . ." Then Jay decides to go on the offensive. "Look, I'm sorry, but I don't see what comes of going into this kind of detail for a day where obviously nothing of interest to you or your federal employer remotely occurred."

Magonis extrapolates the obvious fact. "You went out with her. This girl at the flower shop."

"What?"

Magonis repeats himself: the flower girl: Jay saw her, met her, hit on her, lied about being engaged, went out with her on the night of the 12th. Statement as question.

Jay throws an embarrassed smile, "Jesus, did I write all that in there?"

"No," Magonis says.

They both permit a discomfiting pause to swell.

Evasive, Jay: "You know, um, I don't really remember what happened, I . . ."

"You met her after work," Magonis says, "you had a drink, you went to her place, and—"

Jay says, "I don't see where this is . . ."

"—you fucked her."

Water.

In liquid shadow two clothed bodies churned in a claw-foot bathtub, the hot water cascading over the sides onto dogtooth tiles, Jay and this flower girl, wet, carnal, gasping, kissing, devouring each other—

"—Hold on—that's harsh—and I didn't—"

"Engaged in sexual relations. Made love. Hooked up. Or at least," Magonis continues, "that's what you told Larry Wilson, in your office."

Larry Wilson, booth-tanned, bullet head shaved clean and a vandyke that squirreled away crumbs, would daily rise up over the wall of Jay's cubicle with two pencils jammed up his nostrils and sing Justin Bieber songs.

"Listen, man, let me just explain something: Larry is not a reliable source for any—"

Magonis cuts him off again: "You seemed to like telling the flower girl story, though, Jay, you told it to, well, everybody.

"Although"—flipping through notes—"you told your friend Vaughn"—and Jay pictures Vaughn, Manchurian Global lab in chaos, as he struggles to secure whisker-thin electrode wires to tiny probes surgically screwed into the skull of an unhappy mouse as Jay regales him with some shaggy-dog saga of sexual shenanigans—"a slightly more graphic version in which the aforementioned Flower Girl moonlighted as an Exotic Underwater Dancer and you engaged in—"

Here Jay closes his eyes hard to conjure:

A Technicolor strip club where his flower girl floated weightless in a huge bottom-lit martini glass; grinding, wearing a blacklight-neon G-string and a shimmery, diaphanous latex flipper tail, pressing albino breasts flat against the glass of the tank. Jay, ringside, stared up at her, mouth open in an awestruck O.

"Jesus." Hands together, leaning forward toward Magonis, Jay asks, "What're you guys, the Inquisition? I mean . . . this is unbelievable. This is my private life."

Or are they just stories?

Magonis nods, not listening, "But, full disclosure here, we found no evidence of anal penetration, so I have to assume your recounting of the event for your friend allowed for a gentlemanly degree of exaggeration, if it's true at all." Then he frowns. "Is there really a bar where young women strip underwater?"

Jay, completely confused, but intimidated, and embarrassed, and angry, stands up. "You know what? That's enough. We're done." He licks dry lips and won't look at Magonis, who quietly closes the day planner. No expression.

"We can be," Magonis says. "Done for today, if you'll just confirm: that your girlfriend—sorry, fiancée—Stacy was away on business, that you asked this flower girl out on a date, and that you went home with her—or went somewhere, it would be really useful if you could remember that, but oh well—and then that you, the two of you, you and the flower girl, had sexual relations. Yes, no?"

"She asked *me* out," Jay says finally, as if that distinction makes all the difference.

Another long silence.

"I'm not here to judge you," Magonis says.

"Can you just tell me," Jay protests, irritably, "what the hell does this have to do with—?"

Magonis talks over him. "We don't know. We don't know. But." He hesitates. "What would you say if I told you the flower girl was murdered early that next morning."

Jay's not sure he heard this right.

Reaching on the desk, Magonis finds and flips an envelope at a dumbstruck Jay.

"Maybe executed. Could have been a professional job. Raising, I don't know, all kinds of questions. As you can imagine."

Jay stares at the older man. There is that uncomfortable stillness that follows truth and recognition, the men measuring each other, one for signs of deception, the other for the tells of intention. Slowly, Jay opens the envelope and pulls out the collection of crime photos he was shown at the hospital among Public's papers: unforgiving forensic pictures of a lurid murder scene: the flower girl floats chalk white in a bathtub of pink water, topless, breasts slack, hair in her eyes, slurred black mascara and filmy underwear, legs colt awkward, arms flung out, shot twice through her chest.

"I think you told the marshals you didn't know the woman in this photograph."

Jay's thoughts clot, thick. "I didn't . . . I didn't make the connection—"

"—Or you lied."

"What?"

"Lied. Made an intentionally false statement."

"Why would I do that?"

"I can't answer for you."

Truly shaken: "What are you saying?"

"I'm saying whatever comes into my mind, Jay. Speculation. But then. I wasn't there."

Jay blinks.

"Done? No." Magonis sucks his electric cigarette and shakes his head. "We've barely scratched the surface."

He's right.

And yes, Jay remembers the flower shop, corner of Melrose and Crescent Heights, cramped, dark, even in midday, fragrant, the special on a dozen roses from the refrigerated glass case, the pools of ceiling pin lights, the exotic tropicals, the potted palms.

He remembers the salesgirl writing, she was left-handed and had that weird lobster-claw way of holding the fountain pen to keep her hand out of the ink. Her letters were looped and forward-leaning.

"I have this second job," she told him. "I work nights. But." She looked up. "We close at two . . ."

She handed him a slip of paper with the address of a Glendale strip club where bright light strobed across Jay as he came in, pushing past the thick-waisted underage frat boys clotted around the bouncer at the door trying to convince him they were twenty-one.

When they had adjusted to the darkness, Jay's eyes lasered to the luminous cylindrical water tank that dominated the middle of the club, glowing like a lava lamp, a naked mermaid curling, languid, swirling bubbles like free electrons and slowly stripping inside.

Not the flower girl.

No, Jay found his flower girl behind the bar in a tight black strip-club T-shirt, pouring drinks; she smiled when she saw him.

He remembers how, later, he and the girl spilled out, drunk, laughing, into an empty parking lot, pale colored lights of the bar slowly flickering and dying as the place closed down and Jay swung her up into his arms and ran with her, legs aching, across the empty street, to the entrance of an apartment building where the lobby was tile and carved moldings and Deco teardrop hanging lights and an elevator cage waiting, the rattle of its gate, the hand-lever control that rotated and the cables hummed and the car rose and ribbons of darkness looped across awkward groping, and the girl had her blouse open, some kind of lacy black bra, the red snake tattoo—and her fingers curled through the latticework of the rising car—

And now this unremarkable Zane Grey Building, office number 204, in which Jay looks at his hands. Magonis waits, his right eye wandering, aimless, as if losing interest.

"Look, it's not what you think. I didn't, we . . . nothing happened. Okay? It was one time, I told a lot of stories, they were bullshit. No sex, we just . . ."

—They stopped, he remembers, outside apartment 3H. Didn't they? Didn't he lean back against the wall, drunk, blissful, the hallway and the whole world coruscating, and didn't she smell faintly of jasmine, Maker's Mark and vermouth, and didn't he let the girl mold herself against him, warm and fecund; didn't Jay brush tears from mascara-streaked eyes as she angled her head and kissed his hand, his neck, his—

"—I didn't know her name. I never asked," Jay admits, senseless.

Magonis quietly closes the planner. Switches his bogus cigarette off. No expression on his face except for those crazy eyes.

| 10 |

Or was the kiss just a brush of lips, chaste, regretful?

Or did she fumble for her keys? Sly-sliding wistfully out from the cage of his arms along the textured wall to the deadbolt, and then opened it, she slipped inside, click of a wall switch, light spilling out as she glanced one last time back at Jay as he turned to go. Dark figures swarmed her as the door closed—he never saw them—shadows and shapes, her swift startled intake of breath, the scuffling feet on the hardwood floor.

Or was everything under water?

Harsh overhead light of the bathroom, tub filled with pink, her wide, frightened eyes as she toppled backward toward the roiling surface, filling, and a gun, aimed at her chest, finger thick on the trigger—

—and the elevator's byzantine prison.

Ascending out of darkness, breaking the surface of water—blades of light cutting Jay into pieces with moving lattice shadows. He gasps for air. Then finds darkness again, above, as the elevator rises rises rises and everything goes black.

He woke confused.

Came awake in a car not his, empty downtown parking lot, framed in *the fork of two elevated freeways gridlocked with morning traffic. Leaden roar of the essentially motionless cars. Shimmer of heat waves, light glinting off glass and chrome, dawn crawling over east L.A., the sun an insult, the air heavy with the brown sick—*

"She wants you to help her with some clouds."

Surfacing from a fitful nap to the inverted face of Helen: feline enhancements resulting from face-painting at an after-school birthday party.

This upside-down cat Helen peers quizzically at Jay sprawled on his sofa, stirring fully clothed and clammy from angry, troubling daydreams.

"She what?"

"Clouds," Ginger says, unseen, calling out to him from the dining room: "For a school play."

Jay sits up, groggy. Helen just stares at him like Magonis does, but both her eyes work fine. It's like she can see right into him. Not through him; *into* him.

"They're doing a musical," Ginger elaborates.

"With first-graders?"

"And Helen is making props." Squeak of wooden chair in the dining room. Ginger's ignoring his question.

Jay shakes the cobwebs out of his head. Not convinced this isn't more dreaming. "What musical?"

"The Pied Piper."

"Guy with the rats."

"Roughly," Ginger says. She's come to the archway to check on Jay and her daughter, who hasn't moved.

"I didn't know there was a musical."

"There is now."

"Look," Jay begins, "no offense, but I'm not really familiar with—"

Ginger explains that one of the teachers wrote it. Book and lyrics. Jay wants to make a snarky observation about grade-school teachers and musical theater, but doesn't even know where to start. Ginger wonders if "ambitious" is the word he was looking for?

"Well—or fucking impossibly *grim*, excuse my French."

"It's German, actually. Sixteenth century. And there's a suitably happy ending in this telling."

She surprises him with this comment. Slowly, their more sustained conversations since Helen's night terrors have been filled with similar surprises. A passion for Korean barbecue. A superstition involving frogs. Jay has grown so accustomed to Stacy's easy two-dimensionality, Ginger's raveled, mercurial presence is alternately scary and exhilarating. Sometimes both.

The sum of this—Ginger—the puzzle of Helen's willful silence, the craziness of his ongoing internment, and the stress of his sessions with Magonis, is that he has never felt so alive.

Again, Jay starts to say something, but Ginger's eyes tell him to shut up, shifting discreetly to Helen and back. Apparently, in another life, she explains, in language she hopes Helen can't follow, the author had Broadway ambitions. But some combination of crystal meth, bad boyfriend, forced prostitution, and involuntary manslaughter has resulted in her being available here on Catalina to share her talents with the children.

Jay, translating: "She's in the program."

Ginger reminds him that they're not allowed to ask.

"How many people on this island do you think are—"

Ginger cuts him off, repeating that they're not allowed to ask. "What difference does it make?" she adds. Then shifts gears, upbeat, "Parents are encouraged to get involved."

Jay decides that it's not worth taking the position that this invitation to parents does not, technically, apply to him. It's ungenerous and, in truth, he's interested. "I don't remember clouds in the *Pied Piper of Hamelin*," he says instead.

"Are you kidding?" Ginger smiles slightly. "Clouds are everywhere," she says. "You'll see."

Clouds.

Clouds, barely moving, in a ghostly blue sky.

Wickedly hungover, Jay leaned toward the windshield, looked out and up, between the curling fat ribbons of elevated concrete freeway, squinting against the gauzy glare of light—

"What?"

"I said the play's a virtual cloud convention," Ginger says. "You're not listening to me."

"No, I am. It's just . . . with Magonis, he gets me in these memory spirals, and . . ."

Clouds.

". . . there was this girl."

Ginger: "There's always a girl."

Jay shakes his head. "I thought I had dreamed her."

Ribbons of darkness looped across awkward groping, the girl had her blouse open, red snake, lacy black bra—Jay's lips skated across the sweep of her shoulder, her fingers curled through the latticework of the rising elevator cage and the girl's eyes fluttered and her breath sweet, hot, thick with Kentucky bourbon.

"Tell me." Her voice is too soft, all the edges rounded off. He doesn't trust it.

"I mean, I really can't be sure if she was . . . I might have been dreaming. It's all a mash-up."

"Of what?"

Of Jay, in the car, empty parking lot, hungover, dead yellow sun spliced through the dirty windshield making his eyes hurt, wondering where the hell he was.

He says, "And then I . . . you know—"

Jay and Ginger, staring at each other. Aware that Helen's eyes are on them from where she's playing on the floor.

"—woke up," Jay says.

Jay leaned toward the windshield. Looked out. Up. Squinting against the glare of the light at the—

"And then what?"

—Clouds.

Jay smiles at her, sheepish. "Clouds," he says. "Everywhere."

Raindrops on noses
and whispers on kittens . . .

"Isn't it whiskers? *Whiskers.*"

So here is Jay in the Catalina Elementary School cafeteria, carving a huge fluffy cloud from corrugated cardboard, while Helen, close enough to be his shadow, uses pale blue paint to outline a cut cloud she's already slathered with white.

One of her classmates is crooning her audition piece, high, slightly flat:

. . . Pink salmon cabbages melt into string
these are two-oo of my FA-VOR-IT thingz!

Night, it's cold, a stiff sea wind rattles the windows. In the far corner, near a freshly built plywood platform stage, boys and mostly girls audition nervously for a couple of sleepy teachers. A chunky woman with hair splayed by a scrunchie plays accompaniment on an upright piano, eyes closed, mouthing the proper lyrics. Three brawny dads with power tools study the new stage and murmur gravely.

Verse mangling continues unabated, as Jay, all casual, makes conversation with his pretend daughter, the selective mute:

"How come you aren't trying out for a part in the play?"

Helen just paints.

Jay is determined that he will hold conversation with her whether she responds or not; in his admittedly limited experience, kids don't say much that's interesting, anyway, and this one, with her sharp looks and droll expressions, seems like she's carrying on one long continuous monologue—or tuneless aria—for her own entertainment, without the complication of words. Jay wants in on that.

"Is it the talking thing?" Jay asks her.

Helen looks up at him deadpan.

Against the far wall, a couple of Spanish-speaking women and Ginger, on ladders, are trying to hang a curtain from a cable on one end of the room, for the temporary stage. It sags, big-time. Ginger keeps glancing over at Jay and Helen with a look that tells Jay she still doesn't completely trust him with her daughter.

"Because, don't get me wrong," Jay continues, "I like a good musical as much as the next fool—well, maybe not—but—I think you could get up there and be, like, really really quiet and not say anything, and that could be, you know, pretty effective. Which is to say good. Dramatically. With the piano and everything."

Helen stares at him.

"I carve a lousy cloud. I know. I know."

She goes back to her painting.

"Helen is a pretty serious name."

No reaction.

"You go by anything else? Shorter?"

No.

"I guess there's not really a diminutive for Helen." Jay finds himself struggling not to fall into the empty patter of the phone jockey: "But I'm just saying. Helen could be very heavy baggage. Woman that brought down an entire civilization, launched a thousand ships, et cetera, et cetera. Troy? With the guys hiding in the horse? And noble Hector and the other guy, the creep, I forget his name. Maybe you heard about it. I think Disney made a movie." He waits again; again, no reaction. "Although, I wikied it on my computer at work, and some Greeks say the whole thing never happened, all a ruse. I guess there's a lot of variations on the story. But here's the thing: in one, Zeus has Hermes fashion Helen out of—guess what— yeah, clouds."

Nothing from Helen.

Jay props his improbable, chop-blocky cumulus against his leg. "Or not. Okay, look. Helen. See, for me? It doesn't matter if you talk, there's all kinds of ways to communicate. Plus," he drops his voice low, as if sharing a secret, "I actually get where you're coming from. Half the time nobody listens to what you're saying, anyway, it's just noise to them, just something they gotta tolerate until they can speak again, so I'm saying it's like, you know: what's the point?

"Amiright?"

Helen bends close to her cloud, so close, like someone incredibly nearsighted, meticulously brushing her blue highlights, affecting total concentration, pretending she's ignoring him.

Simple chords bang from the piano. Jay's heard this one before. Another hopeful audition begins to murder the lyrics of a beloved Broadway warhorse:

Somebody will shout, tomorrow
I will betcha a dollar . . .

"I mean," Jay is saying, "talking is words, and words are . . ."

. . .

March third," Magonis says, the datebook falling open to another apparently random calendar page; squares of sunlight, the smell of warm leather, crackle of Jay's planner with its helter-skelter scrawlings, as if someone (not even Jay) wrote in it while on a roller coaster.

March third.

He can't take his eyes off the bad hairpiece. He expects at any moment for it to leap out into the room like a scruffy flat rodent. But at least it distracts him from Magonis's wandering eye. Is it taped on? Glued? What unfortunate individual sacrificed the hair for it, and how much were they paid?

"Are you married?" Jay has asked him before, in elusion. What kind of wife would allow him that rug?

"Love is a complex neurobiological phenomenon," Magonis had replied, thoughtful. "Dopamine, vasopressin, oxytocin, serotonergic signaling, not to mention endorphins and all these weird endogenous morphinergic mechanisms." He shook his head. "There are benefits to the romantic love concept, mostly sex and reproduction. But psychologically? It's a toxic stew." In short, "No. Like nature, I abhor the vacuum."

Jay has no idea what happened on March third.

And he's still upset by what he saw before he came for this appointment.

Jay spent the morning sitting behind the counter at the video store watching *Savage Messiah* and Googling information about Catalina Island and Avalon and tidal reports and how long it would take to swim to the mainland, but discovered he still cannot log in or access any social networks, or Skype, or post anything or shout out into the worldwide void; his ability to upload is, like his physical egress from the island, somehow globally blocked, wherever he logs on.

Nobody ever comes in.

Two women hurried past on the sidewalk around eleven, hair jacked by the sea wind, one of them waved in at him and smiled, and Jay thought he recognized her as part of the U.S. Marshal team at the Santa Monica safe house, but Jay sees U.S. Marshals in pretty much everybody now.

He locked up early and went for bad coffee at Big E's, never making it there because as he rounded the corner he saw a cluster of boats on the horizon line, one of them with a flashing light on it like a police patrol car. Standing on the seawall, he watched them come in to the pier: two civilian fishing skiffs and a big old trawler, trailing behind a sleek harbor patrol boat that tied up on the pier near the harbormaster's office; there was a man lying in back who they lifted carefully and handed to dockworkers, and that was when Jay realized that the man was Hondo, the boat-rental guy, and he was dead.

A shattered fiberglass kayak followed the body from the back of the patrol boat to the pier. It looked like someone had crushed the side of the kayak with a sledgehammer or a baseball bat, and it continued leaking enough seawater that they had to lift Hondo again and move him out of the spill.

A compact ambulance rumbled out of Avalon from the fire station, no siren. The EMTs took over and the fishermen and patrol officers stood around for a while, arms folded, saying little, until finally the fishermen separated and came walking down the pier and Jay could overhear them talking about it as they passed him:

—*I wonder what coulda done that to the kayak.*

—*Rock. Or rocks.*

—Before or after he got shot in the head?

—Coulda been he hit his head on the rocks. Caught a swell and it dropped him right on 'em. There's all kinds of worrisome shit below the surface of the San Pedro channel you don't want to think about.

—Looked like a gunshot wound.

—As if you could fucking tell.

—I'm just saying.

—You watch too much CSI.

—Okay. Okay. But you saying he couldn't tread water? Wearing a life vest?

—Maybe it knocked him out. Hell, maybe it broke his ribs, turned him upside down. The point is, we don't know.

—The fuck was he doing way out there?

Paddling for the mainland, was Jay's thought.

—Drowning.

He recognized Island Video's favorite Francophile customer Sam Dunn walking with them, but Dunn's eyes were down, and he didn't look up, and when they went into Big E's their conversation went with them.

Jay gave up on his bad coffee; he was late for the Zane Grey, Magonis, room 204. Arriving, he asked about Hondo, but the federal shrink didn't know anything about it, and added, somewhat tetchy, that he was on the island only for Jay.

And, presently, whatever it was that happened on March third.

"PCW?" Magonis reading, head tilted slightly, Jay assumes, to favor his useful eye: "That's all you wrote here. You wrote: 'PCW.'" Magonis looks up. "What is that?"

PCW. Paper Clip Wars.

Insurgent response to the tedium of phone sales.

SuperSmash Melée in the bullpen, moving low and fast through the milky white maze mouselike to pop up over the half-wall and poise, rubber

band stretched back slingshot between his fingers and thwak lets fly with a
silvery paper clip that just misses coworker Larry, who dives away, war
sweeping through the office, six, seven players, light jittering off bent-wire
projectiles that spin glinting and ricochet off walls and windows, shoulders,
backs, and asses, bodies jerking to momentary safety, twisting, stumbling,
falling in passageways, and laughing.

    Phones ring unanswered, lines light up, flashing, data streams across
LCD screens, noncombatants cowering low at their desks with their head-
phones and monitors and keyboards uprooted.

    Jay shakes his head. Somehow he doesn't want to give the shrink
the satisfaction of admitting he was part of such a pointless diversion.
Doesn't want to acknowledge that he spent hours calculating a full
range of arcane statistics: win/loss, yield, ordnance economy, weapon
accuracy, overall efficiency, splits, rankings, vulnerability to low, middle, high attack, kill ratios, value added, fail rates and speed charts.

    "It's just, it was, I don't know, business as usual. Sell sell sell," Jay
says. It's not enough, Magonis keeps waiting for the answer, and Jay,
vamping: "So, I mean, PCW, it—PCW stands for partial . . . so, it's
like an acronym: partial collection, um, of . . ."

    "Not so important," Magonis says.

    ". . . warranties. Warrants."

    Until somebody—was it Larry? or Timmerman?—took a paper clip
right in the eye and folded over, hands to his face, screaming Ow SHIT
jesusshitow ow ow and blood spritzing through his fingers and Buddy
DeLuca had to be told, which led to a private conference and reprimands and
penalties and overtime and Larry or Timmerman came back with a shit-
eating grin and thick gauze over one eye and no permanent damage and,
supposedly, a prospective date with a smoking-hot ER nurse, but it was game
over, End of War.

    ". . . part of this kind of insurance program we had," Jay is saying
with all sincerity. "For sharing net losses."

He can't tell if Magonis believes this or not.

March third.

Hondo was still alive then, somewhere. Of that much Jay is certain.

Cliffside on Chimes Tower Road, high above a sun-stung winter Avalon, after school, the Beacon Realty golf cart that no one seems to notice Jay borrowing for another joyride struggles upslope, Helen on the seat beside him, hands folded nicely in her lap, back straight.

"We can't work in a vacuum," Jay tells her. "We've gotta do some cloud research. Like, immerse ourselves in cloudiness. Just go completely cloud."

Not even a smile from Helen. It's after school, they should be making more props for the *Pied Piper*, but over breakfast Ginger announced she wouldn't be there and wondered if Jay could bring Helen home, getting him to promise he wouldn't forget, so Jay figures he's got a Get Out of Jail Free card for at least a couple of hours, until they're due home for supper. And while it's not something that he'd admit willingly, taking her on this excursion is something he's been looking forward to all day.

"Because your mom is right," he says. "Basically, this whole play makes or breaks based on its clouds. Lotta people think it's just rats and kids and a guy in lederhosen playing a flute, with some very, very timid plague allusions." He shakes his head. "But once you get past the singing and dancing"—he makes a vague gesture here, both hands leaving the wheel of the cart, and it veers momentarily toward the edge of the road—"there's nothing but air and water. And vapor is our middle name, baby." Jay grabs the wheel, they curve away from trouble and cruise up onto the rolling, empty expanses of the high plateau. Narrow, dark creased coulees stubbled with mountain ma-hogany and scrub oak and mission manzanita zag like scars down to rocky, surf-sprayed escarpments, the whitecapped ocean stretches magnificently to mainland Los Angeles shrouded, as always, in its aetherlike womb of air pollution.

"Can't have your happy ending if the sun doesn't break through the, you know."

No fog today.

Just clouds, white, cartoon, scattered like cotton Morse code from horizon to horizon, a dotted ceiling that floats, 3-D, beneath the canopy of pale blue sky.

Helen's heels kick the bench in a distracted rhythm. One-two, one-two. Fretful or bored. Hondo's body was gone from the Green Pleasure Pier by the time Jay left Magonis. The shattered kayak was propped up against the shuttered kiosk where the ex-con had worked. What happens when someone who's been erased dies? Does anyone notice? Can a made-up life matter?

Jay clips through the low brush and bristle grass, the hard-packed dirt road dipping and rising as Helen clutches the seat rail and leans out from under the canopy to stare up at the clouds, mesmerized, mouth agape, eyes slitted, the wind in her hair until Jay swerves and bumps and jerks to a halt just off the sloping shoulder, in a riotous field of knee-high wildflowers spanning a table of land that sweeps west to a rocky escarpment on the Pacific side of the island.

"Coupla measly cardboard cumulus ain't gonna make it," he tells Helen, and jacks the brake with his foot. "Not for us."

She hops out of the cart and shrugs off her backpack and runs into the tall flowers, arms angled high, her eyes raised to the blissed-out heavens above her.

Julie Andrews, Jay thinks, and slides off the bench seat into the sunlight. That was a good musical.

He looks northeast. Another couple miles distant, rising above the island's angled steppe, a small airfield where mainland charter and commuter planes can land offers a single dusty scar of a runway made feasible by beheading two peaks and using the resulting rock, clay, and debris to flat-grade the gaps. It cleanly bisects the leveled mesa and simply ends at the edge of a bluff. There's a collection of modest terra-cotta terminal buildings with a Runway Café sign glowing green, half a dozen parked planes, and an almost empty parking lot where park service pickups squat in the latticed shade of a brace of mahogany trees.

A Cessna four-seater is taxiing to position, the drone of its engines burring loud out of the wind like a giant locust, wings waggling. At the end of the runway the plane curls to face the mainland, then stops, the cockpit door catches sunlight as it opens and light splinters off it. The distinctive figure of Sam Dunn emerges, wireless headset and a pair of mirrored sunglasses Jay can see from where he stands; Dunn runs to the rear and tugs impatiently on the elevator trim tab until it unfreezes from the horizontal stabilizer.

The plane creeps forward, threatening to take off without its pilot, but Dunn runs back to the flapping door and climbs inside.

The pitch of the engine rises, and the plane rolls forward, picking up speed, but not nearly enough, it seems, before it runs out of airstrip and drops off the plateau and disappears from sight for a startling moment. Then it catches the channel updraft, air under its wings, reappears, steady, rising, and soars back high up into the dappled sky of cotton-ball clouds, propeller droning drunkenly as it hurries toward L.A.

Jay shades his eyes, lost in thought, watching it go. Dunn is not part of Public's game. Jay is sure he would have known it from when Dunn first came into the shop. No. Dunn is a wild card.

Possibly a trump card.

A joker that flies.

So lost in thought, Jay can't be sure he's heard, under the worbling whine of the Cessna, a little girl's voice announce matter-of-factly: "She's not my mom."

And Jay turns, startled. Helen is staring at him, intent.

"What?"

Helen says nothing to him. She gives no indication that she's said anything. Did he imagine it? Jay takes a couple steps toward her.

"What did you say?"

Nothing from Helen. Only the steady gaze that she's perfected.

"Just now. You talked."

Her expression: open, innocent, inscrutable, unyielding.

"You said . . ." Jay's voice trails off. He balks, adrift in doubt, and it spooks him.

Helen draws a wedge of hair out of her eyes and lazy-skips away, trailing her hand lightly across the tops of the golden yarrow and mariposa lilies, back to the golf cart, where she climbs up on the seat and slips her arms into the loops of her backpack and waits for him, and for the long ride back to town, attending to only what's ahead of them.

11

GINGER CONFUSES HIM.

What is that trope people recite? Mystery inside a riddle wrapped in—or wait. No. Shit. Enigma is part of it, though. And a riddle.

Jay has never been any good at riddles, plus Ginger is thorny and complicated in a way that Jay nevertheless finds more beguiling than he thinks he should.

And then there's the whole killing thing, which, yes, he's already dismissed, but that's the history with which she's been saddled, and the questions linger, chief among them: *Why would Public want me to think that?*

Ginger may not scare him, but the Feds still do.

A night out sans Helen is Public's idea. "You two kids need to act like you're a normal functioning couple, so no one gets suspicious." Jay thinks this, too, is bullshit, since he's convinced that everyone in Avalon is, in one way or another, either working for the Feds or cowed by them.

For his part, Public is the White Rabbit, mercurial, always darting just ahead of Jay—seen passing on a golf cart with Barry, at the end of a street bracing a couple of local working men in coveralls, on the back of a big yacht at anchor with day-trippers from Balboa, but seldom where Jay needs him to be to ask myriad new questions he has about Ginger, Helen, what really happened to the unhappily departed Hondo, and whether Magonis is really a doctor, or just another federal agent playing make-believe.

"Don't assume," Public likes to tell him, when Jay does manage to cross his path. "People assume the serial killer next door is just a regular guy. People assume the child molester couldn't possibly be the favorite uncle. People assume that if they live right God will reward them, but only one guy's come back to tell us about it, and he's family, so we can assume he's not entirely objective.

"Assumptions are the enemy of truth, and truth is all we're after."

Jay doesn't know what this means, but he assumes that Public is jerking his chain because the reedy smile that follows this homily is a kind of flesh-and-blood emoticon, human spam. And Jay has noted with an uneasy curiosity how Ginger will put herself between Public and Helen whenever Public is around.

Happy hour at the Garrulous Parrot, crawling twilight shadows calling for the tea lights and candles that lend a low-rent *Pirates of the Caribbean* ride vibe to the otherwise mawkish glassed-in *terraza* nestled in palms and gum trees, back up the canyon on the road to the Wrigley Gardens. The dim light helps ease the awkward silence resulting from Ginger's preoccupation with her smartphone. Helen is home under the watch of Sandy, their pretend friend and next-door neighbor, a tired-looking twenty-something with a hay bale of frizzy pulled-back hair, and Helen has the *Toy Story* DVD trilogy and their home phone speed dial programmed to Ginger's.

Sustaining a conversation is still trouble for them. Jay's on his second Buffalotini, a frozen concoction of bison milk, vodka, Tia Maria, and bitters that the cocktail waitress Penny recommended before either of them says anything. Ginger has slapped on some edgy red lipstick and false eyelashes for the occasion, making it impossible, when she declines her head to her phone's screen in what appears to be a furious texting session, for Jay to read her eyes. Collared shirt and chinos, he doesn't know what to do with his hands, so he makes a mosaic with the beer nuts, and wonders aloud, finally, "You can make outgoing calls?"

She looks up at him, expressionless.

"My phone," he clarifies, "if I try to call the mainland, somebody comes on the line and tells me to hang up and try again later. Or can't be completed as dialed."

"Angry Birds," Ginger explains, unapologetically, and shows him the game app alive on her phone.

"So you can't."

"What."

"Make calls."

Ginger shrugs. "Who would I call?"

Jay leans forward, on both arms. Feels heat from the candle, and its glow pushes Ginger's face farther into a gauzy otherworld of the bar's dim shadows. "So what do you think? How does this work?" Jay asks. "Are we a happy couple? Why did we move here? Are we apathetic Gen-X or just complacent? Is Helen adopted, or maybe the result of some kind of baby-making science, your eggs and store-bought sperm, which has left me feeling kind of . . . evanescent."

Ginger tilts her head, doesn't answer.

"I know, right?" Jay says.

"I don't know what that means."

Jay sits back, allows that it probably doesn't matter, and starts sweeping the beer nuts back into the dish.

"You're odd." Ginger puts the phone down and sips her drink, then reacting, making a face. "Ohmygod. Yeeg."

"It gets better once you get past the taste and the texture."

She doesn't even smile. She studies Jay for what seems like a long time. "Well, how do you think this works?"

"I have no idea. That's why I'm—"

"And what makes you think it's supposed to work at all? It's an arrangement they've made more for their convenience than ours. Safety protocol and redundancies and whatnot. Short term, nonbinding, trivial in the long run. You know?"

Short term settles on Jay like a funk. *Clinical trial, but without a control.*

"I worked in this lab for a while," Jay says. "My friend does experiments with animals, mostly mice, because they're crazily close to us, genetically."

"Mice."

"Yeah. I know. Gives, like, a whole new wrinkle to that old challenge, 'Are you a mouse or are you a man?' But. There was this one thing they were doing, trying to combine old memories and new ones by jacking with the neurons in their brains, giving them hybrid memories that were part real and part fake."

"How can they tell mice are remembering anything?"

"I'm glad you asked. See, what happens is memory is laid down, or maybe stored, in neurons that are firing when that memory is taking place. Later, if you can find and trigger those neurons, you bring that memory back. On command. So what we did was put these certain genetically engineered mice in a test chamber with a specific color and smell, and let them crawl around for a while so they'd remember it. And—don't ask me how—they—the egghead science team my friend is part of—they figured out and marked the neurons where that memory was stored.

"Then we dosed the mice with this chemical that activated those neurons, and put the same mice in a distinctly different test chamber: different color, different smell. And zapped them with electric shocks."

"Nice," Ginger says, a little bored, fiddling with her phone again.

"It's called fear conditioning. The whole floor is some kind of conductive metal. You zap a mouse and it gets afraid of the place where it was zapped—"

"What a surprise, really," Ginger says drily.

"—and when you put that normal mouse back in that place later it will freeze up, what they, the scientists, call arousal, but, hell, it's pretty much just abject fear—terror—it won't even move, because it's not only remembering, it's remembering the terrible stuff that happened there.

"But these experimental mice were all messed up. They had the memories of the first chamber flooding back on them while they were being zapped in the second chamber—which created a hybrid memory, and now they would only freeze up when we put them in the second chamber and activated the memories from the first chamber."

"Okay, I'm lost."

"Otherwise they went about their business. They couldn't recall being zapped in the second chamber unless they were also having the false memory of being in the first chamber. The false felt real."

Ginger shakes her head. "Somehow I don't think you're explaining this right."

"You can make someone remember something that didn't happen."

"Okay."

"It is possible."

"Somebody been zapping you?"

"Not exactly, but—"

"You're just saying."

"Yeah. I guess." He's no longer sure why he even brought it up. Vaughn once accused him of being obsessed with the mice. "Dude, stop projecting," he told Jay. "They're not metaphors, they're just furry mammal vermin teetering on the low end of the food chain." Vaughn tended to suck the romance out of everything.

"I don't know. I get the feeling you aren't trying to remember, you're trying to forget," Ginger says pointedly.

Jay sits back.

And the awkward silence between them returns.

It's quite a while before Jay breaks it. "There was another one, clinical trial, I mean, where they let this one mouse get really, really good at running a maze. He knew every turn. Then they chopped him up, and fed him to a bunch of other mice to see if, by eating him, they could acquire any of his talent for running the labyrinth."

Ginger seems appalled but strangely interested in this one. "Did they?"

Jay says he quit before the results came back. It's a lie; he got fired. And he knows the numbers by heart, because he tallied them for Vaughn.

"Grim." Ginger shudders.

"Do you have meetings with the guy with a bad toupee?" Jay shifts gears. "This shrink named Magonis?" Jay knows she doesn't. He's followed her, more than once, during the day, to see where she goes, and it isn't to the flat-roofed office building where Magonis holds court in 204. There were errands: groceries, drugstore, the band of a watch that she needed to get repaired. Once she played tennis with the neighbor who calls herself Sandy, and two other women at courts near the golf course clubhouse; afterward they disappeared inside and stayed for a long time.

But Ginger spends most of her time alone with her thoughts, sitting on the front porch of the bungalow, or on a canvas sling chair at Descanso Beach, or at a tin table outside the coffee shop, Big E's, on Crescent Avenue, watching the moored boats rock in the harbor. And Jay's watched her, like a voyeur, or a jealous husband. She's sorting through something, trying to make sense of whatever architecture of events brought her here, to Catalina, witness protection, with Jay. Her fragility, or his sense of it, when she drops her guard and thinks she's alone, makes his heart ache. This cold, complex woman with the little girl who won't speak to her.

He understands what that's like, trying to make sense of the senseless. He wants to tell her that it's futile, but knows this is something she will have to come to on her own.

And then what?

The sound of Angry Birds bleats from the smartphone between her slender thumbs like some weird insect's call. He stares at her. Of the dozen or more patrons in the bar, more than half of them have phones out, glowing, demanding their attention, drawing them away, the siren call of a pointless connection to a virtual life.

And clouds, Jay thinks. Whole worlds floating in the empty space between here and there, tethered to this world by a tenuous signal and PIN-code prayer. Jay has nothing to put in the clouds. Nothing worth saving, nothing worth remembering.

Except that Helen spoke to him. And Ginger doesn't know.

"You want another round? Nachos? Guac and chips?" It's Penny, their waitress. She's dressed vaguely cocktail wench, Wonderbra and fishnet stockings, but the green-and-blue tattoo spilling down her shoulder to her elbow is a lively array of obscure Japanese anime.

Jay looks to Ginger: nothing.

"I think we're good," he tells Penny.

"Date night?"

"What?"

She winks. "I got a third-grader, Max, I seen you at school with your little girl. Helen?"

Ginger says, "That's right," softening, and puts the phone away.

"Me and my husband, Cody, we do a date night like every other week. I can always tell. We got nothing to say to each other, either. Dr. Phil says it's important, though. You just move here?"

"We did."

"It's nice," Penny says. "Slow. But nice. You know. What do you do?"

Jay hesitates. "I have the video rental place on—"

"Gabe's?"

"Yeah."

"That was weird. How quick he cashed out."

"Was it? I don't know anything about it. Never met him," Jay adds. "We used a broker."

"That weird guy." Penny's hands flutter uncertainly in a gesture that somehow exactly conjures Public. "My friend Tina had kissy-face with him one night after last call." She lowers her voice. "He's got a tongue thing." Ginger's thumbs poised over her phone, but not moving, she's listening. "Next thing I know Tina's gone, some Hispanic family is living in her place."

Jay doesn't know what to say, but Penny doesn't seem to need him to comment.

"Well, good luck with it. We don't rent videos. We got a dish."

Jay shrugs. "Okay."

"Very private guy, Gabe. My husband thought maybe he was one of those people have to register as a sex offender, but Cody, he watches way too much reality television, you know what I mean?"

"What does your husband do?" Jay asks, just making conversation, being polite. Ginger has gone deep in her game again.

"Boat babysitting," Penny says. "Here and Two Harbors. You'd be surprised how many people got boats they just leave, never use, never come. I guess they probably intend to. So Cody keeps them all gassed and ready, anyway, like he runs the engine for a while, checks the battery, oil, hoses, does the upkeep, you know. Thing with a boat is you don't use it, the ocean wants it, bad. Weekend people don't think of that. It's not like a vacation cabin you can just shut up and turn off the water and power and come back next summer and everything's pretty much like you left it. Cody, he says boats are living things, you don't show them a little love, they get sick and die. So."

"Sounds like a good gig."

"Yeah, well, and he can smoke his stinky bud all day, nobody gives a hoot." Penny grins. "Hey, whyn't I bring you some nachos? On the house."

"No, don't." Ginger, too quickly, the cold Ginger. She and Penny trade quick, hostile looks. "We're leaving," Ginger says. "Thanks, anyway." She touches Jay lightly on the arm, pushes her chair back, and walks out. Jay can't tell if her pique is honest or a performance. Either way, he doesn't understand it.

Penny watches her go, eyes dark. "I hope she's got an upside."

"She does." Jay puts a twenty on the table. "But I guess we do get what we deserve," he says automatically, "right?" and wondering why he's even said it, because it means nothing, just makes Penny blush.

Ginger is waiting for him outside, arms folded. No expression, no hint of any emotion except an apparent impatience to drop the façade and get back home to Helen. But she takes him on a detour to the tiny grocery store. Glare of white fluorescence, a new flat-screen TV mounted over the cashier counter with murmuring advertisements and infomercials on some kind of continuous feed.

Entering the store, she inexplicably takes his hand in hers and mines, from some other Bizarro Ginger, this weird flirty smile for the young Latina behind the counter, Floria's daughter, and then, in

Spanish, asks with pitch-perfect flustered self-consciousness where the condoms are.

Turns out they're under the counter, discreet, in a teak display box that reminds Jay of the way some high-end restaurants will bring a selection of exotic teas to the table at the end of a meal. Ginger buys half a dozen, sharing gentle quips with the daughter and flicking smoky eyes to Jay and back, shy, still smiling—Ginger hasn't smiled this much the whole time he's been with her—and slips her hand into the back pocket of his jeans as they walk out with their purchase.

In the darkness, it all falls away. No smile, diffident expression, her hands to herself again.

Streetlights haloed with night mist coming in off the channel.

Jay has to ask, "What was that about?"

"Couple of drinks at the Parrot, date night, we don't want your friend Penny to think I'm not accommodating," Ginger says. "Men have needs. I bet she and Cody go home, get baked, and have at it. Lack of chitchat notwithstanding." She stops at a public trash can and empties the condoms into it.

"Live the lie," she says, and looks hard at Jay through the dark, false lashes, drilling deep, to his vacant soul.

"Helen's adopted," Jay says. All of a sudden he feels the need to play a trump card, he's tired of losing every hand.

"Are you fishing, or did somebody tell you?" she shoots back, subdued. More of Public's Machiavellian shit. "Can I give you some useful advice? Don't trust him. Ever." Then, defensive, "She's my daughter, Jay, does it matter?"

It surprises him, when she says his name. There was an ease to it he's not sure she intended.

"I just . . . I don't know. I need to know what I'm dealing with. Everybody's got so many secrets."

"What you're dealing with? You're not. Dealing. With anything.

You're here to tell them what they want, and we're together until you do or they get tired of asking or somebody comes and whacks you—which, I'm sorry, is not my business, either, unless you bring that down on Helen or me, whether she is my biological issue or not—and in the meantime—" She stops, surprisingly emotional, and looks away. Jay, chilled by her choice of words (*Whacks me?*) considers for the first time that she could be even more adrift than he is. And worries again about what she knows that he doesn't.

Ginger starts walking up the hill to their house.

"—In the meantime, live the lie," Jay says, finishing her thought, a step behind.

"Yeah. Can you manage that?"

Jay nods. "It's my specialty," Jay tells her.

12

A CLEMENT DOMESTIC STASIS SETS IN: breakfast (cereal and milk), comics (Helen wants him to read them to her, although he suspects she can read them herself), walk to work, coffee from Big E's (black, bad), bag lunch, the two o'clock with Magonis, dinner (Ginger can cook), homework (phonics and basic arithmetic), play (Barbies or board games), and bed (the sofa beginning to sag, his back stiff and electric with shooting pain; when he's asked for a proper bed, Magonis just mumbles about budget cuts and the paperwork). The ineluctable presence and puzzle of this girl and this woman, this faux-family, the easy rhythms, like a heart, beating, like breathing. Reflexive and essential.

He makes friends, sort of. The old actress he should remember but whose name he's afraid to ask for fear of insulting her; she holds happy hour court at the Parrot bar claiming to be the friend Natalie Wood and Bob Wagner were visiting on their tragic trip to Catalina back in the day. The pensioned Frenchman of the *Brigade des Forces Spéciales Terre* who lost his leg to an IED in the *Côte d'Ivoire* and does Tai Chi on Abalone Point at dawn, but who Ginger insists is a Belgian con man selling Herbalife to the unsuspecting. The shave-ice man, Ruben, whose shave-ice kiosk is never actually open.

A noontime basketball game with a couple of busboys from the Seaview and Anacapa hotel kitchens, the soul-patch hipster who runs Island Zip Line, and a rotating lineup of Conservancy interns from UC Irvine regularly devolves into a primal brawl that leaves him bruised and sore for the entire week that intervenes. Zip Line, who the busboys have nicknamed Tripod based on his apparently legendary physical endowment, which, they swear, has been posted on YouTube by one of his recent conquests, reveals himself to be one of Public's Feds when, after a particularly hard disputed foul by an intern where they both tumble off the court, he pulls a gun from an ankle holster and straddles the terrified intern and shoves the barrel of the .22 into the college kid's mouth, screaming, "You want a piece of this?! You want a piece of this?!" like something out of a bad cop movie. The intern did not want a piece of anything. It took a while for the busboys to talk the Fed down.

Later, over a beer at the Parrot, Tripod confesses to Jay that, "This whole WitPro detail is not what I signed up for when I joined the marshals, and it's kinda starting to wig me out." Jay tries obliquely to ask some questions about Public, but Tripod just smiles and wags his finger and asks how many condoms Ginger has left from her big grocery-store buy. "I'd give my right nut for a little of that moist comfort." Tripod leers, and Jay wants to hit him, but isn't eager to taste the metal of the gun.

Maybe they're testing me again.

In the corner, magazine, pint of beer, feet kicked up, is the puddle jumper pilot and chop-socky superfan Sam Dunn, and Jay considers using him as an excuse to get away from Tripod until it dawns on Jay that what Dunn is flipping through are pictorials in some pornographic publication from Southeast Asia, crazy Thai alphabet screaming in lurid colors from the cover photograph of a nearly naked clearly underage girl in a bomber jacket and nothing else; this may explain why Dunn's sitting alone. Meanwhile, Tripod is asking Jay for what he calls a "who's hotter bake-off": Ginger vs. Stacy: "The government-subsidized gash or your old girlfriend?" Jay stares, numb. "Stacy by a mile, amiright?" Tripod's drunk, on a roll, and launches into a semi-lewd tribute to Stacy's "rack and back," which, he insists, made the surveillance of Jay on the mainland well worth the hassle. Ginger, Tripod muses, "I would think is kinda bony." But he allows that could be awesome, depending, and then waits for Jay's response with a completely serious expression.

When, before Tripod shows up for the next game, Jay tells the busboys, who have often expressed a shy and genuine awe at Jay's cosmic good fortune to have been paired with such a quality individual of the female persuasion as Ginger, about this conversation, they fall quiet, don't say anything, eyes hooded, reaction indifferent, but the first time Tripod goes up for a rebound one of the busboys low-bridges him, and, when he lands hard, the other one steps on his arm and breaks it cleanly.

"They're DEA deep-cover guys," Public explains gravely in the Emergency Room where Tripod gets treated. "They don't mess around." Public has shown up unsummoned, and Jay can now assume that the Feds are watching one another, as well as him. "Things got hairy and they got extracted and parked here until the situation chills. MS-13," he adds, as if Jay should know what this means. "Mara Salvatrucha. Salvadoran gangs, East L.A.?" Public shakes his head. "Miles should know better." Miles must be Tripod's real name.

So it's like that.

He knows he needs to get out.

Jay tells himself he can't afford to relax, it's all a trap. But he's missed this. Family, community, context. He can't remember ever having it, not even in boarding school, where he felt the safe, claus-

trophobic intimacy of adolescence, and the odd parenting of the in-
structors and coaches, and the structure of college prep, but never
trusted it because everyone else went home to their families while he
was, perpetually, the charity case, the lost boy, the invited guest who
put everyone on their best behavior because they pitied him and, on
some level, congratulated themselves not just for showing empathy,
and offering kindness, both of which were, he knew, often sincere,
but also because they were not him.

Here, now, on Catalina, he has found dry land in the vast ocean
of his disconnection.

"You're holding back," Magonis tells him.

"I'm not," Jay lies.

"You're hiding things. You have secrets. Let go of them." Magonis
makes a sudden shift in his chair, like something bit him on the ass.
The faint sour bloom of middle-aged gas followed by a feeble grimace.

"Supposing I was, and I'm not saying I am, how would you suggest I do that?"

In the strange limbo of room 204, Magonis traces circles in the air
with the unlit cigarette scissored between his fingers. "Begin with a
very thorough, and careful—even though it may be painful—analysis
of your own attitude toward your life before you came here."

What life?

*Those days Jay would park in his cubicle at Buckham & Buckham and
float, eyes dead, as all the LEDs of his phone lit up and lines chirred
unanswered?*

It was float or drown.

Is that a life?

"Follow that with a careful analysis of your attitude toward other
people in that life."

*Nights passed, indistinguishable, in tenebrous clubs and coffee joints
and sports bars, the empty thicket of Jay's friends, the small talk and petty*

grievances, arguments, betrayals, and recriminations, bands that played so deafening he would bend at the waist, fingers to his ears, riding a kind of willful oblivion; the drinking, chiding, laughing, and Stacy (or Lisa or Aly or Emma before her), lovely, perfumed, draped across him, sloppy drunk.

And he floated, forward moving, alive, at least.

"Then follow that with a very careful examination of your attitude toward self."

Was it self-defense or damage? Even in his most reflective drunk, he never cared to ask himself. Jay held fast to his unexamined life because he believed examination was unnecessary; there was Jay, and there was the world: singular, plural: he was in it but not of it. Too much to lose. Too much lost.

"And when all of this is done, inquire of your own self concerning *why* this attitude, and *how,* and *by what process* has it been allowed to take possession of the mind."

Hum of the air conditioner kicking in. Jay shifts in his chair, impatient. "Okay."

"After that," Magonis says, then waiting, waiting, drawing his hesitation out for, Jay guesses, some kind of dramatic emphasis. "After that, go into silence."

"Can we take a sec and go back and talk about the flower shop girl?" Jay gets up, antsy, and paces.

Magonis says that it's fine with him.

"In the spirit of me being helpful and all," Jay continues, "I'm just—it's—" He starts over, "What you're looking for—are you saying it's somehow about her?"

"Who?"

"The flower shop girl."

"Should it be?" Magonis furrows one brow. Evidently they, too, are independent of each other. "I thought we were talking generally about your life and your, I don't know, diffidence?"

Jay hesitates and asks the question he really meant to ask: "You guys don't think I had something to do with what happened? I mean, to her."

"Flower girl."

Jay doesn't think this merits a response.

"No." Magonis uncrosses and re-crosses his legs, stiffly. "Did you?"

"No." Jay is irritated. "I don't, didn't, like I said, even know her name." He's at a loss. "Look, I'm sorry I lied about it. Or . . . whatever. It's just—I was—" catching himself, "I am engaged, I stepped out, I didn't want to . . . you know. Because: my girlfriend. It's not something I'm proud of, and I'm not being a jerk about this, I want to help you, I want to get back to my—" He stops, caught short.

Back to my what?

"—you know . . . and I've been racking my brain for what I might have, what I possibly could have—you know—seen—and it's just, at the same time, with all these questions and coded implications and the daily 'What did you do on August fifth?' and 'What does this mean when you wrote this on the first Monday in May?' I mean, god-damn it," the frustration boils over. "Shit." He gestures at Magonis but the words are slow to follow: "I mean. What if. Maybe I didn't see anything. But you want me to think I did. Think I've seen something. Right? Okay? Or. What if this whole thing, all of it . . . is a charade, is about getting me to think I remember something I never saw—"

A single image seared into Jay's memory: liquid night, and he's in it, running across an empty expanse with a mermaid cradled in his arms.

"—so that I'll put it all together in a way that convinces even me that I actually witnessed something that never happened?"

The air-conditioning kicks on with an angry moan, and stale cab-bage air floods the room.

"That is exactly what we're being very careful not to do, Jay." Magonis heaves himself and opens a window. "That's why we're here."

"Is it? I don't know anymore."

Magonis just looks at him and waits, untroubled by Jay's accusations, expressionless. Jay stops pacing and closes his eyes and runs both hands through his hair, trying to squeegee his brain.

"Or what if you're just messing with my memory, trying to mix me up so that I *can't* remember something?"

"What if we are?"

"You'd be assholes," Jay says.

For a moment, Magonis seems to consider this as a possibility. Then he says, "All memories are false, you do understand this? Re-experiencing the experience is, by definition, a distortion. We don't remember anything exactly the way it happened because we aren't *there* anymore, present in that particular moment of being. And the pieces we do remember, we will add to, or subtract from, over the course of time, in order for us to make sense of them. We rewrite," he stresses the word pointedly, "usually to make ourselves look better."

Jay studies him. "But what if you take away one of those pieces—take, like, a piece that actually makes what you remember make sense—"

"It all crumbles," Magonis agrees. "The memory itself becomes, well, mutable."

"Mutable?"

"Unreliable. Quicksand. In which the truth can simply sink and disappear."

"Okay. And then, what? You, me, we, can't know, you can't know for sure . . . that any of what we think we remember really happened?"

Magonis's slight shrug is equivocal. "We're just talking, Jay. This and that."

Jay sinks back in the easy chair and puts his head in his hands, frustrated. "I don't know what you want."

"No," Magonis says. "You don't know what you want. That's what's really holding us up here, isn't it? The hard truth, as I've said, is that nothing we perceive is ever actually in fact exactly the way it appears." He pauses to let this sink in. "And since reality is consensual, what if *everything* you've just said could be true, depending. And we're just waiting for you to pick a place to start?"

| 13 |

"EEEEEEEEEEEEEEE—"

An awful, thin, shrill, inhuman sound brings Jay rushing into the bungalow kitchen to discover Ginger holding a flaming frying pan, struggling to transport the roiling grease fire from the stove to the sink.

"EEEEeeeeeeeeeeeeeeeeeeee—"

Helen, quailing in the corner, paralyzed, is the one making the scary high-pitched shriek.

"Oh—no, hey, no—whoa—" Jay has an inarticulate panic-induced brain freeze and can't find the words to say what he needs to stop Ginger from making the next mistake: water from the tap.

"EEEEeeeee—"

Foom. A plume of fire volcanoes up from the pan, Ginger loses her grip, overcompensates, the fryer tips and a river of flames cascades backward across her oven mitts and splashes onto her sweatshirt.

"Oh boy," she says, distant, with that vacant remove that sometimes attends catastrophe. She's on fire.

Helen is rigid with terror.

The tablecloth blurs off the breakfast table as Jay yanks it loose and envelops the flaming Ginger in its folds, and the whole smolder-ing package in his arms. Later, he'll wonder how he even knew what to do with a grease fire; later, when he thinks of it, if he dreams about it, Ginger will melt and he'll be helpless to stop it from happening.

Thick black smoke is everywhere. Jay falls back, twisting Ginger down to the floor on top of himself, cushioning her descent, and holds her there, smothering the flames with his embrace. She's coughing and shaking, stunned eyes, framed by the creases of the heavy, smol-dering cloth, fixed on Jay, in shock.

And then Helen is on top of both of them, tears spilling, leaking the noise of her wordless weeping, trying to wedge her way under Jay's arms to get next to her mother.

"It's over," Jay says. "It's okay, it's over, we're good." He kicks out at the smoldering frying pan where the grease has burned down and flips it upside down, killing the last of the fire.

For a long time they lie in a lump on the blackened linoleum.

Honey ribbons onto the reddened, largely superficial burns on Ginger's blistered arms. Jay kneels beside her, on the bed, in the darkened bedroom, one hand already slick with honey, the other delivering it to Ginger's right hand and forearm from his fingertips, the honey scooped from a big open jar.

"Lemme know if this hurts. It's not supposed to hurt."

Ginger just watches him, shivering. She smells of smoke and per-fume. The faint white salt of dried tears trails down from her smeared, raccooned mascara. There are two rolls of toilet paper and a Scotch tape dispenser between Jay's crossed legs.

"This was my mother's big miracle home remedy," Jay says about the honey. "I remember she was always burning her hands on these shitty aluminum pots we had when I was little and that my father claimed over and over would give us all Alzheimer's, all the while smoking two packs a day."

"Is that what killed him?"

Jay looks at her strangely. "How do you know he's dead?"

Ginger blinks. "Your file."

Jay asks her how it says his father died.

"It doesn't."

"And my mother?"

"It doesn't say anything in there about your mom."

Jay wonders why. Ginger wants to change the subject, to the honey: "It's cold."

"Yeah," Jay says. "Weird, huh? That's it, working, apparently. Bee magic."

Helen, exhausted, has crashed on the other side of the bed in a tumble of stuffed animals and her thumb, to which the little girl sometimes regresses, Ginger has explained, when things get especially stressful.

"I can't really cook at all," Ginger admits ruefully.

"It's that the honey seals the air out," Jay says. "Or maybe there's something in it, biochemically, or maybe just that it's naturally sterile, I don't know—but now we have to wrap it with tissue or"—he points an elbow to a waiting roll—"toilet paper and leave it on overnight. By morning, the honey'll be gone and the burns will be pretty much—"

"Doctor?" Ginger interrupts.

"—gone."

"I'm dripping."

Sure enough, honey is starting to sheet off Ginger's arm. Slow-motion waterfall. Both his hands are presently engaged and therefore useless, so Jay's at a loss. "Okay. Okay . . . I um . . . sorry about this but—" He bows toward her, lowering his head to her arm, and licks the overflow off the nape of her wrist, gently.

"Oh. Oh, wait—now you've got"—Ginger gestures to a smear of honey on his forehead—"something, here." She tries to squeegee it off with her one untreated pinky finger, but, failing that, just pulls him back toward her and licks the honey off his head.

There follows a very uncomfortably wired moment; an intimacy has enfolded them and neither one of them knows what to do with it.

"Thanks. For putting me out," she says finally.

"The fire? Yeah, well." He makes a vague gesture with one hand. "But what was the alternative? House burns down, and all my stuff is in here."

The joke is lame and slow-dawning, but Ginger shows him the possibility of a smile. Jay eases away from her, uncrosses his legs, slides off the bed and goes into the bathroom, flips the faucet on, water splashing, washing the honey off his fingers.

"Okay so lemme just . . . lemme just . . ."

He dries his hands, hurries back, and stands beside the bed, unfurling toilet paper to make long, narrow, padded bandages the way his mother would, careful and compact, her hands a blur, her eyebrows angled, serious, riot of hair pulled back and knotted to keep it from getting into the sticky stuff.

She was his original rock.

"Is this an important part of the treatment?"

"You better believe it. All of a piece. Kleenex is the preferred medium, due to its superior absorbency, but any two-ply will do."

"Mm." Ginger watches him with an expression he can't unpack, but it's not blank, not indifferent.

Jay positions the completed bandage pads on Ginger's honey-sealed burns, and he holds them in place with more toilet paper unrolled liberally up and down her arm and over her hand, forming a kind of soft cast that winds in and out of her fingers and over her palm and back up her arm, where he fastens it with Scotch tape. The pink tips of her fingers are stark against the white. Honey bleeds up through the tissue but doesn't surface. The room smells of bacon and sweetness.

"Your mom's still alive?" Ginger asks.

Now it's Jay who changes subjects. "Can I ask you something? What the hell do you do all day? I mean, while Helen's at school and I'm cleaning returned discs of the Matrix trilogy or some other incredibly important video-shop chore?"

"Me?" She meets his gaze. "You've followed me, you would know."

Jay's face gets red, but he doesn't back down. "Okay, sure. Once. But—"

She cuts him off: "I float."

Snap: strip club aquarium, Ginger in the mermaid suit, silvery sequins glued to her hips, breasts weightless in their sea-green halter, hair fanned in lazy tendrils, stares emptily out at Jay, eyes searching his, hands flat against the glass.

Jay frowns, squints. "You what?"

—No.

"Float. I do all the household crap my mother did and which I swore I would never do. I surf the web, 'Page Six' and *TMZ*. I listen to music. I read trashy mystery books at the library, sometimes." She hesitates. "And I think about my old life. I float over it. Wondering what went wrong. And if I give a shit."

"Your old life."

"Yeah."

"With your boyfriend and everything."

Sad, Ginger looks down at her papered arms and hands and says, "Husband," like she's underlining it. "He was my husband, Jay, we were married." She shifts her weight and leans away from Jay and scoots back against the wall. Creating some distance.

Stacy could never get close enough to him, it was like she wanted to crawl inside of him, but it was all about body, not soul. Even this far away he can feel Ginger's heartache as she whispers, "We were cops. Did Public tell you that? So it's not as if . . ." She stops again.

Jay wonders: *As if what?*

"And we're not," she continues, voice thin, "I mean, it's not . . ." She lets the thought drift off. Does she blink back tears? Jay can't tell, still wondering: *As if what?*

"Somebody out there gonna miss you, Jay?" she's asking, changing subjects, and doesn't wait for an answer. "I think about that part, too, don't you? With this disappearing stuff. Witness protection. One minute we're in Kansas and the next, poof, Wizard of Oz. Tap tap. Gone. And all the people we knew . . ." She's wistful, but she's fishing, too: ". . . A steady girlfriend or something?"

"That detail wasn't in my file?"

Ginger shrugs. Jay just swims around it. "What's your real name?"

"I like the name Ginger, actually. They let me decide on it." She rotates her arms and studies his bandaging. Avoiding his eyes.

"You won't tell me?"

"I won't. I can't. I'm sorry."

"Well, I'm really Jay."

"Okay. Is that important?"

"Yeah."

She doesn't say anything, then.

"What about Helen?"

"You think that there's another name she's not telling us?"

"So Helen is real, too."

Ginger, stubborn, returns to her talking point: "No girlfriend?"

Jay's sure that she knows, so why is she asking? "Fiancée," he says, flat.

"Oh. When's the big date?"

Jay suggests that his present situation has put a kink in any plans, but Ginger isn't buying it.

"So there was a date on the books."

"Well," he admits, "no."

"Huh." Ginger stares at him. "Commitment issues?"

"Personal freedom issues," he says.

"Oh." But: "So I guess . . . this is all . . . kinda ironic, then. Considering."

"Yeah." Jay is suddenly uncomfortable. "Look—" He stands up. "I'm here—"

"—by mistake. I remember."

"You don't believe me, either."

"No," Ginger admits. "And it's just that I'm not. A mistake. I mean, my being here isn't one. So."

They look at each other for a long time, then Jay nods and leaves Ginger frowning at an empty doorway.

In the kitchen, he takes in the damage: not too bad: burned grease everywhere, the charred tablecloth, the sour funk of the burned bacon. He picks up the overturned frying pan from the floor and clatters it in the sink. He unrolls a few feet of paper towels, drops them, and mops grease with his foot until it's thick and cloudy and pooling up, then he's down on his knees, sopping it and throwing the sodden towels into the trash. The linoleum gets bright shiny, reflecting hard overhead light. He finds some 409 in the cupboard and, with another length of paper towel, manages to cut the grease and scrub the floor clean to its scuffed, worn, dull natural state.

Standing at the faucet, lathering his hands, he looks absently up through the window at the lit window of the house next door. Tripod—the prodigiously endowed asshole, Marshal Miles—is gazing right back at Jay from Barry and Sandy's kitchen. Shit-eating grin.

Exaggerated thumbs-up gesture, his arm cast all squiggled with best wishes and crude cartoons.

Jay frowns.

Tripod puts his tongue against the inside of his cheek and makes a lewd hand gesture suggesting, what? Masturbation? Oral sex?

Blow job. Or whatever. It doesn't matter.

Something in Jay snaps.

He's out of the kitchen, out the front door, into the darkness and braced by a cold wind off the bay before his next thought registers, if he's thinking at all. He hurdles a short hedge, goes up the front steps of Barry and Sandy's house onto the wooden porch and kicks the front door in, splintering the doorjamb just like in the movies and making a crazy racket.

The floor plan of this bungalow is pretty much the mirror image of Jay and Ginger's, but the tiny living room where Sandy is just standing up from the recliner where she was doing her nails and watching TV when her front door caved in is divided from the entry by a low wall decorated with a collection of ugly china figurines, so even if she wanted to intercept Jay, she couldn't.

"Where is he?"

Sandy, fingers outspread, nails drying, cotton balls wedged between her toes, can't seem to decide whether first to shout or to move, so Jay keeps going, murmuring under his breath, "You're all assholes," just as the man they've named Barry comes out of the kitchen, calling to his partner: "Sandy?" He sees Jay, and sputters, "Whoa. Jimbo. What the hell are you—"

"He kicked the door in," Sandy repeats unnecessarily.

"Where's Tripod? And where's all the surveillance stuff you're using to spy on us?" Jay asks, brushing past Barry and heading down the hallway. "In the bedroom?" Barry is hot behind him. "You have cameras in every room of my house? So you can watch me? Record me and Ginger and Helen?"

"Hey," Barry says, reaching for Jay's shoulder. *"Hey."*

"Why didn't you come over and help put out the fucking fire?!"

From behind him, somewhere, Sandy: "What fire?"

The bedroom: normal: single bed, cheap pressboard dresser, some clothing draped over a chair. No Marshal Miles. Jay shouts, "PUBLIC?!" although he's pretty sure Public is not in the house.

"What the fuck is wrong with you people? She could have been seriously burned. I thought you were on my side. I thought you needed me to volunteer whatever it is I know. I thought that was essential."

As Barry tries again to grab him, big hand on one shoulder, Jay shakes violently free, swings wildly, his fist deflecting off Barry's hands as they reflexively go up to shield his face.

"Easy, Jim. I have no idea what you're—"

"I want to talk to Public."

In the back bedroom there is another bed, another cheap dresser, a big taped-up David Hockney poster that passes for artwork, and Jay finds himself for an instant wondering resentfully why Barry and Sandy got two bedrooms while he's in the one-banger sleeping on a shitty sofa.

"Get a grip on yourself, man," Barry says, as Jay pivots and tries to move back up the hallway, past him, but Barry blocks his way, and things quickly turn to an awkward, ugly kind of stand-up wrestling, something Jay is not very good at and would like to escalate into a full-out fight that he would be even worse at, but evidently Barry has instructions not to hurt him.

"Christ on a cracker, man, will you—will you—just stop— c'mon." Barry tries to corral Jay's whirling arms and fists. "We're not

watching anything but your back, you moron. We're here to PRO-
TECT you—stop stop stop—stop fighting—us—"

"Where's Tripod?! Ask him about it. I just saw him in the
window—"

"Just. Take it—easy—"

They spin. Jay slips Barry's grip, steps backward, and, sensing
movement behind him, pivots, swings, and hits Sandy, just arriving,
right in the face.

She sinks, hands crossed over her nose.

Barry wraps his arms around Jay from behind, jams him down to
the floor, and pins him there. "Calm the fuck down."

Between her hands, Sandy says something neither of them can
understand. Back against the wall, knees to her chest, painted toes
lifted, head tilted back. There's blood running down her chin.

"I just want to talk to Public," Jay says, played out, as Barry lifts him
and holds him against the wall with one big forearm up under his neck.
"This is all—I saw that asshole Tripod—I just need to talk to Public."

Sandy rises and lets her hands fall away. Her nose is skewed and
bleeding. Her chin set hard, mouth a straight, angry line. Head cocked
back, she looks down at Jay from her angled eyes. And then hits him
so hard the back of his head makes a crater in the plaster lathe.

In office 204 the next morning, everybody's present and accounted
for: Jay (crazy black eye and a surplus of regret), Magonis, Barry
(weirdly cheerful), the young marshal called Sandy (ruined nails and
her nose set, braced, and taped), Tripod (hair gelled and malicious
smile unshakable), and John Q. Public (serene and dapper in his
cream-of-wheat sport coat and teal club tie).

"I saw him in the window," Jay says.

Tripod insists he wasn't there.

"He's lying."

"And nobody saw any fire," Barry adds.

Magonis suggests they move past the petty argument, that Jay's explosion was borne of more than just Tripod making lewd gestures in the window, which Tripod again, like a fourth-grader, forcefully denies. The shrink has left his walker somewhere, and seems to be fully ambulatory without it. Is the limp an affectation? Is everything and everyone on the island perpetually in flux?

All Jay's paranoia has come rushing back.

"Okay. Then explain to me the point," Jay asks Public, seething, "of three U.S. Marshals sitting in that house watching me like some kind of reality TV show." *Or test subject,* he thinks. The mice, again.

"Watching me, watching Ginger, watching Helen—" *Always the goddamn mice.*

With a shrug, "Got to have eyes on you," Public argues. "It's part of the security protocol. More concerned about incoming than outgoing, though. Truly."

"Watching me in my house is protocol?"

Public shrugs. "If we were, and I'm not saying we are, most people might say it makes them feel safer."

"Anyway, it's not even your house, is it?" Tripod drawls, nettling.

"Jimmy, there's no cameras," Barry announces, defensive. "We're not peepers. Miles's just jerking your chain."

Jay just looks at him.

"Not your real house, not your real life," Tripod sings. "Maybe he's getting confused."

Jay has reached a point where his outrage has been trumped by his situational impotence. He looks to Public, the diplomat, who says that while there aren't any cameras, they could loosen their surveillance a notch, if that's really what Jay wants—

"Yes," Jay says.

—and if Ginger agrees to it, Public continues. "There's the little girl to consider," Public says.

A new thought dances into Jay's head: maybe Helen is the protected witness, and Public's lurid story about Ginger is just another layer of cover.

Magonis is talking about the imperfections of artificial constructs engendered by protective custody, the sacrifices one has to make sometimes for the greater good, and everyone's safety, and Jay, surfacing from thoughts about Helen-as-witness, reminds them that he didn't want to be here to begin with. Tripod drily suggests Jay try paddling a kayak to the mainland, see how that works out. Barry chokes down laughter, and Sandy tells them both to shut the fuck up.

"He keeps trying to call his girlfriend," Barry complains to Public. "Not to shift gears, but. I got phone logs from all over Avalon: bars, hotel reception, day-tripper's cell phones he's been borrowing. He needs to put on his big-boy pants and stop dicking around." Jay doesn't deny it, although it was only the one tourist, a spur-of-the-moment thing when he was standing outside his shop. He got that squalling sound, like an old-fashioned dial-up modem trying to connect.

He hasn't tried to make another call in over a week.

He looks around the room. A veneer falls away.

Just people doing their jobs, he realizes. Buckham & Buckham with badges. Flawed, petty, distracted by personal problems, judgment clouded by personal prejudice, professional but disengaged.

Vulnerable. Just like Jay.

"Is she really a girlfriend," Tripod muses, trying to scratch under his cast with a pencil, "in the deeper, emotional sense of the word?"

"Are we finished here?" Magonis asks, bored.

"Cameras and microphones out of my house," Jay confirms. "Now. Today."

"Sure." Public nods. "It's already done, since there aren't any."

Divide and conquer. This is just another workplace maze, and Jay instinctively presses his advantage: "And I want Tripod off my case. Literally."

Magonis and Public trade looks.

"No way," Tripod says. "Don't let him—"

"Can I just say," Barry jumps in, "this paranoid thing where he's, like, we're all voyeurs peeping into his private life is fairly insulting to me and Sandy. We're professionals," Barry adds. "We've done everything we can to try and make this situation as constructive and comfortable for him as—"

"All I want is some privacy," Jay says. "You treat me like a zoo animal, we're not gonna get anywhere."

Tripod talks over everybody, dagger eyes on Jay, unable to contain himself: "I know what this is about. I know: I hear Ginger sucks pole like a pro. And he don't want to share."

Sandy explodes, lunges at Tripod; fortunately, Public manages to catch her before any damage can be done, because she looks like she could kick Tripod's ass. Barry and Public pull her away while Marshal Miles dances just out of range and taunts, "C'mon. Bring it."

Barry, forgetting in the moment that their relationship is a fiction, tries to intercede, spousal, "Sandy—"

"Shut up. You're a shithead," Sandy tells Barry. "Don't defend the little bastard." She won't look at him. "Jay's right, ship him back to L.A."

"Jimmy," Barry points out pointlessly.

"Easy does it," Magonis says to Sandy as, sandwiched between the immobile old shrink and a surprisingly hard-bodied Public, she stops struggling. "Breathe. Breathe."

They look for Jay, but he's already walked out of the office with his small victory.

The hallway is empty. A cold slurry light glares through the un-washed windows in the stairwell at the far end.

No one follows him.

And he makes it a point to be down by the seawall when the last boat back to San Pedro leaves the ferry landing. Tripod is on it, with his duffel and backpack.

Jay waves good-bye.

| 14 |

FOUR WEEKS IN, Jay thinks he's got the Magonis thing under control.

His hands hang from the loops of the chain-link fence as he stares through the hatchwork of wire watching Helen play with her classmates. Chasing each other around, freeze tag, their long shadows crisscrossing on the asphalt. A normal little girl except that she doesn't make a sound.

There's no more discussion with the federal shrink about the dead flower girl or strip-bar mermaids; Jay has successfully steered the daily dialectic in 204 to safer territory, which is to say anything, everything, else: the endless stretches of days and weeks and months in which his previous year's life has played itself out, soberingly colorless, but, full disclosure, as far as Jay can tell, no different from the featureless year of his life that preceded it, or the year before that one, back and back and back.

It's growing colder; the sun crosses the island lower in the sky, shadows deep all day.

Helen is clearly in charge of the handball game, gesturing, her face a riot of free-flowing emotions, and none of the other kids seems to mind or even notice that she's not using words.

Sometimes Jay worries that this recent past he's unwrapping, day by day, with the odd-eyed shrink, which presents itself to Jay as one sad sustained serialized failure-to-engage, would, in the eyes of another man, read as normal and fine, recalled with a wistful fondness and satisfaction. Would he, in a different context, stripped of the need to provide the key, the clue, to unlock a young woman's demise—the flower girl—if that is in fact what the Feds are hoping he'll give them (that is, if she really died—and he has only their forensic photographs as testament to it and which the mere existence of Photoshop renders inconclusive without other corroboration), would he look at himself and judge his past year differently: with empathy, with forgiveness, absent prejudice?

Autonomic arousal (and, remember, arousal = anxiety) in mice is a biological reaction triggered by the nervous system, including raised heart rate, pupil dilation, changes in breathing. The sympathetic response.

Electrocortical arousal in mice is a change in brain wave functioning, changing frequency, speeding up or slowing down, and probably linked to Eysenck's reticular activating system, about which Jay has never understood squat.

Behavioral arousal is a change in observable mouse demeanor, including restlessness, fidgeting, trembling, or tension.

Even as he's settled into his fragile new made-up existence, the tectonic shift Jay's experiencing by facing down his old one remains unnerving. He wants to ask Ginger if she feels the same way, but he's afraid of the answer.

Assuming that a mouse (or its genetic cousin, the hominid *Homo sapiens*) would actively try to escape an adverse, a.k.a. stressful, stimulus, the tail suspension test dangled, in air, a subject facing downward above a solid surface, with adhesive tape affixed three-quarters of the distance from the base of the mouse's tail (duct tape, unsuitable, will tear hair and skin; attach too near the tip and the mouse will come loose and plummet down), for six or more minutes. Mice will typically panic, and struggle vainly to face upward and climb to a solid surface; when the animal stops moving he's considered to have given up. This resignation to immobility is characterized as depression and submission, which is usually the goal of the TST, but some strains of lab mice can skew the mean due to tail-climbing behavior and unusual leg clasping, neurological abnormalities, or a streak of just plain ornery.

Despite Manchurian Global's ongoing effort to identify and isolate unsuitable subjects, such outliers continued to show up on test day, because it was suspected that one of the lab technicians was sneaking in after hours and releasing them back into the general population.

A quilt of clouds skitters inland.

Helen drops a wicked topspin lob past the outstretched arms of a hapless little towhead, point and game.

If Jay's going to try to escape, and disappear, he senses he has to do it soon.

S ome days Jay runs.

Some days he skirts the seawall where Leo, the one-legged French (or Belgian) putative *Brigade des Forces Spéciales* casualty is preparing for yet another unsuccessful abalone diving mission (there are no abalone in the waters off Catalina, Floria informed Jay one day as he bought cereal and bananas, because the withering foot syndrome wiped them out in the early '90s), past the picket of palm trees and the big casino, across Descanso Beach, up to the Hamilton Cove condominium complex that hangs from the near-vertical, northern escarpments of Avalon canyon, overlooking the sea.

Some days, following the switchback streets between the bungalows and vacation homes, sun on his back, to the crest of the high
plateau, where the buffalo came out of the fog and the road leads ten
miles to the airport-in-the-sky and, some days, even from here, Jay
can catch Sam Dunn's Cessna shooting out from between the hills,
over the eastern cliffs where the channel current crashes against the
rocks, out over the whitecapped water, rising, rising, banking gently
up into the sky and heading for Los Angeles.

He'll slow, and check his watch, looking for patterns, a schedule,
and by the time he looks up into the sky again, the Cessna is but a silvery checkmark in the sweep of blue.

And some days Jay will cross town after his session with Magonis
to wait outside the schoolyard for Helen and walk her home. It's pre-
arranged, there's no pattern and no predicting when, Ginger schedul-
ing him at breakfast, never saying where she'll be or why she can't do
it, and Jay never asking, because he likes doing it, and is afraid if he
asks too many questions she'll change her mind. Despite her denial,
he assumes she has something like his appointment with Magonis,
only with someone else. Relating to what *she* remembers, knows, saw.

Or didn't see.

And Helen, well, Helen's not talking.

Not yet.

After school, after watching the playground through the chain
link and agreeing to one more turn on the monkey bars, Jay and
Helen walk home. If she's happy to see him she doesn't give it away.
Her expression is just short of serious, businesslike, in a friendly but
distracted schoolgirl way. He's no longer a stranger, but not quite a
friend. He doesn't want to admit how thoroughly she's crawled under

his defenses. He takes long strides, she has to skip every few steps to catch up, and Jay pretends not to notice.

There are two principal routes they can take, neither one direct. He lets Helen decide. One loops through downtown Avalon, past the shops and restaurants and along the serpentine seawall to the casino ballroom, then up to their bungalow on the steep streets that stitch the canyon's north slope.

The other route involves cutting across the golf course, which Helen seems to enjoy because they're always finding things in the rough. Not just the lost golf balls, either, but tees (white, natural, and in colors), quarters, dimes, nickels, ball markers, pencils, hats, visors, a V-neck sweater, a broken six iron, one running shoe, and an inside-out umbrella. Helen especially likes the hot-pink and chartreuse high-vis golf balls, and the white ones Sharpie-marked with golfer hieroglyphics: lines (straight and wavy), circles, dots, curlicues, crosses, diamonds, squares. Once they found a dead bird and Helen wouldn't leave until they buried it deep in a sand trap.

He's stopped talking for her; where once he carried both sides of the conversation like a homeless schizophrenic, now he's content to let language go: the sound of their feet, the wild conversations of the birds, the channel wind across the golf course, sharp punctuations from construction sites or distant machinery, or the low murmuring of golfers on other fairways, whine of their carts, rattle of clubs, a ball struck well, a dog that won't stop barking, there's plenty to hear.

He's considered that maybe it isn't that she's not talking, it's that she's busy listening for what might be coming for Ginger.

This clear afternoon the bay sleeps vitreous in the long, cool shadow of the barren hills, and Jay is pushing farther ahead of Helen by lengthening his strides without quickening them. The fairway grass is damp and winter-length, and their feet leave twin trails of dark ovals that shimmer in the occasional shaft of sun. Her little backpack slips off one shoulder as she struggles to keep up. She's frustrated. He seems not to care. It's a long shot, but one he's been working toward for several days: their nebulous relationship means she can't be sure that he'll look back for her.

In the fourth fairway rough, in the dipping swale that rises through a stand of scraggly manzanita to the seventh green, Helen pulls up, cross.

And shouts: "WAIT."

Wait.

Jay stops walking, hesitates, and turns around, slowly.

Helen glares at him: clinging obstinately to her silence, flushed, furious, wordless.

"Did you say something?"

Trapped, she fights back tears.

"Are you talking to me," Jay asks, as if innocently, "or . . . ?" He looks around the empty golf course, purely gestural.

"Or maybe it was somebody else," Jay says. He waits for a moment. Nothing from Helen. He turns his back on her, and takes a step forward. And another. And another.

"It wasn't," Helen sparks.

There. He stops again, turns again deliberately, and they stare at each other for a long time.

"It wasn't," she says again.

She looks into him, defeated. Her defeat becomes his loss, added to all the rest that he's lost, and the sudden weight of it after years of denying it rocks him. "I'm sorry," he says softly. "I just . . ."

Helen opens her mouth, and nothing comes out. Tears flow, she's crying, shoulders heaving, losing it, and any lingering chance Jay may have of self-congratulation for orchestrating this moment is stripped away by her expression of raw vulnerability.

Shit.

He walks back, kneels down next to her, and slips the pack from her shoulders. "Hey," he says softly. "It's okay. I'm sorry. This wasn't supposed to . . ." But guilt overcomes him because, yeah, he calculated everything for just this result, and he knows that she probably understands it or will figure it out over time and, like any parent, even a fake one, he wonders if she will forgive him.

"You tricked me," she says.

"Yeah." She searches his face for the reason, and he should say, *Because I've been there, Helen. I don't know why you stopped talking, but I've been in that place, where everything goes dead, where you want to just curl up and disappear, and I know what happens when you stay there too long.* Instead he just shrugs and shakes his head, struck dumb, like her.

She collapses against him. He has never felt so low.

"I won't tell anyone," he promises.

Ginger is out on the porch waiting when Jay and Helen come up the hill to their bungalow, hand in hand. Her tears are dried, but Helen's cheeks are flushed and her eyes rimmed red, and he feels a tiny, worried tightening of Helen's grip as they tromp up the stairs and Ginger, smiling, squats down to take Helen's backpack and feels her forehead and speculates that there must be pollen in the air and then asks her daughter, as she always does, about her day.

Helen's eyes stay on Jay, level, waiting for the double cross, despite what he's told her. She's said nothing since the golf course. But Jay gently disentangles his fingers and goes inside, keeping his promise.

Suddenly this is the most important thing to him, keeping his promise to this little girl he still barely knows.

Later, blades of street light through the curtains cut ribbons across Jay when he rolls onto his back, startled, eyes open and staring up at Helen, who stands over him; stands very still, just looking down at him, holding her pillow and her blankie crushed against her chest until there's a flutter of light in the dining room, and Ginger appears, silhouette in the archway, rumpled in a sweatshirt, long legs bare.

"She's scared," Ginger says, sleepy. "She wants to sleep in here."

Jay's fuzzed brain takes a moment to register this: "Oh." He frowns. "Okay. Lemme just—" He tries to push himself upright, but he's all mummified by the sandwich of sheet and blanket. "She can have the sofa, and I'll sleep on the floor."

"No," Ginger says, talking over him, "with you. She wants to sleep in here, on the sofa. With you." She emphasizes the words precisely, letting her question fall between inflection and tone.

This does not, to Jay, seem like a good idea, given Ginger's not-so-guarded curiosity about why Helen might be asking this, out of the blue, not to mention that it would be impractical, given the narrow beam of the sofa. "What?" He looks at Helen, realizes that the little girl is dead serious, oblivious to Ginger's fears; Jay understands that it's important, and part of some unspoken bond he's formed, he and Helen, and not to be easily dismissed or trifled with.

It's a test, and Ginger and Helen are looking for equal and opposite correct answers.

"Oh." Jay blinks. "Um"—uncomfortable, wishing Ginger would help him out here, knowing she won't—"I don't . . . think that's . . ." He looks up at Ginger and squints. ". . . gonna work—comfortability-wise, I mean, look, hey, I know: why don't I sleep in your room, on the floor or something?" He starts to gather his bedclothing. "And that way you can sleep in your own bed . . . but I'll be . . . right there. With you." He glances pointedly at Ginger, adding, "On the floor."

It takes a few minutes for Jay to get relocated and arranged in a corner of their bedroom: cold, mostly uncomfortable despite the stuffed animals Helen has generously donated from her small collection—it's a hardwood floor. He shifts and tries to find a neutral position for his hips and legs, and feels the unforgiving flatness, staring out into the soft darkness where Helen has fallen asleep again and where Ginger sits, cross-legged, staring down at him with her dark, unreadable eyes.

Jay shifts again, trying to find a better position that he's pretty sure does not exist.

Waiting for Ginger to look away.

But hoping she doesn't.

Ginger, on the bed, is waiting for him to settle, she has a message for him; when his eyes finally meet hers again she raises her hands slowly, like a magician, rotates them, to show both ivory-pale forearms. Her lips form words Jay can't hear but understands: I'm cured.

Jay nods.

His mom's honey has worked its miracle.

And something in the way she stares at him is different: eyes unlocked and searching, as if she thinks maybe she can figure him out if she just looks long enough.

Jay pretends to close his eyes and sleep. Ginger smiles faintly before she lies back on the bed, rolling to her side, tucking her arm over Helen and settling in to the catholic stillness of the Catalina night.

Jay, though, remains awake. Unable to sleep. It doesn't bother him.

Maybe he's slept long enough.

| 15 |

"*THEN SHE SAID she sensed a million orange-and-blue tears lapping up the sides of my body.*" It's Jay's voice, thin, a recording: "*You know: fire. Which she likened to a half-formed sexual feeling.*"

Laughter, static and nothing, and then Vaughn's voice, made distant by the telecommunications matrix of modern phones.

"*Ooooh, baby. This is what you get for walking into a place with a neon hand in the window.*"

But Jay is not laughing. "*Shut up, Vaughn, this is serious. I mean, I felt this kind of . . . shame, you know? because, I really . . . I was hypnotized by it. By believing it.*"

The plastic cogs of a vintage Nakamichi cassette deck pinwheel as, listening, Jay considers the bulky, '80s-vintage entertainment center of cherrywood and glass in the bookshelf of office 204 and speculates: a consequence of underfunding or is Magonis just going for the high hipster irony?

"*This storefront psychic say whether you, like, die in this fire?*" Vaughn is asking.

"*Well, you can't . . .*" Jay's voice sounds stressed, drifts and phase shifts between sources. *"I don't know if it was literal. Or maybe the timing wasn't . . . specific. I don't remember."*

"But has any of it come true?"

"No. Not yet."

Jay turns away from the console and regards Magonis with incredulity. "You recorded my phone conversations."

Magonis leans forward in his chair, fussing with his electric cigarette.

"Don't you need, like, a warrant?"

"We had what we needed," Magonis says elliptically. "The NSA is our friend."

"Except for Los Angeles," Jay's voice on the tape continues, and repeats: *"Except for L.A."*

Jay remembers the conversation: hurrying toward the Hollywood/Vine Red Line escalator in the W Hotel, sidestepping the Swedish tourists in skirts and T-shirts and jorts and fanny packs and unisex sandals, phone-cams held high like penitents' icons, Jay with a Bluetooth wireless in those days, his voice compressed and city noises filtered. *"And you think she'd be answering the standard questions, you know? Work stuff. Success, failure. Who'm I gonna marry, will I get a raise?"* His laugh is forced. *"No. She gives me a bag of what look like peyote buttons and a year's supply of Mexican Darvon. Enough to melt snow, I mean . . ."* There's an awkward pause, and Jay remembers he dug for his Metro Rail fare TAP card. *"So much for predictions."*

"The hell were you doing at a fortune teller, anyway, I guess is my question," Vaughn says.

The sound of Hollywood Boulevard slipstreams away, sucked into white noise as this Jay-on-tape walked into the W: Jay-on-Catalina conjures a mental slide show of the *cirque* of junkies and prostitutes and businessmen and tourists he left behind under what was likely to be a gauzy, too-hot sun.

"*Stacy,*" Jay's voice answers.

"*Oh. That explains it.*"

"*I know, right?*"

"*But um, just to be clear—does this lady tell you how it's gonna turn out? Kids? Cancer? House in Calabasas?*"

"*Not exactly.*"

"*Well, did she . . . know about, you know: girl, flower shop?*"

Emphatic: "*God, no.*"

"*Not so clairvoyant, then. When it comes right down to it.*"

Then nothing, tape spinning, spinning.

Jay's head is down, he's standing beside the bookshelf, waiting for more, watching motes of light-spackled dust coil up from the carpet, and speculating on why this phone call would be of any interest to the Feds.

"It's kind of like that movie, *The Conversation,*" Jay decides.

"Not really."

"I watched it in the shop the other day."

"That was directional microphones, and all the cross-fading and noise reduction and filtering comes later. Technology from, basically, the Stone Age." Magonis sucks on his cigarette, but nothing happens, and he scowls. "No. We're slightly more sophisticated than that now," he says. "But less artful. The blend is real-time, the feed is sourced. We're in the satellite, the network, we're in the exchange, and we're in the cell site, and we're in the chip in your phone."

"*I have this friend,*" Vaughn blurts, on the recording, his words splintering slightly with digital drift. "*AlwayAlways—psypsychic—parties. RaRaRabid. But—loves the future.*"

Jay's voice: "*Wherever that is.*"

Cell reception falters and fails as Jay goes down the escalator to the underground platform, where thousands of film reels are stuck decoratively to the ceiling of the station, black and white wall tiles stutter through shadows, and the source-surveillance of Jay and

Vaughn's phone connection is suddenly riven and corrupted by a vast sea of unmoored voices:

"—*interesting. You can't*—"

"*God*—"

Shriek of static, then there's Vaughn again, crystal clear: "*Jay? Can you hear me?*"

A stray voice, female: "*When he knows I crave things*—"

"—*lost lines of childhood sing in your head,*" Jay's voice cuts in. Then lots of static.

"*Jay?*"

Jay has been watching Magonis put a new nicotine cartridge in his ridiculous cigarette, and now he says, "There's a point to this?"

Magonis holds up his free hand: "Shhhhhh."

A stray voice, sobbing: "*I've been so lucky.*"

Then Jay's voice, dry as if through a tin can and a string: "—*things you're supposed to do, or be, or apologize for, or whatever*—"

Dead air.

"*Jay?—I lost you.*" Vaughn.

The distinctive low rumble of the Red Line train entering the station. A fragment of AM Spanish-language radio. The hiss of doors opening. Jay imagines himself stepping onto the train, eyes tracing over two city college students, slumped in their seats with their earbuds, eyes like black sparks.

"—*forgiveness. Redemption*—"

Jay asks Magonis to turn off the tape. "It's just me and Vaughn shooting shit."

On the tape, Vaughn, waxing: "*I know, it's something you don't . . .*" His voice trails off, then picks up a new thought: "*and even if you actually live here, I mean: angels? What the fuck?*"

"*They exist,*" Jay's voice insists. The *biiiiing* of the departure warning. In the flutter of the car's fluorescent light, he imagines himself grabbing the overhead bar to brace for the train's moan of acceleration.

Vaughn: *"What do you mean, exist?"*

Jay: *"What?"*

Dial tone. Disconnect.

It seems incredible to Jay that he even got reception all the way through the station and into the train. Underground. There are stretches of Olympic in Beverly Hills where calls drop like in a third world country. Maybe there's a whole cell-tower thing in the W Hotel atrium, hidden behind the hanging ferns.

The tape deck stops, reverses, rewinds, all by itself. Magonis drifts, deep in thought.

The clock on the wall reads five minutes to three. This session is nearly over. Jay asks, finally, impatient, "Um. So now what? You gonna go hunt down the psychic and talk to her?"

Magonis looks up at him oddly, his gaze bidirectional. "We already did." He rolls the phony cigarette between his fingers and gestures with it, like some character in a Noël Coward play. "Masie Del Rio. Little storefront on La Brea and Waring?"

He gets up, moves to the desk. "Ms. Del Rio told us if you've survived this long, you're going to live forever"—opens his desk drawer—"which is ironic"—and takes out a Chiclet-size flash drive nestled in a plastic foam protective case. "Exhibit B." He holds it up high between his thumb and forefinger for Jay to see. "Ten gigabytes. Plenty of memory. Which might, for example, hold an encrypted comprehensive highly sensitive list of names that existed on one and only one other highly secure mainframe storage device in the temperature-controlled vault of a Virginia private contractor that not coincidentally was hacked and purged and corrupted so that this flash drive of names is a unique repository. Names of people who, were the list to find its way into the wrong hands, well, these people named might very well be compromised, if you get my meaning. Because. Of what they know. Or who they are. Or what they represent. You see the significance?"

"Confidential witnesses and informants?"

"Just for argument's sake."

Jay shrugs. "Well. You've got that copy. You know who they are, you can move them."

"This? No. Let's say this one is blank. But the real one looks exactly like it."

"Is it?"

"Is it what?"

"Blank."

Magonis shuffles around the desk, hands the flash drive to Jay, and sits down on the arm of his chair, knees creaking. "Seen it before? Familiar?"

"No."

"Take your time."

"Has anyone on the list been—?"

"We can't both be asking questions."

Jay nods. "No. Okay. It looks a little fancier than the memory stick I use to back up my iTunes. Which is maybe one gig. What happened to exhibit A?"

"You." Both of Magonis's eyes sync and settle on Jay. "You're exhibit A."

Jay was pretty sure this was the answer he'd get, but it still has a troubling chill to it. He flips the flash drive back onto the desk. "What about the flower girl?"

"She's deceased."

Jay walks to the window, buying himself time to sort these details, then turns, thoughtful. "You guys think I have the list?" Suddenly it all lines up: the someone who broke into his apartment was a Doe, or a Public: Feds. Looking for their list. When they couldn't find it, they grabbed him, they expected him to come clean right away, and when he didn't, this, the island, the safe house, the questions, Magonis. Convinced somehow that Jay has it and/or has hidden it and/or knows where it is.

But Jay wonders, again, ineluctably, *Why?*

"I don't know that you do or don't," Magonis responds without inflection. Then, thoughtfully: "If you pressed me, I'd say you didn't. But some of us think you do know *why* we don't have the list anymore.

"And herein lies the irony of your fortune teller's prediction: Unless you remember? You and I will be here, on this rock, in this room, Prometheus and an old walleyed eagle, doing this, this crazy headshrinking rondel, *hoping,*" Magonis adds, coldly, matter-of-fact, "that, God forbid, nobody gets it into his tiny paranoid impatient bureaucratic mind that it might be a whole lot easier to put a bullet in your head and disappear you in the rocky depths off Jewfish Point and hope that the list is never found."

16

THE RESERVOIR, filled to capacity for so long, now tapped, empties of all the words Helen's held hostage.

It turns every walk home into an aria.

Each afternoon, from the schoolyard to the bottom of the hill that leads to their bungalow, the little girl serenades him with a steady outflow of eight-year-old chinwaggery, like some midget castrato AM radio talk show host on Red Bull: Barbie, Ariel the mermaid, puppies, unicorns, musicals, playground etiquette, the magnificence of Miss Healy (best second-grade teacher ever), peanut butter vs. Nutella (close call, but only one comes in crunchy), Jenny Humbert's hair (all the way down to *here*), ocelots, the possible extinction of the narwhal, clips vs. scrunchies, green-tea ice cream (how weird is that?), *Charlotte's Web* (it's true, animals can talk to one another and we don't understand them), why there are words that sound the same but mean different things, triangles, counting by threes, Movies I Know I'd Like if Mommy Ginger Would Let Me See Them, Arlo the Shaky Kid's struggle with quiet time, ponies and horses, good cat names, state capitals, mysterious possible barf under the play structure, favorite food (Chinese chicken salad), and why the Chumash people ate grunions. Every afternoon Jay and Helen take their downtown Avalon loop through the cool winter shadows of the bay-facing businesses. Water slaps against the seawall, sailboat riggings rattle, and Helen talks.

"—I've always wanted to live in a village like Belle and have all the villagers say hello and sing and I'd walk to school instead of going there in the car, so, yeah, like this place, I guess, except it's not really where we live, is it? In the place where I used to live it wasn't a village, really, it was apartments and not so many trees, bigger and kind of scary and I couldn't go outside because of the bad kids and mean dogs and stuff. But Mommy says nothing is like a cartoon, and I know that, everyone tells me it's not real, but it *could* be, couldn't it?"

Jay doesn't disagree.

"And there could be magical animals and spoons that can talk. And there could be a Santa Claus even if he doesn't come to my house. And my friend Jenny who I don't know anymore was nice and gave me a hair band that had real jewels but I lost it. The jewels weren't actually real, just real for me, but. I don't miss her. Jenny. Sometimes she was mean."

The maze her mind runs never fails to enthrall him; eight years old, the same age as was Jay when his life disassembled. They never talk about why she quit talking, or whether she's who has a secret the Feds want to protect, and not Ginger.

No one follows them.

The busboys have left the island, evidently their cooling out completed, and the Wednesday game has been bolstered by new faces: a pale, frightened, hair-challenged man who says little and does nothing but jack up long shots that rarely hit; a short young woman who must've played in college and trash-talks the Conservancy interns until they're crippled with laughter; a Fed, Jay can tell he's a Fed, who works out of the island bank and fouls hard.

"But shouldn't everyone have, like, a village, and friends, and magic?" Helen is asking. "And there wouldn't have to be some guy with a flute like in the *Pied Piper* we're doing, luring the children off into caves because the mommies and daddies won't give him his money. A safe place for a family. Because kids have to be safe so they won't mind how tough things are, later, when they get older, because they're sort of like, I don't know, they get real, real . . . well, tired? for one thing." Sometimes she loses the thread. "So they don't give a hoot? And need to take a nap and then, when they get up, they can have a Harvey Wallhanger or something and then kick back and forgetaboutit!" She cracks herself up, and laughs too hard, and they have to stop, and Jay waits for her to calm down, pretending he's found something interesting in the dusty antiques store window that reflects their mirror images back at them.

Behind Jay, a spectral Catalina ferryboat idles out at the transparent jetty, taunting him, as always, with escape and freedom. If that's what he still wants.

"—I'm just being silly." Helen catches her breath.

Jay says, "Harvey Wall*banger*, not—"

"My old daddy liked them," the girl says absently, leaking something from that private part of herself without even realizing it. "I think they taste like cough syrup."

"Old daddy?"

Helen frowns then, made cautious, and doesn't answer him, as if two worlds have collided and canceled each other out. "Nothing," she decides finally.

"What was he like? What did he do?"

"I don't know," Helen says too quickly. "They're not for kids," she observes. "Harvey whatevers. Are they?"

"No."

"I'm only ever talking to you," she reminds Jay gravely. "Nobody else."

"Only ever. That sounds like a long time. Why? Why not your mommy, or—"

"Mean," Helen says out of nowhere, and it takes Jay a moment to understand what she's talking about: the old daddy. "He was really really mean." She stares up at Jay, in the window, abruptly saddened, and then goes completely expressionless. She's learned to turn her emotions on and off; at the age of eight Jay found the off switch but had a more difficult time finding the on. "Everything is hard to understand."

"You're not wrong," Jay says.

"Does that mean I'm right?" This cheers her; she announces, "The rule from now on is there always has to be a mommy and a daddy."

Jay doesn't know what to say to this.

"I decree. In my land. It's like if you have food on your plate, you have to eat it. And you're the daddy, right?"

He looks at her reflection, shimmery in the glass, angled, slightly set back from him, in the shade, with the sunlight bright behind her. The ferry is heading back to San Pedro, a slurring slash of white in the window-glass bluescape.

A man who looks a lot like Sam Dunn stands on the pier with a new boat-kiosk guy, both with arms akimbo, legs wide, like cardboard cutouts. Dunn should be on his plane, making his afternoon mail run, Jay thinks absently. Is it not a daily flight? He files this away, with the other bits and pieces he's collecting: the Realtor's unused golf cart, the coming and going of delivery trucks from the north island, the faces of locals who pay too much attention to him and tourists who return with regularity but no firm purpose, the slow relaxing of federal vigilance that he's felt more than observed.

"You're the daddy. That's what Mommy said," Helen adds to fill the silence, less sure of herself.

"I'm not, though," Jay says, so regretful that it surprises him. "Not really."

"Yes, you are." In Helen's tone he hears Ginger's familiar *Don't contradict me*. "You are," Helen repeats. "That's what you are now, and Mommy's Mommy and I'm . . . me. Helen."

"It's parts in a musical, isn't it? Just for the show. You can't make something so just by saying it is."

Helen looks at him fiercely, with a small child's intractable conviction. "You can if you want to."

"And if I don't?"

"What?"

"If I don't want to make something so just by saying it is."

Helen is quiet. Then, in a pretty good eight-year-old's imitation of Jay: "Yeah, well, but once you get past that—"

Jay laughs. "—Clouds?"

Helen nods, solemn but pleased: "Clouds."

Behind them, the sun is, in fact, curtained by a cloud and the light level dips and their reflections dissolve and now Jay can clearly see the baroque cerise velvet chaise longue featured prominently in the front display. He muses: *Who on this island would buy that?* He thinks: *If everyone here is like me, hiding, holding back, trawling through the murky waters of their past for memories someone else needs, and tending to pointless businesses existing only to give legitimacy to the lie—*

—how is that different from real life?

The ferryboat horn bleats a faint, last good-bye as it clears the speed buoys, its dark, departing shape barely a punctuation on the seam between the sea and mainland. Dunn and the boat-rental guy have gone into the kiosk.

Helen steps up next to Jay, and takes his hand and presses her nose against the window and makes a low animal noise in her throat.

"Why did you tell me Ginger wasn't your mom?" Jay asks, fishing. "The other day?"

"I don't know." Helen probes her nostril with a wiggling finger, and then gestures royally to the chaise with the other hand. "That's pretty. It's, like, for a princess, from a castle. I'd want to have it in my room and lie on it. But not be Sleeping Beauty. And I don't like the color. Do you think it can talk?"

Jay is still back with her reveal: "What did you mean, Ginger's not your mom?"

"What?"

"Helen—"

"I don't know. I just said it."

"Who's your real mommy?"

Helen takes her hand away, won't look at him. She breathes out and fogs the glass and draws a circle with two dots and cat ears before the condensation evaporates. "You don't want to be my dad?"

Jay no longer has an answer for this, everything has become so involute. So layered and confusing.

Gold-brocade curtains cascade around either edge of the chaise. A neon sign that tilts down overhead past the awning from the second-floor hotel spells VACANCY backward and gleams and trembles in the pair of filigree mirrors bookending the chaise.

After a while, Jay wonders aloud what color Helen thinks it should be. Helen says she doesn't know, but suggests pink, her color default.

Jay frowns at the chaise. "That is pink."

"No. It's just light red." Bored: "Can we go now? I think Mommy's making cookies."

"Ginger?"

"Mommy." She looks at him, challenging him to deny her this. He won't.

The sun behind them blazes again, cloud-free, and Helen, as if quoting (Ginger, probably), turns away, declaring: "Family is every-thing." She walks out into the sunlight and away down the street.

Jay stays for a moment, staring at his reflection, which seems, suddenly, a stranger to him. By the time he moves, Helen is marching off, small, happy again, singing at the top of her lungs and tunelessly: "Family is everything," with the chorus, "that's the way it's going to be."

"You got it all figured out," Jay says.

"Yep." Helen skips ahead, turns, and walks backward, facing him, smiling. "It was really really really hard. But you know what? It doesn't even matter what I say, because things just are what they are," she sings, making up her own musical, "and they're not what they're not—that's what I say so it's so," after which she launches into another monologue about good Jenny and bad Jenny that takes them all the way to the end of the street and around the corner.

| **17** |

SMOKE FROM A BARBECUE, thick and black, roiling, eddies alchemical around John Public and his snorkel, mask, and tongs, flipping chicken and pouring some of his beer on the red-hot coals of the Weber grill, causing even more smoke, smoke so dense it drives even the few nicotine diehards and their ringleader, Magonis, back into Jay and Ginger's bungalow from the patio behind it, where they've been communing with a pack of Kools.

The little house overflows with guests: some federal agents (known and not), and a potpourri of island full-timers (in-program and oblivious to it) Public has encouraged Ginger to invite; a casual neighborhood housewarming party for all appearances, good form now that they've been here for more than a month, with music blaring, white and red meat, potato salad, a potluck of appetizers, much beer consumed, pretzels and crackers and chips and trail mix getting macerated into the floor and the Fed-who-calls-herself-Sandy making frozen strawberry margaritas nonstop in a blender, her sneakers starting to stick to the linoleum.

In the kitchen, Jay and Helen leak tears while carefully chopping tomatoes and peppers and the offending yellow onions under the watchful eye of garrulous Barry Stone, who's been tasked with wrangling the avocados for the guacamole but is concurrently giving a lithe, hard, leathery Avalon divorcée in a black tennis skirt the bum's rush.

"So, you know, I'm thinking—and, well"—shifting his weight so that his shoulder angles closer to her—"frankly, it's a thought that comes over me in so many situations involving a gathering that parties, you know"—he leers— ". . . wild."

Heavy-lidded, she furrows impossibly pencil-thin brows: "You think this is wild?

"I sold a house," the woman confides, dropping her voice to a murmur, "to a famous celebrity—I won't say who—recently, I can't divulge details, but let us just say that men *and* women, girls really"— she plucks a grain of mascara from her eyelash and studies it—"in the infinity pool," she adds, "the only infinity pool on the island, but you can't see it, totally secluded, so . . ." She smooths her skirt and crosses her arms under her breasts, lifting them. "Completely naked and unabashed. Men with augmentations and women labially sculpted in the spirit of what my plastic surgeon calls the Barbie. 'Libertine' is a word you might use. Wild," she concludes, and then, husky, "you have no idea."

At the sink, Ginger, watching everything, eyes bright, shucking the husks off corn: the odd angles of Barry and his assignation as they pose and posture like fashion models, mid-shoot: the protective curve of Jay's back as he helps Helen: and through the back doorway, Public darting in and out of its frame, grill smoke blowing off-patio now, and Public, mask up, snorkel dangling, in deep consultation with Leo, the French special forces vet. *"Transi de froid"* is what Leo keeps barking.

Jay watches Ginger watch.

Barry smiles faintly. "We are what others decide we are. Right? I mean, hey, reality, it's consensual. Right? What the doctor says. And vice versa. So, it's like, from their point of view, au naturel, plumped and tucked in the amniotic embrace of the watery infinite . . ." He shrugs and lets his murky insinuation hang.

"Well, no," the lithe woman disagrees. "Some real is not negotiable. I'm a Realtor, whether you or anyone else agrees that I am or not. It's not up for discussion, it just is. I don't believe in body modification. And my current Realtor's reality is somebody keeps stealing my golf cart from behind the office. It's annoying."

"Stealing is a consensual relationship." Barry's chin goes sagely up and down. "Isn't it? And for whoever's doing the taking of your cart, I dunno, their reality might be more in the vein of you lending and them borrowing. Wouldn't you agree, Jimmy?"

Jay blades away onion tears with the heel of his hand and looks at them, caught short, wondering if it's possible the Feds know about his inner-island sorties, or if this is just Barry stumbling around in the dark, running into things.

"I thought your name was Jay," the Realtor says, twining long brown legs and rising up on the balls of her feet like a dancer.

"Well, yeah. In almost every reality but his."

Barry laughs. "J. J for Jimmy," he tries to explain. Then, gesturing to the onions piling up in front of Helen on the cutting board, "Mince, don't chop. Mince."

Jay holds Helen's hand and guides the knife until she finds the rhythm of it again.

"Maybe you shouldn't be letting such a little one handle that big sharp knife," Barry parents.

"Have you met Bob's wife?" Jay asks the Realtor, gesturing to the blender, and hardworking Sandy. The lithe woman has not; she smiles emptily and abruptly drifts sideways as if she'd been meaning to do it for a while now, opening up the space between her and Barry.

Dropping the last of the corn into boiling water on the stove,

Ginger, watching this, too, locks eyes with Jay and then walks out of the kitchen.

"Ball and chain," Barry jokes, brittle. "And my name's Barry," he tells the Realtor, "he's just—" Spell broken, the Realtor keeps sliding away.

Jay nods, "—Confused." Then, softly: "Bob?"

"Barry." Real anger palpable now behind that easy grin.

"Whatever." Jay jerks his head to the doorway, and Barry follows him out like a puppy into the narrow hallway, where it's dark and cool, and beyond which the living room blooms with flaxen shafts of eventide sunlight, and in which a group of the locals is starting to form a limbo line.

"What the fuck?"

"I don't know, Barry. I just thought, as long as we're going to pretend to know each other," Jay says evenly, "why don't we pretend that we're at a barbecue together? You know—hot dogs, hamburgers, potato salad, corn on the cob, Feds up the ass: *barbecue*."

Barry laughs too hard, his smile a conceit, eyes darting to make sure no one has overheard this. "Feds! Jesus, Jimmy."

Jay murmurs, "Feds swarming in the backyard like summer fireflies."

"They're getting tired of your little game," Barry counterpunches, desperate to reclaim the higher ground. "You know that, right? The thing is, they're beginning to think that, yeah, maybe you don't know shit, in which case—"

"Bullet in the head, disappeared into the ocean? Magonis already used that." Jay's swagger is a charade and he can't sustain it. "The thing is, it's not a game. Whatever 'they'—or you—think 'it' is."

Jay waits and watches while Barry tries to process the honesty of this, and, finding that he can't, just discards it and resumes his clumsy role as blunt-force *provocateur*: "Public's gonna fuck you up. Just wait."

"Okay." Jay looks into the bright light and the limbo line. "I guess nothing else to do, then, but have a safe-house-protected pretend beer. And dance." Jay hands him an icy, dripping Corona from a cooler on the floor. Barry takes it, his broad up-with-people friendliness abruptly vacuumed into a tight, sinister half-smile.

"Beer looks real enough to me, James," Barry says. He holds the beer high, tips it, as if in a toast.

"Yeah," Jay says, "no doubt. But I'm newer at this. You ask me who's on first and I still say: everybody. Everybody's on first." And with that he slips past Barry, and goes down the cool, dark hallway where the teacher who wrote the *Pied Piper* book and lyrics is all dolled up and explaining to the actress whose name he's afraid to ask (and which Ginger has told him, because *she* asked, but he immediately forgot it: Jean, or Joan something. Bennett? Falcone?) that "Goethe wrote a poem based on the story that was later set to music by Hugo Wolf, and he incorporated references to Faust, but I didn't think that was grade-appropriate, so I made the rats friendly and the kidnapping an object lesson in fairness." Jay feels the actress squeeze his arm with her bony fingers as he slips behind them, so close he can see the faint threads of multiple surgical scars behind her ears, where someone took up the slack in her face and left her with the smear of edamame-shaped smile and tissue paper cheeks that turn to him, his uneasy reflection twinned in her pale blue eyes. He doesn't hear her response, but knows it's gentle and, to the best of her ability, heartfelt, whatever it is. Nodding in acknowledgment, he finds himself looking back down the hallway, where Barry has disappeared, but in the sliver of open doorway that exposes the bedroom he can see Ginger talking to Public, animated, unhappy, gesturing with her hands, the whole language of her body resistant to whatever he's asked.

Now the limbo line snakes out onto the front porch, back through the living room into the dining room, where, furniture pushed aside, bongos pop and bodies shimmy in the hands of the new zip-line twins from Altadena, a bamboo pole is strung between two Avalon yacht club weekender swingers, and who but Sandy, slithering, back bent, is underneath it, knees wide in her baggy cargo shorts, bare feet duck-flat and what appear to be saline implants tenting her Hawaiian shirt like mini-Matterhorns, while Magonis, caged by his chrome walker, leans and sings:

Put de lime in de coconut, she drank 'em both up
She put de lime in de coconut, drank 'em both up—

Then it's Public under the horizontal pole, arms winged, pin-wheeling, spectators howling, clapping, his sensible federal man shoes scuffing panicky until finally he just falls back on his ass.

Said, "Doctorrrrrrr . . ."

The party warps and whirls, a carousel of bodies and emotion, a rousing success, its odd moil of Feds and informants and islanders and artifice well matched to the fade and muddle in Jay's head and yet concrete and real in a way that worries him, in a way that rattles the foundation of everything concrete and real that's come before.

Barry under the limbo pole.

Stoic Leo tucked in a corner with the Realtor, her bare heel hooked around his fake leg, her skirt clinging static to his hip, he's murmuring French into her ear as an excuse to get his lips that much closer to their goal.

Magonis in a syncro-shimmy mambo with the old actress suddenly, their gray eyes locked, her teeth perfect, his hair jumping like a small animal up and down on his head.

And Helen in the kitchen doorway, watching, archiving, ever-vigilant even as, behind her, Sandy powers down frozen margarita directly from the blender itself.

Someone wraps her arms around Jay from behind, and whispers, lips soft and breath hot against his ear, and he turns in to Ginger's tight embrace, surprised, astonished, really, the strange familiar closeness of her, not at all sure that he's heard what she said. And Public joins the howling shrink for the song's refrain:

—*you drink them both together,*
and then you feel better—

Jay is searching Ginger's face for a clue: she's tentative, ashen-faced, grim. Jay asks, "What?"

"You need to get out."

"What?"

"It's not safe for you here. Go." She keeps looking away, anxious, keeps track of Public, in the crowd, his back turned to them, arm around Magonis, singing.

"Where?"

She kisses him, suddenly, hard, on the lips, with longing and desperation. Her smile is heartbreaking, her eyes dark, fierce, decisive.

He wants to ask her what she and Public were arguing about, but she can't seem to bear to look at him afterward, and she's dead serious when she says, end of subject: "Anywhere, Jay. Go. Please. Just run."

Much later, shock of the stillness, the quiet darkness, the party finished, food eaten, sharp miasma of smoke left on everything, sticky floor, guests long gone, bags of trash heaped on the back porch and the house left empty except for the three who live there.

Just run.

Deep in the unlit front closet, Jay quietly rummages through the boxes stored here, looking for and finding a box within a box. He opens it and removes his old wallet and some keys. Behind him, Helen walks back and forth through the bright frame of the kitchen doorway, helping Ginger clean up, as Ginger gently murmurs to fill the odd quiet Helen carries with her.

Just run.

He puts the wallet in one pocket and the keys in another and steps out of the closet, softly closing the door.

In a soft glaze of the next morning's sunlight Jay's eyes slit open to the sound of Ginger and Helen leaving for school. He rolls and turns and stretches up to look over the back of his sofa: through the rippled glass of the bay window he can see distortions of the girls descending the hill flutter, flatten, refract, and disappear like a *fata morgana.*

Showered and dressed, he sits at the kitchen table eating cold cereal and smells the faint remainder of Ginger's perfume and stares at the many crayon drawings of clouds fixed to the refrigerator with magnets.

He shivers with a gathered melancholy that surprises him.

Mid-morning the bell over the video-store door jangles and sunburned Sam Dunn flip-flops in to drop a big cardboard box on the counter, dust shedding from its sides. His guayabera shirt reeks of Humboldt shaggy. The day is hot already, a hard, grinding, disquieting winter heat blowing off the high desert and across the channel.

"Asian Trash Cinema," Dunn announces. He spills the contents—mostly Chinese pirate DVDs—on the counter in front of Jay. "I picked these up in Thailand coupla years ago. *Blood Maniac, Innocent Nymphs,* and *Leech Girl. Freedom from the Greedy Grave. Twist. Pom Pom and Hot Hot* with Lam Ching-Ying and Bonnie Yu"—he sorts through them quickly—"this one, *Green Snake*—which for some reason is called *Blue Snake* in Hong Kong—it's about snake sisters who want to be human," and then, as if he anticipates Jay's reservations, "Hey, Maggie Cheung and Joey Wang give each other *baths*. Damn." He steps back, hands up, switching to a soft-pedal. "Okay okay okay, yes, they're mostly just plain kick-ass chop-socky films, but some are modern classics, and so I'm betting more than a few of these island yacks'll go for 'em big-time, and you and me, dollar a disc, we split the rentals. Pure cash profit."

Jay says, "What?"

"Fucking hot weird shit out there today."

Jay nods.

"Santa Anas. Earthquake weather."

"Mmm."

Dunn puts his hands flat on the counter. "Okay, look, here's the pitch: I can see what you're up against. That's all this is. You gotta do something or you're gonna go broke. This stuff, you'd be surprised. People get into it? Can't get enough. And these are titles you can't find anywhere else. Hell, I know a guy, we'll make a website, you can do online rentals like Netflix, only specialized, I guarantee there are a herd of film nuts out there who will jump on this."

Jay says, "I don't know."

He's been casing Dunn for a couple of weeks, double-checking the regularity of that mid-afternoon Cessna out from the Airport in the Sky but unable to pin down Dunn's return after dusk. Sometimes Jay suspects the pilot stays on the mainland, but then there are mornings Jay will open the shop and look out into the bay to the patchwork old teak cabin cruiser Dunn calls home, moored beyond the short-timers, laundry on the rigging, hull partly painted, windows dim-glowing with a smoldering glaze of dawning sun and Dunn in a stern hammock, faint firefly glow of a fatty that ebbs and wanes as he smokes it down to nothing. Some nights the cabin windows stay dark, but other times they glow and soft shadows form and flutter inside and the sound of a woman's laughter comes jittering across the harbor like seabirds' calling, light, high, strange. And some mornings the rear deck stays empty, Dunn's dented aluminum skiff tucked and tied up under the pier, but the Cessna is waiting mid-afternoon for its run, flies out, as if Dunn is only an occasional passenger, unnecessary for the task. But always, the cruiser is lifeless on weekends, making it difficult for Jay to find a way to cross paths.

"Fine, you take sixty, no, seventy percent." Dunn is twitchy, he keeps angling his eyes to the street, running his hand through his hair, restless. "All your highbrow French flicks are just sitting there getting slowly degaussed, my friend. Or whatever happens to discs. Nobody's watching them. This is a win-win sitch."

Jay only vaguely understands what Dunn is offering, but the video business is a sham, so, fuck it, let Public sort this out; he nods and agrees, "Sure. Okay. Great."

Now it's Dunn who demurs, backing off, as if this went too smoothly. "What? You sure?"

Jay was half hoping Dunn would show up at the barbecue, but no; and yet, now, here he is, walks right into the shop, just like that, with a harebrained business proposal, and so Jay quickly tries to figure the odds of this being coincidence as opposed to some twisty federal ruse, but then just as quickly decides it doesn't matter. It doesn't matter. Ginger's admonition to run thrums through his every calculation.

If it's Doe or Public pulling strings, setting him up, the worst that can happen is they catch him, and his situation remains exactly the same.

But if it's not? If Dunn is legit? He's looking at an exit plan that may not present itself again.

Jay asks him, knowing the answer, "So do you fly to the mainland every day?"

"Yeah. Do you really think—?" Dunn stops short, looks from the pile of DVDs to Jay, and elaborates: "Weekdays. Mail run. USPS budget cuts have cut out weekend delivery, in case you hadn't noticed. I used to skywrite for walking-around money, but the whole spelling thing was a big problem for me." He cocks his head. "Hey, you really, you really want these—do you really think it's a decent idea?"

"Yeah."

"Awesome." Dunn's grin is childlike. "Epic."

Jay tries to make the next thing he asks sound as natural as possible. "Hey . . . Sam . . . do you think, could you give me a ride to L.A.?"

Nodding, Dunn: "When?"

18

AT TEN MINUTES TO TWO that same afternoon, a couple sweat-soaked delivery guys will have a protective-plastic-shrouded cerise chaise strapped end-up on a dolly truck when Ginger answers the door.

The men could complain about the hill before they say anything. They'll have forgotten how steep it is. They'll catch their breath and ask for Helen Warren. They'll say they've got her lounger, using the accepted American mispronunciation.

Ginger will be completely confused by this. Why would Helen be getting a delivery, much less furniture? She might frown. She will ask to see the invoice.

The men will trade looks, and the senior one will take from his pocket and unfold a printout to show to her. The address of the bungalow, Helen's name, Jay's signature. Even sideways the chaise will look to Ginger like something out of a New Orleans whorehouse.

The sweaty men will wait, patient. They have more deliveries to make, and the longer this one takes, the fewer of the remainder they'll have time to do.

Ginger will scan the invoice, beginning to understand what it means, then perhaps step farther out on the front steps and stare down the hill, to the rooftops of the Avalon shops facing the harbor, not so much surprised by this development as (perhaps) regretful that it happened so soon.

But the gesture of the chaise longue itself will stump her.

Finally, she'll nod, distracted, step out of the way of the men, and open the door wide for Helen's long chair.

At half past two, Magonis will be sitting motionless in his chair, smoking his disagreeable electric cigarette, listening to the Chimes Tower ring and staring irritably at the half-open office door and sweating in the unseasonable heat, because the air-conditioning is being repaired.

He will check his watch. He will check the clock on the wall. Both will, more or less, give or take five minutes, announce two-thirty. But the tower is never wrong. Smoking, his irritability morphing into a kind of disquiet, he'll listen for the sound of someone coming up the hallway to suite 204.

Jay has never been late to their appointment.

At some point, before the hour is up, Magonis will dig in his pocket for his cell phone.

At quarter to three, as the tower chimes on the fifteen again, Public will come walking briskly down Crescent, and cross the street to the window of the video shop where Jay has posted the plastic sign with a clock that once had moveable hands someone long ago ripped off their pivot point, leaving the BE BACK AT: forever inconclusive.

Public might screw his mouth up the way Jay has noticed he will when he gets agitated, step back into the street and find himself unable to choose his next destination: looking first to the empty ferry landing, then north to the big casino on the point.

In the absence of any facts or real knowledge, Jay has convinced himself that nobody knows how many protected witnesses are on the island. He believes that different marshals are each in charge of their own small group of assets, scattered among the four thousand permanent residents, ninety percent of whom live in Avalon, the rest in a few tiny unincorporated settlements bounded by the vacant sprawl of protected Conservancy land covering most of the seventy-four square miles of long, thin, craggy Catalina Schist rising out of the Pacific, southernmost part of the Channel Island archipelago.

This would ensure that any breach of the protection program would be limited. Unless a full list of witnesses was to become exposed.

It also means that each lead marshal is the ruler of his own tiny kingdom.

Susceptible to the vagaries of such license.

Accountable, like any king might think, only to his legacy.

Wilting in the blast of heat mid-island, Sam Dunn bangs out of the back of the Buffalo Springs Station terminal building lugging two big locked canvas mail sacks to his Cessna, waiting on the apron of the runway. He opens the cargo door, throws the bags in, goes back to the terminal, and rolls a four-wheel dolly piled high with UPS and FedEx packages out to the Cessna, where he quickly stacks them around the mailbags and some other L.A.-bound cargo. A short, fat man waddles out to retrieve the dolly, grunts something at Dunn, and disappears into the air-conditioned terminal, slamming the door shut.

Dunn is sweating.

Big half-moons bloom on his shirt under his arms, his hair dank, he drops his Revos onto his nose and climbs into the cockpit, where Jay is all folded up low, in the passenger's seat, so that nobody can see him. He hasn't been waiting for long.

"Hi," Jay says. "Go."

For weeks Jay has been perfecting this plan to slip out of Avalon without anyone (Feds) noticing. Even as they began to back off their watchful surveillance after the incident with the marshal everyone called Tripod, taking a golf cart, Jay decided, was infelicitous due to the probability someone (probably a Fed) might quickly notice it missing and the certainty he'd be spotted (by Feds) on the long snaking road to the airport. All those jogging circuits that took him along the ridge road suggested that the airport was probably too far to run to; not to mention there were a series of brutal ascents after the initial one; today the heat made this option even doubly difficult, had he chosen to take it. No, getting to the airport seemed impossible until he noticed the Catalina Conservancy truck bringing fresh water to several tin troughs for the buffalo and mule deer on the mesa. It made its circuit twice a week, mid-afternoon, driving up from the staging yard and the back of the canyon, past the golf course, on roads Jay had run, and proceeded to the farthest watering station first, a spot half a mile south of the airport, then snaked back through the wild rye and rattleweed and coastal sagebrush. He had actually practiced hopping on as the truck rumbled past him jogging, and then rode for a while tucked between the water tank and the back bumper, where nobody could readily see him.

Knowing that this was potentially the most vulnerable moment of exposure, he had learned the best place to catch his ride was a hairpin turn thick with fennel and scrub oak just before the old burn area near the canyon's lip. He knew that Monday and Thursday were water days, and this day was a Monday, and so Jay had decided, driven by Ginger's warning, to make his break.

No one saw him go, he kept looking back as he ran, the roads were empty; he was fairly certain they hadn't seen him. But when he leapt off the truck he'd stumbled and rolled his ankle, felt the sickening pop and the rubbery fold of foot underneath him. Pain came, slow-building, visceral; first the tingling rush of adrenaline from the shock, then a touch of nausea, and it made the half-mile trip uphill to the airport just that much more difficult. A shuttle bus from Avalon rumbled past on the gravel road; he stayed low in the seams of the rolling terrain, climbing, the side of his shoe cutting into the puffy flesh where his ankle was already swelling. Heat rose off the island clay. He circled wide around the head of the runway, then simply emerged from the brush into the baked, treeless, graded flats, and limped straight-line to Dunn's waiting Cessna. An employee of DC-3 Gifts & Grill stood in the shade of the terminal, smoking, staring at him, but not seeing him.

He climbed into the plane and hunkered down behind the seats and waited, sweating in the stifling oven of the cockpit for Dunn's arrival.

Three o'clock sharp, the Cessna shudders as the propellers find speed. Dunn releases the brake and eases out onto the runway. Cool air leaks into the cockpit from circulation vents. He catches the bubble lights of a couple of Avalon sheriff's station SUVs juddering through the scrub oak, fishtailing up the airport road. At the runway's end, Dunn sharply pivots the plane, pushes the throttle forward, and hurtles toward the open sky at the tarmac's opposite end.

Dunn glances, insouciant, at the arriving sheriff's vehicles as he whips past them. They've gone past the terminal, to skirt the runway, their sirens Doppler for a moment in the plane's wake and—

"What was that?" Jay asks, staying low.

"Nothing," Dunn says after a beat.

—a man in a federal suit tumbles out of the back of one of the Avalon station SUVs to watch helplessly as the mail-run Cessna floats off the headland cliff, dipping, then catching the ocean updraft effortlessly for a power-climb into a torrid day's poor excuse for a sky.

| 19 |

"*DOUBLE FATTINESS* IS ANOTHER GOOD ONE."

Blue sky and the laboring whine of the Cessna climbing fast.

"*Dreaming the Reality.*"

"What?"

Blue sky. Smear of whitecapped water, a sliver of firmament. Blue sky.

Hurtling through empty space on a diagonal, gravity's drag—what do they call it?—g-force, makes Jay's eyes ache in their sockets, and his fingers tremble.

"Guy in a maze," Dunn explains, no stress in his voice. No sign that he's mid-loop of some inexplicable aerobatic maneuver involving roll, pitch, *and* yaw; he could be sitting on the seawall by the Tuna Club, sucking on a warmish microbrew and watching the sun set over East Peak. "Guy in a maze confronts kickboxing killers, prostitutes who can crush watermelons with their thighs."

Jay's muscles tighten and his stomach flips.

"Everybody's lying," Dunn says.

Blue sky. And the angry whinge of the plane:

"There's a warlock with an army of female zombies brought to life by pounding spikes through their skulls—"

A sense of spinning, but with no horizon to reference, it's like a crushing onset of vertigo until an upside-down cockeyed world slides into Jay's field of vision and hangs there, sky, ocean, and the litter of civilization with which Los Angeles tumbles off the continent—but in reverse order—

"—all these nests of worms and centipedes that grow under the skin—"

—and Jay, eyes closing, cheeks sheet-white—

"—a magician," Dunn revels, "who drinks human milk to keep from aging—"

—the plane twists, flips, and swan-dives earthward, toward blue-black whitecapped swirls of sea, gaining speed, a death dive, and—

"—not to mention all the usual exploding bodies, love potions, amnesia, hysterical blindness—"

—through a gathering gossamer fume that seems to be spun out of nothing, a pillow of dreams—

"—crocodiles slit open to release snow-white doves, fireballs, and this really confounding subplot involving—"

—g-forces blading Jay's cheeks like rubber—

"—a lost little boy who rebels against his well-meaning but slutty mom."

At the last minute, Dunn pulls back on the yoke, the Cessna arcs up and strafes low across opaque sine waves of indigo water that foam and fall away.

"Epic."

They rocket into white blindness.

Dunn chortles: "Marine inversion from the Santa Ana situation.

Hodeeho." He eases back on the throttle and pops his sunglasses up onto his head, squinting into the impenetrable fog.

"Soup," he says. "Technical flying from here on, ladies and gentlemen."

Jay shifts in his seat, swallowing the acid regurge that rose to high tide in his throat.

"Skywriting, sometimes you'd go through a fat letter you just laid down and get somesuch like this. Only for the moment, though. Like you forgot something. Then it'd . . . clear."

Jay feels delivered into abeyance. No sense of movement, or direction, just the steady hum of the twin engines and the thwop of the propeller blades in the moist air.

"Can't we just climb up out of it?" Jay asks, whereupon a jumbo jet breaks through the brume, its belly huge, jet turbines roaring. Dunn's prop plane pinwheels and barely avoids crashing into it.

"Whoa, Nelly!"

The noise is astonishing.

The jet vanishes almost instantly, it happens so fast Jay doesn't even feel the panic until it's already gone, leaving a whirlpool of turbulence and wind shear that has Dunn fighting with his throttle just to stay aloft.

"—I don't think so, no," he says to Jay. "We're kinda splitting hairs between LAX and John Wayne flight grids here."

Jay thinks: *No shit.*

They're in the fog for a long time. As if someone painted the cockpit canopy opaque white. For a long time they don't speak. Jay wants Dunn to concentrate.

"It's like we've been erased," Dunn announces finally. Fluttering shadow geometries glide past. Buildings?

Erased. Dunn has no idea how that resonates for Jay.

A Milky White Maze, Jay thinks.

"A what?" Dunn asks.

Jay's surprised he said it aloud. "My friend runs experiments with mice in mazes," he explains. "I used to work with him. There's one, it's made of translucent plastic, sometimes it's even suspended in water, lit from all sides. The rats have no visual points of reference. The world is a blur."

A canyon of huge buildings looms dead ahead. Massing from nothing. The Cessna, jacked sideways by Dunn's sharp reflex, banks gracefully and slips through unscathed, swallowed again by the stubborn marine layer.

"What's the point?" Dunn asks, meaning the maze. He turns to look at Jay, his face lit cold and white and surreal and edged green by the dull glow of the instrument panel.

"I don't know," Jay says, sorry he brought it up.

"Maybe," Dunn suggests, "it's so they won't remember how to get back to where they started. So the rats gotta, you know, always go forward."

"Mice, but yeah." But Jay's mind goes elsewhere. Back to where this journey started. Vaughn and the lab: experimental neurosis. "To the doors." Consuming themselves, in their choler and confusion.

"The what?"

"Doors," Jay repeats. "Forward to and through the doors."

"Oh." Dunn, nodding as if he understands.

Crackle of static on the radio, some airport control tower, comprehensible only to Sam. Dunn asks why Jay quit that job with Vaughn. Jay recalls the day he was tasked with shaving two dozen rats' heads, placing them in a clamplike restraint, using a glorified drill press to puncture tiny holes just behind the ears into which thin wires were cemented and soldered to solid-state microprocessors the rats wore like football helmets, chin-strapped on, blinking teal LEDs and a whip antenna, and then Vaughn's project leader, a sun-starved psycho-behavioral post-doc goth goddess with violet-tinted contact lenses and a tangle of ginger hair and a filthy lab coat, tapping steadily on a wireless tablet keyboard sending messages to the rats that had them gyrate tilt-a-wheel until their eyes bled and they convulsed into comas.

"I got let go," Jay says. "Funding issues."

A dreamworld flickers in and out of existence as the squawk of air traffic control harmonizes with the drone of the plane. Parallel rows of halogen lights beckon them forward, skewed in the cockpit windshield.

"Jeez. We're cockeyed," Dunn says, and fusses with the wings to straighten their orientation to the runway guides as the Cessna gently falls to its impending landing.

Then: a muddle of flashing red lights: another phalanx of patrol cars, this time police, racing along on either side of the runway to keep pace with the plane.

Unnerved, Dunn says, "Shit—what are—FUCK. Cops." Jay, of course, assumes it's Public's guys, Feds, waiting to re-collect him, and starts to mentally resign himself to it, but Dunn throws the throttle forward, and the engine complains because: "Oh, man, and I got twelve kilos of pot in the luggage bay. SHIT. SHIT."

Twelve kilos of—what?

Landing gear toes the tarmac, the tires skid and the plane bounces. Directly ahead of them, at the far end of the runway, are more cop cars and emergency vehicles and lights flashing spectral through the fog. The Cessna, powering up, accelerates toward the blockade, landing gear touching twice more before leaving the tarmac for good and barely clearing the hardware below, men in fire suits and uniform frozen, watching as the plane careens over them, one strut clipping something with a sickening metal shriek of a wheel torn loose, and the plane is tugged violently sideways, Sam Dunn screaming as he tries to hold his plane from nose-diving left: "LOSE THE WEED! LOSE THE WEED!"

The Cessna lifts wildly, knifes into the fog, and the police dragnet vanishes behind them. Muffled cry of the engines peaking and then simply cutting out. Stalled.

Silence.

"Initiating plan B," Dunn mumbles, numb.

Jay is afraid to move. Waiting for the impact of a crash . . . that doesn't happen. *Plan B?*

Dunn is fighting with switches, trying to will the engines to re-start, and yelling at Jay: "THERE'S A—I'M—DUDE, helpmeout . . . LUGGAGE HATCH! IN THE BACK! IN THE BACK! THROW— THE WEED—OUT THE DOOR—BEFORE I PUT THIS FUCKER DOWN! I'LL . . ." Dunn doesn't finish the thought.

Scrambling back through the cockpit only because maybe then Dunn will shut up and concentrate, losing his balance, catching him-self on the bulkhead, Jay gropes at the prominent handle he finds on the floor in the back of the cabin, twists and yanks the compartment hatch open, revealing: nothing. No dope. Just the mailbags. He braces himself to turn, confused, frowning, and say something to Dunn, but Dunn is no longer at the Cessna's controls and as Jay's brain struggles to process all these incoming contradictions his world explodes be-cause the plane finds ground.

The noise of the impact is so deafening Jay registers only the change of pressure in his ears. He's thrown violently forward, feet-first, but somehow catches and braces himself between the backs of two seats while the fuselage fishtails and carves like the bow of a boat through turf and mud that sprays helter-skelter into the cockpit be-hind a bright curtain of shattered windshield glass as the plane finally impales itself on the low branches of a huge tree, bark and greenwood erupting scattershot, the smell of burnt wood and jet fuel and a gray

darkness that grows a muffled silence, fingers of fire reaching upward, smoke gathering, the sound of Jay's breathing, coughing, his
own heartbeat, the sound of his shoes banging on metal, the searing
pain that shoots through his ankle and then a perfect oval punches
out of the darkness as the Cessna's door falls away and a shadow
passes. Chalky light spills in on Jay, the weblike fractured branches of
the tree crowd the cabin, but he's been sheltered by the seats.

The Cessna's torn and buckled metal tick tick ticks with stress
points released. Hacking up the acrid smoke, Jay tumbles out of the
plane, onto the cold, wet grass of a small city park. Fog hangs curtained across a bright green field bordered by trees that seem to be
holding the formless drapery aloft.

He rises onto his hands and knees, looks back at the plane. Tangled fingers of oak have punctured the cockpit like an iron maiden
where Sam was sitting. Tongues of flame lick the broken cockpit glass
still held in the windshield's warped frame. Reflection of tree, sky,
fire, and the exquisitely fractured safety glass prevent Jay from seeing
inside.

Sirens, distant, mournful. Growing louder.

Jay gets up, his ankle fat, aching. And he runs. Like Ginger told
him to.

Often, even after years, mental states once present in consciousness return to it with apparent spontaneity and without any act of the will; that is, they are reproduced *involuntarily*. Here, also, in the majority of cases we at once recognize the returned mental state as one that has already been experienced; that is, we remember it. Under certain conditions, however, this accompanying consciousness is lacking, and we know only indirectly that the "now" must be identical with the "then"; yet we receive in this way a no less valid proof for its existence during the intervening time. As more exact observation teaches us, the occurrence of these involuntary reproductions is not an entirely random and accidental one. On the contrary they are brought about through the instrumentality of other immediately present mental images. Moreover they occur in certain regular ways which in general terms are described under the so-called "laws of association."

—HERMANN EBBINGHAUS (1885)
Memory: A Contribution to Experimental Psychology

| 20 |

HIS KEY IN THE DEADBOLT LOCK.

His lock.

His apartment door, which he's unlocked at least a thousand times. Jiggling metal against metal, but the deadbolt won't budge and a woman's voice calls out querulously from inside: *Who is it?*

Who is it? For a moment he's confounded, and he steps back to make sure that he's at the right door, even though he knows he is, this door he's opened and closed and gone in and out of without thinking about it, instinctive, but after a month in the shifting sands of witness protection, his senses are dulled again, his compass broken. Anything could be true. Or nothing.

The tiny security peephole in the door ripples with the black-and-hazel smear of a tiny, distant eye pressed against it. Jay removes the key from the lock and steps back.

Jay says that this is where he lives.

The voice disagrees, and points out that, in fact, *it* lives here, evidenced by the fact that it is inside and Jay is out in the hallway with a key that doesn't work.

Erased.

Embarrassed, he corrects himself: he used to live here: there is no response to his apology.

His body still aches from the impact of the Cessna's crash landing, his legs are dead from running, he reeks of smoke and sweat and maybe, he considers, he's been concussed, because if he was thinking straight he should never have come here to begin with, should have known that his apartment would be emptied and re-rented as part of the deletion that Public claimed was foundational to the program.

Jay puts his head to the door and asks if he could just, for a moment, look inside and see it again. He wants to know that something he remembers is true.

He hears the woman, farther back in the apartment, moving around, calling out to him to go away before she calls the police.

His Los Angeles, washed-out, uninviting, dour. Mid-city, disgorged from a 720 rapid bus, it feels to him like a foreign country. The squat, blunt, tawny sage hills rising above the crazy quilt of architecture, malignant scatter of stucco boxes, and the intermittent cluster of high-rises or skyscrapers, louvered parking structures, the theme-park shopping malls, the food trucks, phone stores, walking Sikhs, cut fruit vendors, hot dogs wrapped with bacon, inflatable toys on sticks. The scream of billboards, branding, half-naked boy-hipped women you'll never know gazing down with hollow promises, someone else's dreams.

The long-shadowed rectilinear moil.

The shimmering rivers of traffic.

The mad, quailing palms.

At the boxy, tan, Beaux Arts Hollywood Y, Jay pushes from bright, flat flaxen daylight in through the side gymnasium doorway, a stark silhouette that resolves into a man, and he stands for a while with hands in pockets, watching basketball players run the court, sneakers squeaking, bark of voices, slap of bodies and limbs colliding, the sharp percussion of the ball on the floor.

There are familiar faces, a couple of heads turn, with partial recognition: the equivocal look, half-nod, but the game flows on. Jay forgotten.

He doesn't see anyone from his old employer, Buckham & Buckham. They're still at their desks, he thinks.

He wants to take a shower, but the Sikh at the desk says Jay's membership has lapsed, in fact, he owes more than a hundred dollars in delinquent fees and there's only seventeen and change in his old wallet, so he turns and goes back outside, where a dim, bloodshot descending sun is still trying to burn through the fog, fat in a nankeen sky.

A CCESS DENIED ACCESS DENIED ACCESS DENIED. A reflection of Jay's resignation in the screen of a cash machine mocks him. There's a short line of impatient people behind him; he punches the keyboard again, sure that his password is right, knowing before he started that federal due diligence would have blocked this path along with all the others, but stubborn, he gets nothing but irritable beeps and denial of service, and finally swirls away as the machine eats his cash card and resets:

PLEASE INSERT YOUR CARD AND ENTER YOUR PIN CODE.

The dead eye of the security camera stares back at him.

A new hire, the security guard in the lobby not only didn't recognize him, but had never heard of Buckham & Buckham, and said the seventh floor was vacant and even confided that building management was having a hard time finding new tenants for several

full-floor suites on account of the stagnant economy and soft commercial rental market and Jay was welcome to go up and look, the
doors were open.

Upstairs, on seven, Jay rips protective paper from a window to let
light fall in on the emptied low-slung span of what was once his workplace. There's nothing here, just the faint impression of the desks and
cubicle walls on the dirty carpet, and the raw guts of an IT system
disemboweled and sprouting out of the floor at junction boxes.

Jay takes it all in. The quiet is awful, and the air is stale. Public
wasn't kidding when he told Jay they'd make him vanish; not just him
but everything that defined him. How far does it go? He's not as upset
as he should be, and he wonders why. His old life feels like a story
someone told him, secondhand, unreal.

He waits, listening for a haunting of voices he remembers but
cannot recall. He wonders, not for the first time, but for the first time
with a kind of clarity: *What happens when everything you've known is
made a lie? And all the lies play true? Are you the sum of your memories, or a
collection of consensual, verifiable facts?*

He still has a key to her apartment, too, but decides to ring the bell
so as not to frighten her, and just in case she changed the locks,
not wanting to repeat the distressing episode that happened at his own
apartment, earlier; he hears the familiar shuffle of her fluffy slippers
on hardwood flooring and, after a moment, Stacy opens the door and
comes face-to-face with Jay. Evidently, it still takes her breath away.

"Oh. My. God."

She looks good. But then, she always looks good, she works hard
at it. Jay says hi quickly, moves past her, into the tiny, single-girl apartment he thinks he remembers, but where now a hard-bodied guy in a

tight black T-shirt and Prada suit stands up from the love seat like a bit character in a failed '90s TV crime drama. Jay can't remember his name; it's the guy he thought moved to Houston.

"Oh my God," Stacy says again, in rising pitch.

"Hi. I'm sorry. I'll explain everything in a second, but first I gotta call Vaughn." Jay cuts his best indifferent look to hard body as he crosses to the phone. "Who are you?"

"Who are you?" the guy asks, standing up. It's the cage fighter: Juan Pablo. He's bigger than Jay remembers, and not remotely South American. But not really a cage fighter, Jay reminds himself, and Jay's pretty certain about it; that was just Vaughn, riffing, stoned. Wasn't it?

Jay glances at Stacy. "Tell him. Tell him who I am." He lifts the receiver from the cradle, and dials.

Stacy still hasn't closed the door. "What are you doing here, Jay? Did they let you . . . out?"

"What? Out of where? I've been in witness protection, you won't believe what I—"

Stacy cuts him off, cold: "Your mom called me and explained to me about the, you know, breakdown, and—"

"My mom can't call anybody, Stacy. I told you that."

"Yeah, well, she said that you'd say that, and that it was all part of your, you know, situation."

Jay listens to the phone ring on the other end of his call. "Come on, Vaughn. Pick up."

"This situation you have—this condition—oh, Jay, why didn't you tell me the truth to begin with? I feel like I don't even know you, I feel like I've wasted—"

Jay, attention divided, "Stacy, trust me on this: my mom didn't call you."

But Stacy's not listening. "You did this, anyway. You were the one who didn't want a commitment. Didn't want strings, take it as it comes, well lah dee dah, Jay, lah dee dah."

"What are you talking about? I proposed to you. We're engaged."

"No. Not really. Never really. I even had to buy the goddamn ring. Here. You can have it back." It's in her hand. She presses it into his palm, and the diamond bites.

"Stace."

"You didn't want it, Jay. That's why we could never pick a date. You know you didn't, and okay, maybe neither did I and now—this— well, I'm sorry but—"

"There is no 'this.' Let me just—why doesn't his machine pick up?"

Hard body looks to Stacy. "Baby, do you want me to take him outside?"

Baby? "GODDAMMIT!" Jay slams the phone down, and whirls on the Prada man. He inexplicably growls, "Back off, motherfucker!" and it sounds incredibly lame and stupid coming out of his mouth.

The puzzled look from Juan Pablo. "Hey, now." Still, Prada man drifts sideways, wary, rolling his shoulders, wiggling his fingers, taking Jay's measure.

"They said that you might do this, too," Stacy says. "They said—"

"What, that I went crazy? Stacy, they grabbed me, they put me into—"

Talking over him: "No, not crazy, just—"

"They?"

"The doctors. After I talked to your mom."

"Wait. Did they tell you, what, Jesus—they've got me in some mental institution somewhere? And you believed them?"

". . . just, more, like mixed up, and . . ."

"TOTAL strangers—"

". . . you know, and kind of delusional, baby, which the doctors said makes you think things are happening that . . . aren't."

Jay, keeping tabs on the cage fighter, shakes his head. "Stacy. Somebody calls you on the phone and says I'm in the mental hospital, says she's my mother, and you go, 'Oh, okay'? SHIT, Stacy, goddammit! I mean—"

"This is hard for me, too."

He tries to stay calm: "Okay. They, U.S. Marshals, took me into witness protection. They think I've seen something, or know something, I dunno, it's insane—the whole fucking thing is one long bad dream—"

Stacy is in her own aria. "—do you think I've slept one night since you didn't come home? I can't stop thinking about you, and how I had no idea you were—your Facebook page? Is *blocked*—"

"Stacy, will you listen? Look at me. This is me—"

"—and I'm just not good at this sort of thing—"

"—You know me. I've been disappeared, and you're one of the only people I can—"

"—but I can't pretend that this doesn't like . . . change everything. I mean. I can't be your nurse, Jay, I'm strong, but not that strong, and you've gotta go back, and whatever it is, whatever dark storm you're going through, let them help you, well, you gotta let them get you well again and let me . . . go—"

Jay stares at her, suddenly hearing her; he's hearing her for the first time.

Tears streaming down Stacy's face. "Jay—? Jay—?"

"—what?"

Her voice soft, soothing, the way she might talk to a child: "They gave me a number. To call. In case. Let me," and she's moving to the telephone, "so let me just call the hospital and tell them you're here, and—"

"Whatever dark storm I'm going through?"

"Jay—"

"No." Jay moves to intercept and stop her, but the hard-body guy grabs him, big hands on Jay's arms, and spins him away.

"Let her make the call."

Jay loses it. "You want to go, Houston, here, now?" The big man lets go of Jay and takes a half a step back, frowning, putting his hands out to either side, empty.

"No. I don't think so. I don't think so, because you do *not* want to be where I am right now, man, because—" Jay turns, hurls the ring in his fist across the room as hard as he can and is astonished when it *sticks* in the drywall like one of those flying oriental nunchuk whirly blades, or whatever they're called.

Hard body grabs Jay and lifts him a little too easily and pins him hard against the wall, knocking what's left of his breath out of him. Stunned, wheezing, Jay tries to fight back, approximating something he's seen in a movie, swings rubbery, but his fists find nothing but air, and suddenly he's stumbling out the door, colliding with the hallway wall opposite and falling to his hands and knees, woozy. Something pings off the side of his head and falls to the carpet, scattering light: the engagement ring. He looks up in time to see the door slamming shut. The man is laughing behind it and Stacy is telling him: "I'm calling them. We can't just leave him out there, he's sick . . ."

Whatever the would-be cage fighter from Houston murmurs to her is muffled, and Jay, in the empty corridor, can't decipher it. He gets up, unsteady. Attends to the sudden quiet, and surrenders to it, and walks away.

| 21 |

A **WROUGHT-IRON ELEVATOR CAGE** descends, byzantine, bottoms out at the end of a narrow foyer, and its manual-draw doors remain shut, the lift empty. Through locked glass double doors Jay peers in from outside the building, his hands laced through the security grille, buttery light bouncing off brass mailboxes queued along one tiled wall.

He didn't dream this.

He turns away, his reflection vanishing into a silken darkness through which a crude neon red-lipped smiling mermaid perched on a cocktail glass glows crazily. Her tail flutters and, in a sequence of neon stutters, she drops inside the glass.

He didn't dream her, either.

Inside the storefront strip club directly across the sleepy street, fixtures rattle with the rapid-fire percussion from calypso music and a tangerine-tailed real-life mermaid rises in the huge glass cylinder that serves as a watery center stage; hair black, skin white, she floats up, arches her back and does a lazy, curling flip, palest breasts roiling, the girl, sinking away again, down, and golden bubbles rise in a burst from both sides of her siren's red-lipped smile.

Half a dozen male patrons, none of them sitting together, watch her swim.

On the far side of the huge, glowing tank, in the darkest part of the bar, Jay looks back at her blankly, nursing a ten-dollar vodka tonic. Swirling the ice. Lost. An uneasiness has been creeping up on him, a nebulous slow-dawning understanding that it's possible the relative ease with which he escaped from custody, or protection, may have been predestined: they let him get away to see where he'd go. Ego prevents him from fully embracing this notion, but he can't seem to dismiss it. It travels with him like a yoke.

The mermaid floats up close to the glass in front of him, dark hair in tendrils, pale skin, glitter mascara, one pink nipple pierced with a gold fishhook. A tiny zipper tag flags from the orange scales at her hip, betraying the rubber tailfin costume this thalassic stripper has zipped herself into.

The dream version of the club, softened, rippled and smeared, looms behind her: the bar, the doorway, the faceless patrons at the scuffed black laminate tables . . .

. . . and John Q. Public strolling through the entrance curtain, followed closely by the Agent Known As Barry Stone. Public scans the bar, the room. The patrons. The tank. Mermaid in slow gyration, gilded in bubbles. Barry circles the stage-front tables, casual, careful, staying in the shadows.

No Jay.

No, Jay is bursting through the door of the upstairs tank room, out of breath from his sprint up the stairs. He slams it shut, looks around for something to wedge it closed. Water rocks free in the big, circular access hole that comprises the middle of the wooden floor. Some spangly mermaid costumes hang upside down from a rack in the far corner like gutted fish.

The pockapockapocka of a tiny air compressor whose hose disappears down into the water. Club music thumps below. An orange smear curls deep in the tank. Jay's desperate to discover a second way out. There's a ladder in the corner that leads to a trap door up to the roof. Fire escape?

Water sloshes up over the edge, darkening the floor, and the orange mermaid breaks the surface, gasping, spitting out her transparent air hose, scaring the shit out of Jay, and then groping for the railing to beach herself.

"Help me out here, willya, I can't"—she extends a slender white hand toward Jay—"this lovely fin suit's like wearing a giant dildo, plus it leaks and fills up and probably weighs as much as I do by the time I'm done." Jay braces himself and hauls her up into the room, and she flops, awkward, wet, tail spritzing heavily chlorinated moisture, frisky breasts going everywhichway. "I HATE IT. I just . . . hate it . . ." She finds the zipper and yanks and escapes, wearing nothing but a bikini bottom, and now she gets self-conscious: "TOWEL?"

Jay finds one, and the girl covers up, shaking the water out of her ears.

"You're not supposed to be in here," she says. Then, squinting at him: "Jurgen?"

"No, Jay."

"Sorry. I'm blind without my glasses and I can't wear contacts in the, you know. Seriously: legally blind. I want to get the laser surgery, but I'm nervous about it. I hear it goes bad. Jurgie's this guy I made a mistake and sucked off about a month ago." She adds, "Musta been life-changing, cuz he keeps following me, and like I'm gonna go through that crazy shit again, uh-uh, I don't even think he's German."

She finds her glasses on a shelf above the mermaid tail rack. Thick rims, retro-chic cat's-eye. She turns and watches Jay as she peels off her bottom, under the towel, and hangs it, dripping, from a hook. "Never wear latex with a Brazilian," she warns him. "You walk like a rodeo cowboy for a week."

"I'm looking for . . ." Jay stops himself. He sounds like a cop. He takes a different tack. "There was another girl who worked here, at the bar. Last winter."

The mermaid gives him a dead eye, teasing: "Oh, sure, okay, yeah, like now I know exactly who you're talking about."

"She worked at a flower shop during the day. This was just, nights, I guess, part time, but, well, something, this bad thing, happened to her and—"

"—Miriam."

Miriam.

The girl is suddenly sad. "Aw, Jesus, what a fucking mess. You were a friend of hers?"

"Kinda," Jay says, but, from memory, a single image: running across an empty expanse of blacktop with a mermaid in his arms.

"Super-tragic," the stripper remembers, "I mean—and she was our best swimmer, too, she was like, I think, almost in the Olympics or something, in that synchronized thing."

"No, she worked the bar. I—"

The mermaid shakes her head, wet hair dripping. "Miriam was a mermaid. Miriam Miller. I wasn't here when it happened, but," she's looking down, distracted, into the water, "hey, is somebody looking for you?"

Jay follows her eye line down through the tank and the warp of the water to Public, hands pressed against the glass, looking back up at him blindly.

"Don't worry, he can't see you," the girl says, shaking out her hair again and starting to twist it, the squeezings streaming back into the tank, "on account of, I think, the surface reflection, or something. Otherwise, all the fappers would be, you know, nose pressed to the glass and drooling—"

Jay explodes through the trap door to the rooftop like he's been launched from the ladder, pivots, his ankle aching, kicks the metal square shut again with his good foot and hop-skips across the roof, bathed in back-bleed from the shimmering cocktail neon hanging over the club. At the parapet he leaps a narrow slot of darkness to the tar-and-gravel of the next building's roof, landing gingerly, weight on one leg, and limps across to the next parapet, to leap again.

One after another, roof to roof, down the block. Vent pipes like punctuation marks, his sneakers slipping here and there on ancient patches. The channeled black scar of the L.A. River squeezes in from the sudden rise of Griffith Park, to the north, as the row of commercial buildings ends in a cross street and Jay can go no farther. He glances back. No one has followed him, and the one sleepy car that crawls past below is heading away from him, east into the Valley scatter.

Jay finds the fire escape and awkwardly scrambles down. Hits the sliding ladder and takes it rattling to its abrupt end—hangs there for a moment—drops to the sidewalk, where he sinks back into the shadows and sits back against the brick, ankle throbbing, catching his breath.

Another car blows past, headlights liquid in the night air, slows at the corner, taillight winking red, and disappears.

The night is electric with the deep hush-and-rumble of the Los Angeles he'd forgotten from his weeks on the island. Across the street, a dead metal security gate pulled across its entrance, is a flower shop.

Jay stares at it dully.

He remembers that his mother loved roses.

| **22** |

HE ARRIVES SO EARLY that he sits and waits for a while in the first light on a bus bench across the street. Visiting hours are nine to six, but the graveyard-shift staff lets him in when he tells them who he is and who he's come to see.

No one has called on her in a long time.

They find his name on the list in a file of preapproved visitors.

A nurse offers Jay coffee. Steam twists and coils from a cup with pop-out handles.

Huntington Hospital has a psychiatric wing called Della Martin, nestled deep inside the grand modern-mission medical complex, with a restful courtyard of grass and garden and trees. While, officially, the ward has no long-term-care program, there is a middle-aged female patient who has been here for as long as anyone can remember.

This woman is ashen-faced, and her dry, short hair is the institutional gray of the walls. Her eyes are dulled by years of lithium and the latest antidepressants and electroshock whenever it happened to come back in fashion.

She hasn't spoken in almost twenty years.

Jay sits on the edge of her bed, across from her worn armchair, dawn light slanting through the slot of window tracing faint promise on the hook rug under his feet. There are two forgettable abstract paintings on the facing walls, which Jay remembers from his father's den; the bureau is covered with framed snapshots of a happy family of five: vacations to Disney World, Christmas, birthdays, summer at the beach, three children, frozen in time: ten, eight, and five.

A larger formal wedding photo rises behind the collection as if attending it, awkward, ungainly; the young couple is handsome, happy and in love, oblivious to the catastrophe that awaits them and their children and all these framed stillborn memories they would not, did not, have the good fortune to ever look back on.

"Mom?"

The female patient is Jay's mother, and the glowing young woman in the photograph is Jay's mother, and there is no resemblance between the two. None.

She says nothing.

This is what he remembers:
    Fear.
Darkness.

His eyes blinking open to a bedroom he knew and sensed was not the same bedroom he'd fallen asleep in.

Something had been added.

Halloween night had been frigid, frost dusting the grass when they trick-or-treated, glistening on their shoes, the ghosts of breath trailing as they ran from door to door. His homemade ghoul costume hung from the hook on the open closet door, glow-in-the-dark viscera painted across it and still faintly greenwhite, slow-fading like memories, and all the candy in a pillowcase safely shoved under his bed.

On the back side of the shake-roof split-level was thick bluegrass that sloped past the covered, peanut-shaped pool to a dry creek bed that ran along a private gravel road lined thick with eucalyptus and pine; the streetlight at the intersection was shrouded by the trees' canopy, so even with the draperies pulled open the room was dark.

His heart was pounding in his chest, his mouth was cotton; he was scared and he didn't know why.

What had changed?

Motionless from fear, he listened. Listened until the quiet turned itself inside out and he became certain that somebody was in the house. Motionless, he listened, hoping for the heavy tread of his father's feet, or the whistle of his mother's slippers, or the slow-sliding socks of his brother, Carl, or his little sister's chronic sniffling. Halloween, he told himself. Halloween is scary, it's just that.

A low murmuring. Drawers sliding out and back in.

A heaviness in the house, extra weight, extra mass. A disturbance in the balance of things. Movement he could sense and not account for. A wicked, crushing, foreboding of otherness.

His father's voice, sleepy, calling out to ask who the hell was making that racket in the kitchen.

And then such an absence of noise, it was as if lives had already been sucked from the house.

He remembers being very confused after that.

He's never been sure how long he stayed in his bed, listening, waiting, dreading.

He thinks he heard his sister, Cara, cry out so suddenly that the silence swallowed it and made him wonder, in his bed, whether he'd heard anything at all.

His ears ringing. His heart pounding.

Shadow among shadows, he slid from the bed and went to the doorway of his bedroom, still listening to the uncertainty of his dread.

Felt the cold of the terra-cotta tiles in the hallway on the soles of his feet. Smelled the pine and eucalyptus outside, wet, sickly-sweet.

A rustle of trees and branches; icy breeze brushed his neck.

The front door was open. A cold hollowing darkness spilling in.

He stopped. Not brave. He wanted to go back to his room, get back in his bed, back under the covers; he was only eight and afraid of all darkness, convinced, once tucked in, that if any part of his body became exposed to the night whatever was lurking out there in it would find him.

Not so much to steady himself as just to feel its reassuring immutability, he put his hand on the wall and looked back down the hallway, to his bedroom, where he saw that the door to Cara's room was yawning in; through the yawning he watched curtains curl, rippling, lit ghostly by his little sister's nightlight, more of the cold bleak gloaming stealing in.

A door that his mother always closed after Cara fell asleep. A window that should not have been open.

And the noise in the kitchen, feet scuffling, half an exclamation of surprise and then a soughing sound and his cowardly indecision: the open front door and its promise of safety and the otherness in the house, the rancid smell of them, their voices, the bloody palm print on the wall: the ominous absence of anyone else in his family awake.

This is what he wants to forget:

Fear.

Darkness.

Everything that followed.

Even now it's a jumble.

There are blank bits that he could fill in, if he wanted, with what he later learned.

Jack-o'-lanterns' rowdy, puddled light from melted candles drew him up the steeply sloping hillside, through his mother's roses, thorns slashing him, pajamas tearing, barefoot, slipping on the frost-cold flattened lawn and leaves, eight years, two months, six days old, blind with tears to the Bruces' house where drunk, adult-size sexy witches and warlocks and vampires laughed shrill and febrile at the cartoon spookiness of his costume (zombie?), the liberal use of lifelike blood (just like a boy, isn't it?), and his squeak—he couldn't speak—the words wouldn't come—

—he was struck dumb—

—squeaking—

—crying—

—help them, help them, help them—

—Abigail Bruce finally found him and understood that her neighbors' son shouldn't have been there after midnight.

He does not remember what he told them. A group of men went together down the hill to the house and came back pale and shaken. Someone cleaned Jay's cuts and wrapped him in a blanket and the women sat with him, quiet, holding his hands, black mascara tears running down high-colored cheeks, sober while the men huddled and murmured with low, regretful voices.

The police found his father in the kitchen with stab wounds to the heart and head. Jay's little sister was suffocated as she slept. His brother. Carl. Struck and killed with the aluminum bat kept next to his bed. His mother, battered, broken, endured. Detectives believed that she came down after Jay fled, interrupted the two men at work on his father in the kitchen, and was caught in the front hallway but somehow survived an unspeakable assault, and the front hallway was where the men from the neighbors' party found her, eyes fixed, mouth open slack; the men in their Halloween costumes and stage makeup, she thought them angels, and the single statement she made to them before leaving this dimension was "Pray for us."

Two homicidal interlopers in 99-cent store masks and black sweats disappeared into the night of All Hallows, two scary monsters in a city of masquerades. They took the jewelry and a couple hundred dollars cash, a Cartier watch that had been his mother's Christmas gift that year, and the lives of five people, two of whom did not die.

Jay has no memory of the funeral.

After the one time, to collect his things, he never went back in the house.

The home invaders were never caught, and because there was a worry that the perpetrators would come back to "finish the job," he and his mother were relocated to California, where the generous insurance settlement cared for them both—Jay in boarding schools, summer science camps, and awkward trips with the Bruces, who were his parents' executors and best friends—what remained of his mother in managed-care facilities and psychiatric hospitals, principally Della Martin, where doctors watched and waited and hoped for a breakthrough that never came.

Twenty years of silence.

Spring semester of his high-school senior year at a Santa Barbara private school, Jay had had a visit from a federal agent who told him that a convict in Leavenworth had confessed to the crime in a letter he left behind to be found in his cell after the man garroted himself with a loop of baling wire in the prison garden one hot summer's afternoon. His recounting was dispassionate, detailed and specific, credible, including information that his accomplice had died of a drug overdose six months after the killings, a bad bolus of Mexican brown purchased with the last of the blood money stolen from Jay's family. It was a waxen day at Cate, the fog off the ocean was gluey and warm and clung obstinately to the hillside. The man gave no reason for the murders. Offered no apology, sought no forgiveness. He had said he hoped this would give Jay some kind of "closure," and that he was sorry it was so long coming.

It was a good story, well delivered. Earnest. Maybe true, sure. Jay suspected, however, that they'd made it up. That it was another sleight-of-hand blithely offered to facilitate his so-called healing. At the time, Jay didn't know how to tell the federal agent that, if he thought about that night at all anymore, it was to wonder why he hadn't stayed in the house with his father, and not run like a little coward into the darkness, where his life and all memory of what he witnessed between the hallway and the Bruces' party fell away and was lost.

There are some doors mice choose not to go through.

There are things best forgotten.

Or not remembered.

At noon his mother rises from her chair, stiff, knee joints clicking, and kicks off her slipper turtles and climbs onto the bed, knifing pale varicose legs under the sheet and tugging it up over the shoulder she turns toward the wall so as not to face him, although Jay, still sitting on the edge of the mattress, wonders if she even really understands that her son, her only remaining family member, is there.

"Mom?"

He feels a strange compulsion to talk to her. He wants to tell her what's happened, that he's been taken into protective custody by federal agents who want him to remember something he may never have seen. That he's broken up with a fiancée his mother didn't know he had, he's been given a false life with a woman named Ginger and her daughter, Helen, selectively mute, and he's developed all these dumb, stupid, complicated attachments and feelings for the woman and coaxed the daughter into talking to him. And it's not real. He knows it's not, but it might as well be, it might well be what he wants, but what he wants, what he wants to know, what he wants to ask, what he wants his mother to tell him, is: What should he do?

"I learned this thing in college," Jay says aloud to his mother's back. "In, I think, philosophy class, this experiment called Mary's Room. There's Mary, this brilliant scientist, who gets locked away and raised in a black-and-white room, where she's given a black-and-white television monitor and the controls for the camera that's directly attached to it, which can, like, float around the world—don't ask—wherever she needs it to. And Mary, who eventually becomes a specialist in the science of seeing, slowly collects all the physical information there is to truly know about what happens when we experience colors: what goes on when we see sunflowers or tropical skies or ripe tomatoes on the vine. She learns the exact wavelengths of light necessary to stimulate the retina to perceive these colors, and exactly how the brain decodes that information and then stimulates the feelings we have and the breath we need to expel and the vocal contractions necessary to say, 'Whoa, look: that sky is fucking *blue*.'

"In other words: she knows everything there is to know about the science of color. Everything. In theory. But when the door unlocks and she finally walks out of that room into the world of color, what? I mean, when she actually *experiences* color. Will she learn anything new?"

Jay's mother says nothing. She doesn't move.

"You can study and shape and imagine what it would be like to experience something—let's say, in this case, a life, a real life—but how do you know that you'd recognize it when it happens to you?

"And what if you recognize it, but it's just a construct? Temporary, hypothetical. A convenient fiction."

Jay's mother says nothing.

He blinks back tears that take him by surprise. He puts his hand lightly on her arm, and the arm draws away from him, in a reflexive recoil.

The lab mouse was invented in 1909 by Harvard track star C. C. Little, who mated generation after generation of field mice until he had a healthy, genetically stable, inbred strain that lived in sterile isolation awaiting any number of unfortunate outcomes over which it had no control. But as genetically close as a mouse may be to a man, mouse metabolism is not human metabolism, and there are a lot of ways of being small and brown. Or white and blind. Or epileptic. Or obese. So a new science of mousing evolved, to make it possible to turn on or off individual genes in mice and isolate those traits linked to diseases or conditions that Big Pharma like Manchurian Global yearn to cure. And with the sequencing of the mouse genome, the lab mouse is no longer a substitute human. Not even a mouse, really. It's something other: a genomic runner negotiating the maze between life and code: offering an illusion of understanding things that Jay knows cannot be understood.

And monsters exist.

And mermaids drown.

And little boys lose their lives without dying.

And their moms lose their minds.

She has no reaction to his leaving. A staccato of anguished voices and the rattle-drone of dayroom television serenades him down the corridor to the front desk, where he signs out. The receptionist smiles sympathetically and asks if he had a nice visit.

Jay allows that he did.

| 23 |

THE OVERHEAD FLUORESCENTS flicker on and slowly brighten Vaughn's Manchurian Global lab, and Vaughn, pulling his card from the reader and looping the lanyard back around his neck, enters to the sharp smell of urine and the startled light shimmying of tiny legs across cages and the insane screaming of a couple of test monkeys.

"Yeah, yeah," he drawls, "Daddy's home."

It always takes a while for the energy-savers to gain their full intensity. Vaughn weaves his way through warrens of mostly unused cages interspersed with stainless-steel examining tables and Plexiglas mazes in various stages of demolition. His desktop computer monitor is on and glows with data; an archived *Los Angeles Times* newspaper article featuring a big lurid color photo of a covered body getting hauled by fire personnel out of the front of an apartment building. The headline:

STRIP CLUB MERMAID'S MURDER

BAFFLES POLICE

In the thick of the body copy is inset a one-column head shot of Jay's flower girl, helpfully captioned "Miriam Miller." Vaughn frowns because this was not on his computer screen when he left the lab last night.

Strewn across the desk are more articles that have been printed out, and tiled, overlapping:

_____

THREE DEAD AT GLENDALE STRIP BAR
D.A. SEEKS SAMARITAN WITNESS TO CLUB KILLINGS

_____

A short intake of breath, Vaughn sinks into his chair, shakes his head, wondering, basically, what the hell?

_____

EXOTIC SWIMMER SHOT IN CLUB,
CARRIED TO APARTMENT

_____

Jay's hand touches his knee. Vaughn yells and kicks back from the desk.

"Vaughn." Jay, rolling out, spectral and groggy, from where he's been sleeping, then hiding (when he heard someone come in). "It's me."

"HOLYcrap," Vaughn says. "I almost—what are you—Jay?" Looking closer: "Your hair looks like crap. You're like, are you a blond now or—?" and finally, "how the hell did you get in here? This is a secure building."

Jay's up and stretching. "I keyed in my old code," he says. "Or maybe you told me what yours was, once."

Vaughn is staring at him.

"What?"

"Did they let you out or did you escape?"

"I haven't been in a mental hospital."

"But—"

Jay, rote: "I'm not crazy, I didn't go crazy, I wasn't in a mental hospital. Feds've taken me into witness protection, they think I . . ."

Vaughn is staring at him.

"Don't. Vaughn? No. Don't do that. Come on—this isn't—this is me. Vaughn, you know me."

"No."

"How can you—"

"I know what you've told me. I know what you want me to know. But, um. Do I know that it's true?"

"Yes. You do."

Vaughn shakes his head. "No, see, that's just the thing—I don't. Not really. After you . . . disappeared? And I got the call from the hospital?"

"There was no hospital," Jay says again.

"It's like I thought about it. You know? I thought about it, us, our friendship, me and you. What I know, what I really know. I thought about it for a long time and I realized: How long have I known you? And I don't know shit."

The lights hum. The animals fidget in their cages, hungry.

"You live lightly on this earth, my friend," Vaughn says. "It's like you don't, I mean, there's no, well . . ." He makes an ambiguous gesture. ". . . not a lot of give and take."

Jay nods, because he actually understands, and wants to explain, "That's changing—"

"But, um."

"—I swear to you, federal marshals have put me in protective custody over on Catalina Island over something I don't even know what it is."

"Rutger Hauer."

"What?"

"In *Blade Runner*." Vaughn indicates, with his chin: "Your hair, dude."

Jay runs a hand across it, absently. "And yeah, I took a runner. I got away from them with this weird guy in his pot plane."

Doubtful: ". . . Okay."

"Seriously. We crashed. I don't know what happened to him. But they erased me, Vaughn. Everything I was. Or thought I was. Buckham and Buckham? Gone. I mean, *gone*. Some lady's living in my apartment, Stacy's shacked back up with that guy from Houston—"

"The cage fighter."

"Vaughn, he's not."

"Okay. Whatever."

"And they told everybody who might wonder where I went that I went crazy."

"Juan Pablo."

"That's not his name. Vaughn: focus."

"They said your family took you home."

Jay blinks. "They said what?"

"After the breakdown," Vaughn says. "You never talk about your family."

"Who? Who said about my family?"

"I mean," Vaughn says, "you talk about being erased, but it's like you don't even exist here and now to begin with. You know what I mean? Maybe nobody notices you're gone because you were never here."

Jay says nothing. Hollowed out.

Vaughn looks away, to the articles, to the computer screen. "What's all this?"

"Vaughn—"

The monkeys are screaming again, and genuflecting in their cages, arms out, heads dipping, long fingers laced through the bars. It's a morning call to prayer.

"They left a number I'm supposed to call when I see you," Vaughn admits sheepishly.

Jay, impatient: "What's your point?"

"Well, um. They left it on my cell phone this morning."

"So?"

"*When* I see you, Jay. Not if, *when.*"

Jay blinks. They knew. They let him go.

But why?

The newspaper articles spill upside down across a swirly Formica tabletop. This downscale Atwater retro café is chrome and black and white and gray. There's a breakfast crowd, mostly locals; the dark eyes of the lone waitress watch idly from behind the register. Jay sits opposite Vaughn in a crescent vinyl booth safely away from the front window, fanning and collating his collected documentation between them to make his case.

"You remember this?"

Deeply engaged with his scrambled egg, chorizo, feta, and cactus burrito, Vaughn can only shake his head and murmur, mouth full between bites, "Since when do you read the newspaper? You always say it's too depressing."

Jay thumbs the head shot of Miriam. "According to my new federal friends, I went out with her—well, yeah, and I did, I think I did, but they knew all about it, they've been watching me for—remember? She worked in this flower shop on Melrose where I got Stacy a Valentine's Day—"

"I remember that." Vaughn bolts some coffee. "Yeah. Your porno fantasy. She—"

"No. I made that part up."

"Really?"

"Or. Maybe I made all of it up. I don't know. I don't know. You're just taking my word for it, anyway. The point is—"

"See what I mean? You're not a truthful person."

"—the point is," Jay continues, stubbornly, "they think I know something about what happened to this woman, what happened in this bar, but I don't. Remember. I was drunk, or stoned, or drunk and stoned, or it didn't happen. I don't know, Vaughnie. I don't remember."

"Yeah, well. Memory, yo, seriously: What is it? The fucking consensus intersect of desire and regret."

"Or what I do remember doesn't, you know, add up to . . . this," Jay says ruefully. "What they're . . ." He stops. What are they saying it adds up to? "It's all . . . I mean, it didn't even happen on the right day." He makes a sweeping gesture to the articles. "They keep talking February twelfth, but according to these stories, February twentieth, February twenty-second, this all happened like, eight, ten days later."

Vaughn, pushing his empty plate away, makes the point that he thought Jay went out with her twice.

Jay: "Excuse me?"

"That I personally know of," Vaughn says, "that you told me about, but, um. For all I know it coulda been—"

Jay cuts him off. "Are you listening to me?"

"I'm just saying."

"They don't even have the right day."

"Oh."

"I would remember. If I went out with her twice."

"Okay."

"I would."

"Hey," Vaughn says blithely. "Maybe you've fallen through a wormhole, man. Parallel universe. Or you went in one and came back out."

The shriek of the espresso machine allows them to sit back and regroup. A waiter refills Vaughn's coffee and clears their plates. Jay hasn't touched his oatmeal. Glancing reflections of traffic fracture through the window. Someone at a table in the front laughs too loudly.

"They walk me through my life last year, day by day, but out of order," Jay says. "Like they're trying to trap me or something. Catch me in a lie. So deliberately random that there's got to be a pattern, certain connections they want to make. It's gotta all fit, I mean, the details, and I keep trying to . . . figure out . . ." His voice trails off, suddenly bleak. "But my life was shit, wasn't it?"

"Everybody's life is shit."

"You're wrong."

Vaughn says that that's why they invented heaven. "Well, oh, and for those few lucky pricks whose lives aren't shit?—the one percent, credit swap bullshit, or those Goldman Sachs sucks, billionaire IPO Net-head geekazoids and maybe supermodels with real breasts and anybody who works at Apple?—there's eternal hell waiting for them, so it all, like, evens out." Vaughn frowns. "What is that?"

Jay's got Stacy's engagement ring out of his pocket; he's spinning it absently on the Formica, lost in thought. "I went out with the flower girl . . . twice?"

"I don't remember exactly," Vaughn lies, and looks away, guiltily, and seems like he's about to try to explain it, but Jay's next soft statement stops him:

"My brother and sister and my dad were murdered when I was eight."

Vaughn turns his eyes to Jay, mind clearly blown. *What?*

"Yeah. They never caught who did it."

Jay watches Vaughn slowly try to comprehend that this is a confession. That Jay is telling him something fundamental. He doesn't move.

"I should have told you a long time ago."

"Probably," is what Jay thinks Vaughn exhales.

"Not that it explains everything, but, I don't know. It was not good. Not . . . good. My mom went catatonic with grief," Jay says. "You know. What they call fugue state or something. She's still . . ."

Jay can tell that Vaughn's mouth has gone dry because he lifts his cup and sips cold coffee, murmurs something soft that gets lost in the diner's din.

"I know," Jay says.

Vaughn offers something else, kind, sorrowful, meaningless.

Spinning the ring like a gyroscope, Jay: "Me, I got away. They didn't get me because I ran. Two guys. Two guys, they took some money and jewelry. It was on Halloween, that was why I never liked . . ." Vaughn knew all about Jay and Halloween, but now knew why. "I had this righteous stash of candy under the bed in a pillow slip. I forgot to get it. When they took me back for my stuff. For the longest time I tried to convince myself that was my big regret. And everything after, it's like I had this life that was predicated on not looking back, never looking back. Can you call that a life? I don't know. But, um," he says, unwittingly mimicking Vaughn, "I got a new one, on Catalina, Vaughnie. Totally by accident, and pretty much totally a construct, I guess, but . . ."

"A new life."

"Yeah."

"But what?"

Behind Vaughn, in the mirror surface of the stainless-steel wall behind the breakfast counter, Jay senses more than sees a movement, a figure, the faint ghost of the street and someone in the front window staring in—

"Jay?"

—the face of Sam Dunn, staring in at them.

Jay swivels in his chair (how did Dunn survive the crash?), spooked (how did Dunn survive?), looks to the front window itself: nothing, nobody there. A shiny slur of traffic through morning sun.

"What are you looking at?"

Jay turns back to Vaughn. Chilled. "Nothing."

The ring wobbles to a stop. Jay covers it with his hand.

Struggling to stay on topic: "Anyway, what I'm trying to say is, somebody holds your past year up like that, naked, particularly a life as sorry and sketchy as mine, it looks . . . I don't know . . ."

He glances over his shoulder to the window again. No Sam Dunn.

"I'm sorry," Vaughn says.

"It is what it is. I didn't tell you because I don't tell anybody. Like I said. I don't think about it."

"Yeah."

"I just—"

"—Okay."

"So. Now you know."

Vaughn sighs, and looks relieved somehow. With a friend's rare kindness, as if sloughing it off, no big deal, "I realize this will probably sound incredibly lame, but, um: it's your life, Jay, you've only got one. I mean. Fuck it. Whatayagonnado? Reboot?" He belches. And smiles faintly, wry. Jay is quiet. He looks down at his hand covering the ring and a life from which he's just now realizing he's been set free.

"Jay. Jay. You okay?"

"Yeah, fine." Jay looks up. "Hey, I'm gonna need some money."

Vaughn blinks. *Money?*

"And a place to crash, just until—" Jay feels the movement behind this time, his head whips to the window, where he catches just a glimpse of a face, a figure, a shape slip out of frame, and abruptly he's pushing up and away from the table. "I gotta check this—sit tight for a sec, okay?" he tells Vaughn and hurries to the front door and out onto the sidewalk, where he looks both ways, up and down the street, not much foot traffic in either direction, and no sign of Sam Dunn.

It's a bright, unforgiving sunlight. The homeless guy on the corner dances, his tinfoil cape throwing off dazzle. Jay moves along the café window, under an awning, to where he thought someone, maybe Sam Dunn, was standing when he thought he saw him, and turns to peer back into the diner at Vaughn—

—who is *gone.*

Struck light-headed with a slow-rising panic, Jay tries not to freak out: there's the table, there's Vaughn's chair pushed back, there's his coffee cup freshly filled. Jay wants to think maybe Vaughn's in the bathroom, and when he gets back inside he goes down the narrow, dead-end hallway to the door marked: GUYS. Barges in. It's unoccupied. But the window is cranked wide, and the sound of a car firing up draws Jay to it, and to look out into the alley behind the diner where a beat-to-hell dark gray S-Class Mercedes is pulling out, fast.

Vaughn's face is twisted toward Jay, one hand pressed to the back window glass, frightened eyes, mouth open and yelling something as the German sedan peels out. Then he's jerked back into the shadow of the interior and the sun's reflection wipes even the memory of him away.

Oh shit.

| 24 |

Out of breath.

Tuneless keytones. 411: government listings: U.S. Marshals office: Los Angeles: main switchboard: the helpful operator: Jay impatient, says hi, needs to talk to Deputy U.S. Marshal Public. First name John. Yes, John Q. Public, Jay says, voice thin, hoarse, words coming in breathless bursts, please don't hang up, he knows what it sounds like, it's the name he was given, the name of the agent, or connect him with Jane Doe. Stupid, yes, but—who's calling? Jay tells them. Johnson. Jay. He tells the operator at the U.S. Marshals office that he's a protected witness, he's in the program, and she hangs up.

The receiver drops from his grasp, dangles on its metal leash. Hands on his knees, coughing, bent double, he closes his eyes. His heart pounds in his ears. He tries to fill his lungs with air.

After he watched Vaughn stolen away, he sprinted back through the diner, into the kitchen, past blank stares of startled fry cooks to the rear exit and burst out into the alley and ran pointlessly after the Mercedes just merging into traffic, as if by will alone he could catch it, down the long, shadowed alley, his legs hitting the pavement so hard he began stumbling forward into heavy traffic on the next city street, cars swerving, honking, as Jay, sidestepping a slow-moving gridlock caused by roadwork at the next intersection, looking for the sliver of dark gray maybe, possibly, just disappearing around the corner—feet pounding, running, running, as if all the running he did on Catalina was training for this one feat—saving Vaughn—which he knew was impossible, knows is impossible, you can save only yourself and, sometimes, even if you do, what's the point?—although this time he's not running away—running, stumbling reckless forward desperate around another corner where finally he saw the charcoal S-Class picking up speed (was that it?) three blocks ahead of him (was it the same car?) and make a merging swerve onto a main thoroughfare, disappearing, Glendale Avenue or San Fernando Road, Jay didn't know, he was all turned around.

But there was this gas station across the street.

Receiver in hand. Dial tone. Tuneless keytones, he tries it all again.

Same result. Institutional politeness followed by exasperated skepticism, impatience, threats of legal consequences for tying up a federal phone line, for making a nuisance, and Jay says fine, fine, send somebody to get me.

And she hangs up on him.

Dial tone tuneless keytones; this time he taps out 9-1-1.

Johnson, he tells the operator. J as in . . . Johnson.

Yes, it's an emergency, Jay says, he's a Federal witness, he's left protected custody, he's exposed, vulnerable, he's out, he's whatayacallit—compromised—and the emergency operator asks him to repeat his name and he does. Johnson, J. B. Jay. Johnson.

A soft voice behind him suggests trying "Jimmy Warren."

Jay spins.

Jane Doe is standing outside the pay phone kiosk, at a respectful distance, not too close, casual; he forgot how tall and striking she is. A navy blue Prius with government plates has stolen up, silent except for the faint bite of gravel under the tires, with waiting doors open, beneath the service station awning.

Tripod is behind the wheel. He grins out at Jay mirthlessly. Lifeless eyes lumped in his face like two rubber stoppers, opaque.

Doe asks, all droll and friendly: "Where you been, James?"

I saw him," Jay insists, although, as he says it, he's aware that he's not completely confident he's right.

Through some ugly ramble of lower Glendale the government plug-in hybrid floats silky, tinted windows set at half-mast. A smog-mantled cityscape roiling and wheezing past like rear projection, the Library Tower and a posse of flattop skyscrapers loom over the palm-stuck hills of Angelino Heights. Jay's thoughts scatter, regroup, flailing for coherence. Piecing together a story he doesn't even know the plot of.

"Dunn?" Doe, in the front seat, with her head barely turned. Tripod driving, unusually silent.

"The pilot, yeah. My ride. After the plane crashed and burned . . . I didn't see him get out, but—" Still laboring to get his breath, though now he's not winded. It's more like there's simply not enough air. Anywhere.

The back of Doe's head angles, wordless, pensive.

"If he got out," Jay says, words knotting up on him. "What, or why, is he . . . ?" Then, frowning at an old thought he needs confirmed and changing subjects: "You let me go." It's a question made statement; Doe is unresponsive and won't confirm or deny. "Was he—" But Jay's not sure what to ask next. "Dunn. I mean—was that why—do you guys know who he is—was—or if he's part of—?"

"We don't know him," Jane Doe cuts in, even-tempered. "The

Cessna he crashed belongs to one of those well-connected private paramilitary government contracting outfits that sprung up in the fertile fields of 9/11, like genetically altered weeds, and now you can't get rid of them."

"Why would they—he, Dunn—or anyone—want Vaughn, when it's me, or at least according to you, I mean . . . isn't it—?"

"Take a breath," Doe says. "You saw something, Jay. This morning. Yesterday. Something you're not sure of," gently, almost solicitous, "if you think about it."

Jay hesitates, knows she's right. "Lately," he confesses, "since I left, since before I left, okay sure: I'm finding it's like, yeah . . . I'm just not so sure of things. Anymore. Which is not to say fucking blind," Jay adds, defensive. "And, yeah, it worries me, because we, I, all of us. We're so easily erased. And you guys—"

"Where does your friend live?" Tripod asks.

"Vaughn's not part of this."

"He is now."

"What do they want? The list? Is this all about the goddamn list? Oh, and Vaughn thinks I was in a psych ward, so does Stacy, thank you very much—"

"Calm down."

"—You told everybody I went crazy? What the fuck is that? I mean. Fuck. It's just, everything, is completely—"

"Jay?"

"—just completely—"

She turns to face him around the headrest. "Jay . . . step by step. Where does Vaughn—"

"—and then he was right there," Jay says, still agitated.

"Calm down."

"Right there. In the window. Outside the diner. Like a ghost."

"Jay."

"And Vaughn—"

Doe's arm swipes over the seat and the back of her hand delivers a moment of fireworks and darkness. "I said—"

Jay's head snaps into the seat, he slumps back, hands going up, bleeding from the nose. "OwJesus."

"—*Doucement*," Doe declaims softly. "We know where he lives, we were just being conversational."

"*What?*"

"*Doucement*," Doe says.

Tripod: "It's French for shut the fuck up."

"No, it's not."

Jay, glaring, is adrift, a flare of rage only serving to choke him wordless. Wet red threads leaking out of his nose, monsterlike; he can see them in Tripod's rearview mirror.

"You need to get ahold of your emotions," Doe tells him. She hands him a tissue and looks at her hand. Her knuckles are red. She flexes her fingers and frowns, as if disappointed in herself.

The tinted windows hum upward.

They veer north on the Hollywood Freeway, the dour silence of the preternaturally mute hybrid car broken by the thump of the concrete seams, low-fluttering: fffmmmphhh fffmmmphhh fffmmmphhh fffmmmphhh.

"This is not a maze," Jay says finally. His face aches, and his nose is numb. Thoughts untwisting: "This particular zigzag gang of angles. This . . . thing you've made for me. Has no outlet. At all. Which means it's not even, at the heart of it, a riddle to solve. Is it?"

Doe and Tripod have no reaction.

"A *true* riddle, or test, has something akin to a door," Jay says. "This, instead. It's like, what, I don't know . . . a zero-sum game. Or a watery grave. Without any hope of exit, unless, well, unless there's a looking glass up ahead."

He watches traffic fall away on either side of them and wonders if Feds can drive as fast as they want. "Is there? I mean. Is there a looking glass?"

"I don't even know what that means," Doe says at length.

"A way to just opt out of this whole thing," Jay explains.

Tripod makes a low guttural noise that is either mockery or disgust.

Jay closes his eyes. "And I wish I could say there was some . . . satisfaction in seeing . . . feeling all this, but there's not, but . . ." His thread unravels. He's beaten. He's got no fight left. He knows it. "You thought I'd lead you somewhere." Nothing from Doe. He no longer cares to know what they want. "Or you'd see where Dunn would take me." Tripod's head moves slightly, as if he's looking for some signal from Doe. And what Jay wants?

Doe's eyes stay aimed straight ahead, "Whatever you say, Jay. Have a party."

Jay lays the side of his head she hit against the window and feels the heat on his skin. "Okay." It does not escape his notice that she's called him Jay.

The Prius slips down an off-ramp, decelerating, and outside Jay sees streamers: plastic triangle flaglets of red white blue flap and rattle like little tropical fish sucking air, as, underneath them: the federal car fragments through the intersection, leaving rubber as it arcs around the used-car lot and merges with local traffic.

Vaughn?"

It's the white door at the very end of the corridor, 440E, and the E is missing; fourth floor of a Deco Irving Gill knockoff residential apartment building just off Las Palmas. Jay pounds with the heel of his hand.

"Vaughnie? You home?"

No answer. An uneasy deadness in the stale air. He looks at Doe, and Tripod. "If they took him," Jay says. "Why would he be here?"

"If they took him." Tripod puts a fat hand on him and draws him aside to let Jane Doe expertly kick the door inward without splintering the jamb.

It doesn't smell right. There's lots of Vaughn in the place, but also something else. Not Vaughn.

Doe has her gun out, but at her side; she leads them through the quaint, pointless quasi-foyer with the small, round antique table Vaughn got from his grandmother and a fishbowl of tetras suspended in still water like a handful of small promises. Vaughn's bachelor apartment is usually tidy, bright, sunny, with a postcard view of the Hollywood sign. But right now everything's been tossed like a salad and the Venetian blinds are rent and splayed and the mermaid Jay pulled warm and vibrant from a strip-club sea just last night dangles dead as anything in the middle of the main room, hung from blue-black duct-taped hands on a ceiling fan slowly turning with an angry hum.

Somebody has shot her in the head.

Even Doe is caught by surprise, and she exhales a soft, sad lament.

Jay turns away, light-headed. He twists and buckles to his knees. His forehead touches to the floor like a penitent praying, and Tripod arcs around him, no big deal, as if to suggest this sort of thing happens in his, their, world every day (which it couldn't) and in so doing establish his, their, professional distance from it (which he can't), cracking wise: "Well, now, okay, maybe he'll believe us. Maybe he'll finally understand the serious, serious shit he's all up in." But Doe just touches the mermaid lightly, tenderly, sorrowfully, and the body sways. "Oh, girl," she says to it softly. "I'm sorry." Then, to Jay, absent of judgment, asks, "Do you know her?"

There's no response from Jay, who has further upset himself with his unchecked, spontaneous, and callous relief that it isn't Vaughn hanging from the fan.

Fuck. Fucking coldhearted shit.

"Jay?" Tripod, impatient. He's pulled latex gloves from his pocket and put them on. *Does he always carry them?*

Shit. Shit.

Did he know her?

Doe looks absently to the doorway, still gaping, but she's talking to Tripod. "Call it in, Miles. Don't touch anything. We're not staying."

Did he, does Jay, know anything?

Finally, Jay finds his voice: "Yes," he answers. "Yes." And then, truthfully: "No."

Twenty-six miles across the sea

Santa Catalina is a-waitin' for me

Santa Catalina, the island of

romance, romance, romance, romance

Water all around it everywhere

Tropical trees and the salty air

But for me the thing that's a-waitin' there—romance

It seems so distant, twenty-six miles away

Restin' in the water serene

I'd work for anyone, even the Navy

Who would float me to my island dream

Twenty-six miles, so near yet far

I'd swim with just some water-wings and my guitar

I could leave the wings but I'll need the guitar for

romance, romance, romance, romance

—"26 MILES (SANTA CATALINA)," THE FOUR PREPS (1958)
Music and lyrics by Bruce Belland and Glen Larson

25

CHASING DUSK, skimming the surface, Long Beach forgotten, the Catalina jet cruiser runs through sawtooth dark water, roiling, rolling, shoved high by one wave, dropping hard into the trough of the next, trailing in its wake a foaming scar of white.

It may be that more than fifty million mice die in U.S. laboratories every year. Jay found the data incomplete, and murky. Laboratory mice succumb to everything from toxicology tests (in which they are slowly poisoned) to burn studies to psychological experiments designed to induce terror, anxiety, depression, and helplessness.

Even C. C. Little's eugenic mice are still mammals with nervous systems much like a man's; they feel pain, fear, loneliness, joy. They become emotionally attached to one another, love their families, and bond with human guardians.

Baby mice giggle when tickled.

Some adult mice have been known to show empathy when another mouse—or human with whom they've bonded—is in distress, and exhibit altruism, will even put themselves in harm's way, rather than allow another living creature to suffer.

Vaughn says this is horseshit, but you can look it up.

They are, however, Jay discovered, categorically not included in the federal Animal Welfare Act provisions that extend at least some hope of dignity to other experimental subjects. While rabbits and guinea pigs, for example, must be provided with pain relief, and labs must prove there are no modern alternatives to the use of these species, scientists are not even required to count the number of mice who perish in the course of their research.

Off and on for more than two hours, from Vaughn's apartment to San Pedro and now on the fast boat, Jane Doe has been murmuring to him, perhaps debriefing him, but Jay can't seem to hold on to what she's been saying. He can't shake the dead girl from his head. They are the only passengers making this crossing; Tripod remained behind in San Pedro. The forward cabin is vacant, Jay is pretty sure there are support marshals with them on the boat, from the way Doe is all relaxed and easy, and sometimes he can feel their eyes on him, but hasn't seen them, and he doesn't care; the Feds think they erased him from Los Angeles, but in truth he was never there.

The dead girl has also discomposed the implacable Jane Doe. Jay can see it in the marshal's face: the tightness around her mouth, a fitful preoccupation in her gaze, even though, once she confirms how little Jay knows about the stripper, she stops talking about it and moves on to other subjects.

Are they worried about Vaughn? Doe wants to know more about him and, like in his sessions with Magonis, Jay is quick to become discouraged by how little he can detail once he gets past a wooly, ballpark résumé and wiki of his putative best friend: valley kid, original Pokémon survivor, North Hollywood High gifted program, biochemistry at Berkeley, fondness for mussels, no interest in team sports, two siblings he talks about, one that he doesn't. Jay keeps telling her, just like he told Public, that Vaughn is collateral to whatever this is, but Doe seems skeptical and the image of the dead mermaid stripper keeps cycling back on them, bleak, final, a reminder that there is a deadly game being played.

By someone.

And Ginger told him that Catalina wasn't safe.

It's not surprising that the more they talk about it, the less certain Jay is that a sanctuary is even possible for him anymore. His nerves are raw, his ambition guarded. After a while he pleads fatigue, leaves the cabin and Jane Doe and her questions, and stands on the forward deck, letting the raw, briny mist soak him, thicken his hair, sting his eyes.

He wonders what's going on with those cardboard clouds.

The dark bump of Mount Orizaba seems to draw no closer for the longest time. It is a peculiarity of Catalina that some days it is a low smear barely visible on the horizon, and some days it rises like the broad back of a leviathan above the livid sea.

He doesn't look back at the mainland.

A canopy of stars drops like a bad scrim, and the cruiser's motors cut, the bow levels, and finally Avalon lights accordion out from the darkness, close. Jay smells the faint rancid backwash of fish, gasoline, and pollution that plagues the sheltered harbor. Water laps at the hull chines. Music rattles out of a bar somewhere. The town seems to have shrunk in his absence. Tired and windblown and wanting paint.

Public is waiting for them, on the Casino Mole boat landing, in a pool of light, hands jammed in the pockets of his coat. He looks lonely, Jay thinks. Small and lost. Public watches the ferry come in and does not change expression when Jay comes down the pier to join him.

He says nothing. His hard gimlet eyes are empty.

The bungalow is dark. Dead quiet when Jay gets the door closed and the sound of the Catalina night is squeezed away. He sags, eyes half-mast, against the front wall. Then opens his eyes wider, surfacing, and . . . becomes suddenly acutely aware of the utter absence of—

—everything—

—everything too spare, in the kitchen dark. The overhead light flickers on at his touch. Spotless. No, empty. Barren. Jay looks across at the blank window of Barry's house and—

—his heart sinks—

—in the bedroom, the bed made up but abandoned, hospital corners and stiff white institutional pillows. Nobody in it: vacant: and nobody expected. All of the odd little-girl toys are missing, along with her drawings, picture books, collected golf-course curios, her tumbled-out shoes, an utter absence of any of Ginger's personal effects on the bureau: the scant jewelry, the cut-glass bottles of perfume, the bullet-like cylinders of lipstick: the closet absent of clothing—

—the one thing he hadn't factored in and now, numb and emptied out, chastises himself for not seeing it, the most obvious thing, right in front of him the whole time—

—they're gone.

Jay's been away a little more than twenty-eight hours.

Ginger and Helen are gone.

26

MISERABLE, he stays up late drinking at the Parrot, unwilling to sit in the bungalow alone. One-legged Leo and the old actress are on the veranda, powering down Rusty Nails and arguing, as usual, about transubstantiation. "Welcome the fuck back, *bienvenue*, James or Jay, whichever." Leo, lapsed Catholic but Pope Francis fanboy, thinks the doctrine is just another eschatological smoke screen, purely semantic, the Vatican Council throws up to cloak its more reprobate, pederastical appetites and transgressions; the actress is old-school Christian Science and convinced that everything is a metaphor.

Even Jay's family's departure.

"The Lord giveth, and, well, you know," she says, and asks, basically, what did he expect? It hits him: she's in the program: a protected witness relocated here to Catalina long ago, maybe even one step short of stardom once, and then, for all these years, derailed. Erased. Reborn.

Peromyscus polionotus, Jay tells them, well into his third (or fourth?) frozen margarita, "is a small, nocturnal mouse found in the southeastern United States. A.k.a. oldfield mice, they're monogamous, pairs mate for life, and both the guys and the gals take care of the oldfield babies."

Leo allows that he doesn't like mice; rodents, in general, creep him out, although on one harrowing mission to Chile he was forced to eat degu (that country's indigenous, brush-tailed rat relation) and, roasted over an open fire and well salted, it wasn't all bad.

"The females," Jay soldiers on, "have a greater impact on the success of the family unit than do the males—but consequently male oldfield mice get better perks from choosing carefully between potential mates who represent potential futures, or like: paths of life."

"Same as it ever was," Leo drawls, David Byrne–like, and, à la Dumas, *"Cherchez la femme, pardieu! Cherchez la femme!"*

The actress raises her glass. "What he said. Here, here."

Jay expands: "At Manchurian Global, we put them in a maze that my friend Vaughn built from scratch, using big pet-store aquariums divided by opaque panels that would isolate the females from each other, but allow the guys to schmooze the girls, individually and privately, so that we could track the amount of time spent associating with each female, and figure out which girl mouse which guy mouse was crushing on."

Leo concurs that these parameters sound reasonable. The actress has mixed emotions about the largely passive role assigned to the "poor ducks."

Some males, Jay admits, "were disoriented at first, and, you know, indifferent to the experiment. Focused solely on getting the fuck out, or literally confused by the parameters of their new situation." The tequila is coursing warm through his veins. "We got mice from all over the country, in order to ensure a kinship coefficient that would not bias the outcome of the study."

Leo grumbles that he doesn't know what the fuck a kinship

coefficient is, and, Flomax kicking in, excuses himself for the men's room. Jay slides his eyes to the actress. Thin white seams of last-century plastic-surgical corrections are ghosting through her carefully applied foundation; the Rusty Nails are making her eyes crazy red.

"As might be expected," Jay tells her, sounding more and more like the paper Vaughn wrote, that Jay typed and spell-checked, "males spent significantly more time associating with, you know: exciting, vivacious, unfamiliar, distantly related females than with more familiar females."

"Men love mystery," the actress says, smiling. "You remind me of something," she adds, drowsy. "From *Peter Pan*, one of those boys who were with him on the island, runaways who never wished to grow up. But more at the end, when they did, when they had to."

Jay confesses that he never liked that story. The actress says she once played Peter Pan in a summer stock musical. "Like Mary Martin, but we didn't have a rigging, so I just had to run around the stage and flap my arms." Her words are beginning to slur.

The oldfield males were subsequently separated from their chosen female, and when Leo comes wobbling back, Jay tells them how he was witness to the corresponding listlessness and decline and full-on depression of the test subjects that made them unsuitable for further experimentation.

He says, "Many just failed to thrive, stopped eating, stopped grooming, stopped moving, and died."

"*Tout amour,*" Leo murmurs. "*Vouloir prendre la lune avec les dents.*"

This mouse melancholia did not factor into the final, official study. "They're just mice," Vaughn had said. "Don't read too much into it."

"What happened to the boys who survived?" the actress wonders.

"Sold to pet stores," Jay says, "as bulk food for large snakes and other reptile predators." And their litters provided subjects for subsequent studies involving experimental neuroses and the Milky White Maze.

The actress bursts into tears, and Leo and Jay can only watch, uncomfortable, while she excuses herself and fumbles for her purse by her chair and hurries out into the comfort of the night.

The Parrot has last call. Leo tells one final, bitter war story entirely in French, and Jay staggers home on mist-slick, black ribbon streets under a smudge of cloud-wrapped quarter-moon.

Home.

The empty bungalow and the bed he's never slept in. Cold, stiff sheets, absent of wordless little girls, just the trace of Ginger's perfume, and the weight of Vaughn and the murdered mermaid still unshakable; drunken spinning lime-and-reposado-fueled dreams of an impossible future to which only a Lost Boy can aspire.

They've been moved to a new situation," Magonis tells Jay the next morning in the video store. The shrink has a new walker, flat black, with big wheels and hand brakes. "You shouldn't have taken that L.A. run."

But would it really have mattered? Jay asks himself, and answers himself: *No.* Slow-witted by a searing hangover, he rings up rentals for a reptilian, leathery-skinned long-timer in bicycle shorts: *Forrest Gump, The Wiz, Ordinary People,* and *Double Fattiness,* one of Sam Dunn's chop-socky classics.

"Movies died in '95," the customer gripes, pretending Magonis isn't there.

"Have a nice day," Jay says. The door jingles out of tune as the shop empties of the interloper. Eyde. Jay remembers her name too late.

"New situation. What is that?"

Magonis approximates a shrug. "A *new* situation—"

"—like, another house on the island? Two Harbors?" Jay feigns calm and logical; he's already decided it's the best strategy (or *ruse de guerre*, as Leo would say) for now.

"No." Magonis puts his hands in the pockets of his slacks and jiggles keys. "A more *permanent* situation," Magonis says. "Long-term. Protection-wise."

"Where?"

"On the mainland. Or maybe not. I'm sorry, it's none of your business. Or mine, for that matter. Look, Jay—"

"You could find out, though."

"It was never to be made permanent. We said that going in. Jay, this witness protection protocol has been around for a long time, with remarkable success rates, based on a few simple principles including 'need to know,' and 'institutional firewalls.'"

"Is that good for Helen, moving her around all the time, is that healthy?"

Magonis stares at him.

"Because I'm just saying. I don't know for a fact, but I'm guessing she and Ginger have soldiered through seven rings of hell long before they got thrown into this one, you and Public and the program, and subsequently you guys go yanking her, them, from place to place, school to school, situation to situation willy-nilly without a thought about how that impacts Helen—and Ginger, but especially Helen."

"Helen's fine."

"I don't think so."

"Jay—"

"No, listen—"

"Jay—"

"—I read somewhere that kids who go through serial relationships, foster care, whatever, can grow up to be sick puppies. You know? Serial killers and stuff. Sociopaths. They've done studies. You must know about them. You guys have a *huge* responsibility here."

"You understand our position, then," Magonis says evenly.

"No," Jay says. He does, but he can't.

Magonis takes the electric cigarette from where he's tucked it behind his ear. Rolls it between his fingers, no intention to smoke, just a prop, for effect. He says, "I thought you weren't the family kind of guy." He looks up into Jay's eyes and holds them, level, piercing, unblinking. For some reason he wants Jay to say it.

Jay drops all pretense. "I want them back," he admits. "Okay? Yeah. You took away my life, I want the one you replaced it with. It's only fair."

"Fair."

"That's right."

Magonis bursts out laughing.

Public is less amused.

"Jay," he says, as a sigh, exhaling it. "This arrangement. It was never intended to be—"

"—permanent. I know. No shit. Well, guess what?"

Public studies him. At Magonis's instruction, Jay has found the head Fed at Big E's, waiting on a triple latte and chatting up Penny, cocktail waitress from the Garrulous Parrot who, from her easy body language and casual sharing of Public's chocolate *croissant*, fingers brushing his, appears to have let the Fed introduce some measure of doubt into her fealty to the boat babysitter husband, Cody.

"Bring them back," Jay says simply, "and I'll tell you the truth."

"This dislocation, your state of flux, it's perfectly natural to form attachments. All the adjusting. It takes time." Public finishes his thought before Jay's offer fully lands. "What?"

"I'll tell you what I saw, everything," Jay says, playing his trump card, and straightens up, stubborn.

Silence. Public is, for once, flummoxed. And skittish: the way he sent Penny off when Jay showed up: brusque, impatient, unhappy. A man in flux? He repeats the offer aloud, frowning, as if trying to make sense of it.

Reading the tea leaves of Public's distraction, suddenly understanding that maybe this has been Public's folly and crusade, and he's gone all-in on it, Jay is gambling that it's the conundrum in the Glendale strip bar that they crave unwrapped: the flower girl: the mermaid: the shooting that happened there: Jay, girl in his arms, running away, running away. It can't be anything else, can it? He's making this up as he goes along, hoping it will be enough, hoping that he can make it enough.

They stand at the seawall, looking out at the rows and rows of boats and yachts moored, white, bright, promising, in the morning sun. The reek of fish and petroleum is almost overwhelming. A brace of high-school kids in yellow kayaks and orange life vests paddles out around the tongue of Casino Mole toward the kelp forests of Lover's Cove.

"Everything," Jay says again, impassive, waiting. "You got me. I give up."

Public tilts his head to one side, a dog hearing a weird frequency, or wondering where you hid the squeaky chew toy. "I don't understand, though. Why were you holding back from us all this time?"

"Maybe you didn't offer me the right incentive."

"But—"

Jay, honest: "I don't know. I don't know."

Public seems to accept this. He's pensive for a while, staring out at the harbor. Then: "What if they don't want to come back?"

Jay says nothing. In this experiment, the parameters are fixed, there are no variables.

"Ginger and her daughter. You know . . . we can't just force them to—"

"—Yes, you can. You can do whatever you want. You're God."

Public doesn't deny it.

27

AN ENDLESS PARADE of whitecaps paints a watery tessellation as far as the eye can see.

Unruly waves swell over the rocks of Abalone Point, sending cotton spumes of mist skyward with a rumbling, hissing symphony of indefatigable yearning.

Then, head thrown back, momentarily deafened by the rotor roar, Jay watches the helicopter arrive and spiral down to the helipad, settle, and go quiet, doors opening to release Helen and Ginger.

They step unsteadily to solid ground. Helen runs to Jay, leaps, arms wide, for him to catch, and she hugs him, hard in a silent bliss.

Ginger hangs back, her hair a mad tangle, her eyes dark and chary with that wacky '90s grunge-rock art-school mascara he's come to expect when she tries to doll herself up, her expression flat and unreadable but possibly pissed off. Her eyes find Jay for an instant before flicking away, and Jay follows her worried gaze to Barry, just turning and stepping, like a forgotten promise, into the shadows of the heliport terminal hangar, where Sandy has chosen to stay. Public declined to attend the happy reunion, explaining he had preparations to make with Doe. Jay doesn't know what he expected from Ginger, but he's understandably uncertain, apprehensive: it's a strange feeling, where something matters.

His mouth is dry, he can feel his pulse in his head. He's spent so long being well defended, immune to loss.

They decide to walk back along Pebbly Beach Road. Everything is gauzy, as though there's been a slow-smoldering fire inland, but it's only the midday brume, hilltops ablur, sky scrimmed slate. Helen takes the concrete stairs down to the shore and throws stones in the ocean, while Jay and Ginger find a place among the jagged rocks to sit, already in the blue shadows of the naked cliffs, and watch her.

"What are you doing?" Ginger asks finally, faintly.

For the moment, Jay stays silent. It seems like Ginger knows what he's doing, she just doesn't want to ask why.

"What happened in L.A.?"

"Pretty much my whole life," he says, tentatively, answering a different question, "I've never really wanted anything. I've never really had the courage to care about anything. You think you float? I invented floating."

Ginger looks unconvinced. "Huh."

"I did what you said. I ran. But that was the plan, right? Did they tell you to say it to me, or—"

"I meant run and keep running. If you'd kept going, what they wanted, or expected, wouldn't have—"

Jay cuts her off. "And I saw what I didn't have. And now my friend is missing, and a girl is dead, and I'm still clueless what these guys want from me, but I decided what I want. I decided."

"You don't know me," she says. "You don't know anything about me." Up on the road, not so discreet, a stationary golf cart holds Barry and Sandy, who aren't talking. Ginger tries to keep her voice low: "What we had was not a relationship, it was not a family, it was, I don't know, what, an accident, a kind of theater."

"I don't care. It's what I want. Can you understand that?"

Ginger watches Helen dance along the water's edge. "I can," she says softly.

"I don't care what the world is, as long as you're in it."

He can see how this rocks her; in truth, it rocks him, putting the words one after another and saying it. Ginger slits her eyes and lifts her chin, almost defiant, and runs one hand through her hair to get it out of the way: "That doesn't make any sense."

"I am way past the idea of things making sense," Jay says. "Nothing makes sense. Emotions are all that's left." He hesitates, then continues. "So, I figure, hell, let them anchor us."

He hunts for Ginger's eyes under the curtain of her bangs. "Let emotions rule."

Helen tosses a huge boulder into the sea, so big that she has to use two hands and almost goes into the water with it, and the splash comes flopping back on her. She screams, happy, and glances back at them. There's nothing coy in her look. Ginger smiles, brittle.

"I'm a marshal, Jay. I'm a Fed. Deputy U.S. Marshal Virginia Blake. I'm part of the team that put you here. And kept you here."

"The inside guy."

"Yeah. Put there just in case you want to, you know . . . confide to me what you won't tell . . . the others."

Now it's Jay's turn to be rocked by her words.

As she says them, as he reacts to them, thoughts rear-ending each other as he tries to re-calculate everything he knows, and expects, ruefully blinking back astonishment he chides himself for feeling because, waiting for Ginger and Helen to return to him, Jay had run through all the variations on the Ginger theme, and Ginger the Fed was one of them, sure, but he'd dismissed it as way too pat and paranoid. It certainly helps explain why she told him to run (or he hopes it does), but it isn't the version of the story he was yearning for. And, potentially, it makes things that much more difficult, going forward.

Or does it?

Ginger stares intently down at Helen, to avoid looking at him, a fragile uncertainty in her cant and posture.

"All that stuff about your boyfriend . . . ?"

"Husband. He's dead. He was an asshole and he's dead, and I don't miss him." She stops there, suggesting she'd decided there's nothing more to explain.

"Did you—?"

"—Kill him? No. Public loves his fictions. I told you. It makes him feel like Zeus. Looking down on us mere mortals."

"And Helen?"

"What about her?"

"She a Fed?"

Ginger can't help but laugh. "No."

"But not your daughter."

There's a long hesitation before she admits, "No. No she's not." She starts to tell him the story, how Helen's parents were bad guys, bad people, killed by some other bad people, Helen saw it, and because of what she saw and because the killers fled the country and are still at large and know she saw them Helen's at risk, and under the protection of the Marshal Service. But Jay hears only half of it; he watches as Ginger sweeps the hair back off her face again, gathers it at her neck, and ties a fat knot with it to hold it there. She doesn't look like a Fed. None of the steady cast of appraising eye, she's all over the place, nervous, shy, vulnerable. She looks like a work in progress, mercurial, a young woman who got to be a mom before she thought she was ready, discovered she was good at it and enjoyed it so much she doesn't want to think about what might happen if someone decides to un-mom her.

"Does she remember what happened?"

"The doctors say maybe, maybe not, she was too young. But she hasn't talked since it happened, either, so . . ."

"Right." Jay can't help adding, for the irony: "Maybe she does remember, and she's just not saying."

Evidently, Ginger doesn't like the easy familiarity of this. She stands up, hands on hips, hair flowing: half a goddess, at least.

Jay stands up with her. "You love her," he says, finally.

"I was assigned to her," Ginger says, evasive.

"Oh. Is that all it is?"

"To protect her."

"Right. Like a mom," Jay says.

"Yeah."

"And one thing led to another."

Ginger snaps at him: "It's not the same, okay? It's not the same thing as . . . this. You and me. It's not."

Jay waits for her to calm. She unknots her hair, and combs at it with her fingers. She smooths her jeans with her palms. There are tears in her eyes, and she doesn't wipe them away.

"They'll take her away from you," he says quietly. "Sooner or later."

It's a cheap shot, and he regrets it the moment after he says it. Ginger goes very quiet. She nods. "I know."

"I just mean—"

"I know what you mean," she interjects, without any bitterness. "Don't make me choose, Jay," she says. "This was a sweet, sweet dumbass gesture, to be sure, and maybe, I don't know, heroic, even, but . . . There's no happy ending here. Not for us. I'm just the inside guy, waiting for you to tell me what you know."

"Why don't I believe that?"

Her smile breaks his heart. Waves lap the rocks, brittle-sounding. Helen has drifted farther down the shore, out of earshot. Jay glances over at the grim Feds in the golf cart.

"What do they want from me, Ginger?"

Jay has to wait again. He's not sure if she's filtering what she's going to tell him, or simply organizing it into a form he'll easily understand. "They? We? Me?" She sighs, big sigh. "Last year we had this . . . problem. One of our guys, an unhappy marshal, went into business for himself. He had this list, of names—"

"—on a flash drive."

"Yeah. Somebody else offered a whole lot of money for it."

"Somebody who wanted to make the people on the list disappear," Jays says.

"Worst case."

"When is it ever anything but a worst case?"

"There was a meet. The deal going down. At the strip club with the mermaids. But our unhappy marshal got himself killed. We got there too late. And the list is unaccounted for." Ginger looks at him. "We—they, Public and Doe, and the people they answer to—think you saw who the shooter was."

"And the shooter will get them to the buyer."

Ginger doesn't appear to feel the need to respond.

Jay absorbs this. "Do you think that's right?"

Ginger says, "I think you should tell them the truth."

The silence that passes between them is thick with a weight of sober understanding, a connection Jay has never had with anyone. He can't explain it. *This is life,* he thinks. *It matters, it's messy, it's ugly, it's an act of faith.* A leap into the darkness.

Jay nods. "Yeah." He wants to kiss her. It's the craziest thing. Her eyes are dead and her hair is a tangle and needs washing. She looks wrung out, he realizes. Someone who's been running an ultramarathon, and there's still hours and miles to go. He asks her where they took her and Helen when they left the island.

"Vegas," she says. "So grim. Hellishly hot. Acres and acres of ambling ghost-town housing developments of foreclosed and repossessed properties we've been requisitioning for the program. Sketchy stucco split-levels with satellite dishes and three-car garages.

"All these displaced people, living lies," she says. And she admits, "I shouldn't be telling you that."

Jay says it's okay, he can keep secrets. *Ask Helen,* he wants to add.

Ginger stares at him for a long time. "The unhappy marshal was my husband," Ginger says then, emptily, and walks down to the water, to Helen.

Jay's mind reels. But he hears himself call after her, defiant, "I don't care."

She stops and turns and pulls her hair back again. Just holding on to it, this time. The sun unforgiving on her face as she looks back at him, puzzled. "What?" she says. She heard him, though. He's sure of it.

"I don't care," he tells her, meaning everything: the bad husband, the lie she's lived, the part she's played in this. "It's okay. Doesn't matter. It doesn't change anything."

She shakes her head and asks him something, but he can't hear her over the surf breaking on the rocks.

"Say again?"

"After everything. After all this," she says. "How can you trust me?"

This, he knows, is the question he should be asking himself. But he's not. And he won't.

Jay shrugs. "How can you trust anybody, Ginger?"

| 28 |

A mermaid, roiling the petite sea of her giant barroom beaker with shimmering bubbles and fractured light, arms graceful, tail coiling. The flower girl; his flower girl. Loin-thrilling, wanton, siren-smiling, unreal. She arcs up, her breasts rippling buoyant. Waves at him. Waves a goofy little girl wave—

"There's a lot of it I don't understand," he says.

In the stolid office, number 204, chairs facing, Jay and Magonis are staged for what Jay hopes will be the last time.

"Nobody expects you to."

To say that Jay has a plan would be generous. He has an intention, a direction, a goal—or maybe just a destination. And an irrepressible, blind, obdurate determination to reach it, by whatever means necessary. "I didn't . . ."

"Just tell us what you saw, Jay. That's all we're asking."

Jay knows that's not true.

His eyes have found the four, small, wireless video cameras: mounted on the bookshelf (high and wide), between the pictures on the cabinet behind the desk (low and wide), in the air-conditioning

duct (side view), and on the windowsill (tight over the shoulder) behind the chair where Magonis hunches, chewing a fingernail, his hat
hair evidently an afterthought today, ill-combed and crooked.

Multiple angles. Discreet placement. Jay's got an audience of more
than one. Doe? Public? Someone they answer to? At Cate, junior year,
he played Banquo in *Macbeth*, but forgot his lines during the dress re-
hearsal and was replaced opening night by Vaughn.

Jay closes his eyes.

"First off—"

He imagines: *Vaughn, plunging awkwardly into the mermaid tank,
fully clothed, lab coat trailing white filaments as if of chalky melt, and tan-
gling around him as he churns his arms and curves upright and peers out at
Jay, scared—*

"—Vaughn." Jay opens his eyes. "He's not involved."

"So you've said."

"In any way. He's an accident of intersect."

"That's an interesting way of phrasing it."

"Passing through," Jay says. "I just want everybody to be very,
very clear about that, whatever happens, and leave him alone."

"Whatever happens?"

Jay worries he's said too much. "Maybe they think they can use
him to get to me. Or they've misinterpreted our friendship to imply
collaboration. I don't know, but I just know, I'm telling you, he's . . ."

Magonis nods. "Okay." But he's evidently not convinced. "Manchurian Global does a lot of government contract work, CIA stuff.
You don't think—"

"No no, this isn't anything like that, it's not spies, man. Jesus.
How cheesy would that be?" Jay says.

"Oh."

There's something in Magonis's tone when he says this; Jay's eyes
narrow. "I mean—or would it be?"

Magonis just waits.

"Spies?"

With his good eye, Magonis studies his bit-down nail.

"No . . ." Jay says, thinking it through aloud. "It's something stupid, isn't it? Like revenge or greed or—"

"Jay."

He remembers, in a dizzying rush:

"—or love."

Liquid darkness of the strip club, thump of bass notes, smell of liquor and desperation, stray light striating across Jay as he drifted in, sifting through the beaded curtain just past the bouncer at the door. The flower girl, tight black T-shirt half-hiding her snake tattoo, looked out at him, amber-eyed, from behind the bar, where she poured out martinis from a shaker. The luminous tank threw its rippling glow across the room, across the lumpen hunched figures in cane chairs nursing drinks, eyes fixed on the show, and, yes, the flower-girl-now-turned-mermaid, naked breasts pressed pale pink flat against the transparent swerve of the tank, and—

boom

The tank exploded. Water and glass.

Magonis, wondering: "Jay?"

Entropy.

Parking lot.

Static crush of cars glinting streetlight, the smell of smog and sea, the deafening hush of an L.A. night, a thin sheen of night dew on the asphalt and the harlequin neon of the strip bar slowly flickering—shorting out—dying as Jay ran from the doorway of the club, across the wet pavement, with a mermaid in his arms—

Jay looks at his hands. Magonis clears his smoker's throat and waits.

"I went hoping maybe I could take her out for coffee or something after, like the last time. Still, I don't know. The embarrassment.

It was a spin cycle: longing, lust, the sweaty entanglement, the slow-dawning shame, then retreat. To Stacy. And repeat.

"That I couldn't get her out of my head, just finally gave way to, after a while, sure, I just wanted her." Jay goes quiet, with some thinking. He doesn't want to go too fast, but it's iffy what he's got under control here and what's simply spilling out in confession.

"I wanted her. But. Strippers." He sighs. "It's not a game with them. You know? Or it's the right game, which, I know, is kinda fucked-up, unless you see it as a romantic thing. Old school. And foolish beyond belief.

"Save the lost girl, with your noble intentions, your roll of money, your fast car. Take her home, make her real. Suburbia. Babies. But, still, after, in the dark . . .

"Ba-boom."

Magonis notes that this sounds like something Jay read in *Esquire*, if it's still in print, or *Maxim*. Jay allows that both are, and it might be, but argues that Magonis is of the generation that produced Hefner and Norman Mailer, so if it is some banal macho fantasy maybe it's generationally immutable.

"Truth is. I was bored with my girlfriend," Jay admits.

Magonis just nods.

"Pissed off at her or maybe just at my life in general, which was, you gotta admit after all you've heard, really one long relentless pointless chore."

Magonis shifts in his chair, trying to find a comfortable position. On the exhale: "Okay. That's interesting and everything, Jay, and we could spend a few years on the couch examining the roots of it, but—"

"—No, it's relevant to this," Jay insists. "Because expectation goes to the heart of what you see, do you know what I mean? You see what you prepare yourself for seeing." He sits forward in his chair, intent on Magonis. "And what you don't expect, can't . . . doesn't . . . hold. We don't really see what we're surprised by. It goes by too fast. That's my theory."

"And?"

"That night the bar was filled to capacity, mostly men, the kind who say 'titties.' Vacant expressions, or hard, or lonely. A couple bachelor parties of frat brothers drunk as pigs. Laughing, reeling, shadowy smears in the dark recesses of the place, hustling the one waitress for a lap dance she wasn't for any amount of money going to do.

"The smell of chlorine from the tank, the pop and hissing of an air compressor, the dreamy unreality of night, and the naked, unedited lust. As if you just—"

The air compressor, upstairs where the mermaids dressed and slipped into the tank, was totally inaudible in the bar below. So as not to break the illusion. Plus, all that fucking rave mix music—

A white lie.

"—stepped off into another dimension," Jay finishes. He grins warily at Magonis, who seems, so far, engaged.

"So. Bad margaritas: not enough salt on the rim and I *hate* that— and Rob Roys—or was it Separators?—which my friend Otto once drank at a brunch, nine in a row, and got eighty-sixed, because you knock a few back, thinking, 'This is nothing,' and two minutes later you're flat on your ass, bitching about the Lakers."

Jay gets up, to pace.

The air compressor hitched and sighed.

A shitty bar band he's just thought of shuffles into this gathering decoupage of his memories and invention, a Jethro Tull cover thumping muffled like a yearning.

"Retro night. Flute solo." Jay smiles. "Christ. Can you believe that?"

Alone at a table ringside to the mermaid tank, Jay drained another Rusty Nail, sloooop, no problem.

Jay takes a pause and concentrates. He can't afford to let this float away. "What I've got, though, remember: it's pieces," he warns. "I'm just saying. And you can't trust that. You know—not completely."

After a moment, Magonis prods him. "Go on."

The shriek of bad music, loud, on blown speakers, the table of Korean businessmen laughing, the chime of glasses behind the bar and a mosaic: the painted nails, the slender arms, tail, swerve, bedroom eyes of the mermaid flower girl.

"Her eyes," Jay says.

The big tank glowing incandescent as she swam and stripped.

"As she swims and strips," he says.

She looked right out into the sea of chairs, into the colloquium of men, and found Jay—or did she?

"And then . . ."

Because, inside the tank, mermaid point of view—he's thought this through—wouldn't what she saw be the arc of aquarium glass reflecting her starkly downlit mirror image back at her? A water world in which she's the only inhabitant.

". . . Through the tank, past the swimming stripper, I could see shapes, kinda like shadows on the other side: these guys: suits, young, old, yearning, sitting, standing, staring, dark, sharp-featured faces suddenly caught in a strobe of light cast from above."

Magonis leans in, hooked.

"Shadows."

Magonis waits.

"Drifting along the singular, curving plane of the tank. Like vertical eels," Jay says. "Flip-book faces, one after the other, smeared and distorted, if only, like a camera, I could just push closer, you know? Zoom in, find focus—almost there, almost a revelation—then: flam

flam flam flam—the shadows kicked off the edge of the tank where they became the bodies of men in black suits moving fast, around the corner."

"Running away?"

"Running away," Jay says. "You feel the gunshot, visceral; it never registers really, not like—"

Silence. No band, no compressor. Smoke pulsing with light.

"Anyway. You don't hear it."

Something instantly shattering the strip bar's raucous, testosterone-fueled tenor: the crowd flinched as one. Shadow fringes slower to react, but middle of the room between two pools of downlight a man was lifted out of his chair, blown backward by bullets and, midair, hit again, by more bullets, body jerking, limp rag doll haloed in a fine mist of expelled blood.

Magonis asks how many shots there were.

"But all I see is the girl," Jay says instead.

In the tank, the water bloomed with eddies of—

"The pink tendrils of blood from her back," he remembers.

A faraway, hollow crackling sound swiftly built to a roar. The glass of the tank was fracturing white-silver. About to burst.

"Her hands pressed against the glass as it slowly spiderwebbed. From the pressure of the bullet hole. And she had this . . . look of . . . surprise. This strange, abbreviated smile . . . issuing bubbles.

"I can't even describe the way that sounds in your head," he says.

"Why did you run with her?"

The confusion.

Front row, Jay turned one shoulder reflexively in defense of himself as the glass of the tank exploded out onto him, water shoving him back. The flower girl flowed into his arms, and they were swept away into the tumult of screaming patrons, swirling tables and chairs.

"Jay." Magonis leans forward, elbows on knees, palms pressed together and touching his lips: "Why did you run with her, Jay?"

Jay doesn't answer for the longest time. His face contorts with an onrushing accretion of shame he has buried and grief he has never allowed himself to feel. There are tears in his eyes, for this mermaid, this girl, this woman, he knew only in the most physical way.

He found the strength to lift her from the floodwaters. Stumbled through chairs and flailing customers, through the beaded curtain, and out the door. He sprinted blindly across the parking lot, holding the dying mermaid in his arms.

"You think, when you see it on television, how fake it is that guys can carry girls, you know? Running through the flames. Big-shot heroes. Because girls, they're actually pretty fucking heavy in real life." He thumbs the tears from his face. "But it's true."

She was feather-light but slippery cold in his arms . . .

"This girl was weightless."

He cannot distinguish anymore between what he's inventing and what he remembers. *Parking lot. Empty street. Lobby. How did he get the front door open? Elevator cage. The groan of gears engaging and cables going taut. Choppy light flickering halos, the dying girl's limp fingers curled through the latticework of the rising car.*

An old carved apartment door that Jay muscled through and carried his mermaid into—

Sun punctures the morning marine layer outside and the office abruptly floods with light. Magonis squints, turns from the window, backlit like some Biblical prophet. His fake hair afire. "The man who was shot, behind the tank, in the bar—"

But Jay cuts him off. "You think you can manage things. You say to yourself: 'What the hell, I'm a problem-solver.' And then you trace back through all of these useless acts. Epic fails. All the blanks you couldn't fill. Helpless. Until you get to the most incredible, inexplicable, abjectly humiliating and utterly, indelicately human one."

Magonis says nothing.

"I put her in fresh water," Jay says. "Where mermaids breathe."

Her colorless body, afloat. The white porcelain tub, holding her in its glare. And Jay in her bathroom, wet, exhausted, heaving, standing over her, fists balled up, disbelieving.

"And then, nothing."

He sank to his knees.

"Test pattern."

And could not find a God to pray to.

"Lights out."

Magonis makes one of his abstracted, empty-handed gestures. "Trauma is this weird thing, Jay." He sounds skeptical. "We cushion the shock. Things retreat. But—"

"You guys. Found me, and moved me."

Magonis nods, confirming it. "Who was in the bar?" he asks again, stubborn.

"I woke up behind the wheel of my car, hungover and thick-headed. I was parked between two freeways. You know where the 10 and the 110 intersect just south of downtown? Near Staples Center?

"A long way from the bar. And so I didn't believe it had happened. I had no proof . . . that it ever happened." Jay thinks about this, then adds, "I didn't look for any proof, either, I know. But."

"You carried her out of the bar," Magonis says. "Your actions were . . . unusual." He grips the arms of his chair and pushes himself more upright. "And as we watched you, on various surveillance cameras in the parking lot and buildings in the area, watched you carry her across the street, into the building where she lived, we thought: it's a hide-and-seek thing. And then we watched you some more. Patient. I mean, it's not like memories are dead. They—"

"They're dead all right. And corpses keep their secrets. Forcing you into," Jay smiles bitterly, "communication with ghosts. That's the only evidence you got that means anything, as far as I can see."

Magonis stares at him. His question unanswered.

"Sam Dunn," Jay says finally.

"What?"

"The charter pilot who flew me out of here. The chop-socky film nut. Dunn." He gestures nebulously. "In the bar. Among all those faces, his—"

"His."

"Yeah. A distorted reflection of him in the glass. I can still see it." Jay could. He made himself see it. "I didn't make the connection until I saw him here, on the island, and even then . . ." Jay lets whoever's listening in try to complete the thought, because he doesn't have anything left.

"So what are you saying? That Dunn was the shooter? Dunn?"

Jay shakes his head and shrugs. "I'm saying whatever comes into my mind. Isn't that what you want?"

"If Dunn was the shooter, Dunn would have the list. People on it would already be," Magonis, catching himself, editing himself, "well, compromised—and he wouldn't be bothering with you or your friend." The federal shrink stares at him, one eye fixed, one wandering, and Jay can't tell which is the one struggling to see through him, or if it even matters now.

"You didn't see anything," Magonis says with an edge.

"Yeah, I've been saying that all along, but the fact is? I saw plenty," Jay tells him. "Just not what interests you." Then asks, "Is that it? Are we finished?"

"You tell me."

"We're done," Jay says. And in the chilled darkness of the make-shift surveillance room that Jay imagines is probably right down-stairs, John Public and Jane Doe will stare blankly at four monitors on which four Jays walk out of office 204.

| 29 |

PIANO PRELUDE, faintly out of tune, and awkward; the deliberate jaunti-ness of a primary-school music teacher aspiring to something like Sondheim, but never making it there.

Jay can't get it out of his head.

He's walking with purpose down Crescent Avenue, in the silt light of dusk, onto the Green Pleasure Pier, where the new Pacific Boats rental kiosk guy, Valario, is lowering the wing flap shutters that secure the counter windows, done for the day.

Jay's come more or less directly from his session with Magonis. As his plan unfolds, resolute, inescapable, he starts to think it's so dumb it might even work. Everything is stacked against his succeeding, and he knows that even in success everything is stacked against what he wants to happen afterward ever working out.

But Jay has chosen his door: he's going through it: tonight.

He's made a couple of stops on the way to the pier, creating his own admittedly improvised, abbreviated, but nevertheless adult-size milky white maze in the hope that it will help obfuscate the obvious and buy him more time: first, beer at the Nautilus, a bar he's never been in before, where a couple of locals who rented *Blue Valentine* for the sex scenes and were disappointed sat at a corner table, playing rummy. Locals. He didn't think they were marshals, or in the program. Then, at the tiny grocery store, he bought bottled water and snacks and three thermal blankets that he threw away in a dumpster a couple blocks later, making sure that no one saw him do it.

He asked Floria about the weather, and she told him it was going to be a quiet night. *No habrá viento.* Calm.

"Yow, Mister-mister," Valario says in his Eurotrash hip-hop way, before Jay even reaches him. He's not exactly in the program, just some collateral damage of a garden-variety drug case that went postal and now the government feels responsible for his safety. He wants to be a deejay. He wants Jay to be a record company R&D guy the marshals have taken into custody, and has half convinced himself that Jay is stowed away here because of testimony he's going to give that will bring down the record business and make it possible for aspiring musicians—or mash-up artists—like Valario to thrive in the feeding frenzy that surely follows. Jay knows that Valario is part of the loose network of part-time amateur spies that have helped Doe and Public keep a rein on him.

He's counting on it, actually.

"I need a boat overnight."

"You can see with your eyes I am closed."

"I promised the kid I'd take her to see the flying fish."

Valario shrugs, looks at Jay with no expression, no judgment. "Better weather tomorrow, my friend."

"C'mon."

Valario shrugs again. Stares out across the sea. Then back at Jay. "Five hundred dollars."

"That's ridiculous." Jay will haggle a bit just for form. Valario expects it. "Your day rate is one hundred."

Downturn of mouth, Valario cracks his neck, and flips the latches on the window shutters with a kind of finality.

Jay looks away, south, and sees, hurrying to the Cabrillo Mole ferry landing, Magonis, going as fast as his old legs and cane will allow him, handle of a small rolling suitcase in his free hand, a collection of books bungee-corded awkwardly to the top. The shrink is boarding the day's last boat, which is idling, impatient, at the passenger pier, preparing to head back to L.A.

They know it's the endgame, Jay thinks.

Even from a distance Magonis looks glad to be going. But then, unaccountably, stops. Turning at a shout to a burst of bright red silk coming at him on strap heels: the old actress, a whirling of pale arms and legs that furls into the bigger man and nearly disappears in his unlikely embrace.

"Two-fifty," Jay offers Valario.

"Four."

"Three."

"And you will bring it back first thing in the morning, clean and spanking, no bilge water I have to bail, full can of gas."

Magonis and the old actress, heads touching, her scarf sailing, her face canted back under his like in the movies, the old ones, before love got deconstructed.

"Deal."

A final ferry horn calls. The odd couple separates, Magonis hustling off, doesn't look back.

The glass-rippling water of the bay judders with the twilight. Los Angeles glisters on the eastern horizon, like an expensive piece of jewelry that someone has stepped on and ruined.

At which, as if cued, the engagement ring, Stacy's rock, comes out of Jay's pocket, worth considerably more than three hundred dollars, but Jay doesn't care.

After the ring has changed hands, operating and safety instructions given, and three life vests produced from a bin at the back of the kiosk, Jay knows that Valario will be in the darkness of his shop, dial-ing his cell phone to report to the *Federales* what has happened, while, out on the end of the dock Jay yanks the cord of a faded fiberglass skiff's outboard engine, kicking it to life.

A nd he imagines:
Jane Doe is staring out a window and into the kitchen of Jay and Ginger's bungalow, where Helen is fussing with Ginger's hair, trying to put a ribbon in it that matches the one in hers.

The girl who won't speak.

The ringtone—the first few bars of "Brick House"—causes Doe to get her phone from her bag: "Yeah?"

The house is vacant. Jay has looked into it, and has seen that a couple cardboard moving boxes are all that remain of the star-crossed fiction that was Barry and Sandy.

As his boat glides across the harbor toward the brightly lit casino façade, Jay imagines Doe listening to Valario's soft reporting, tapping to end the call, and pushing her coat aside and adjusting the gun that he has never not seen strapped to her hip.

In the mirror on the mantel he imagines she looks back at herself and, perhaps, for a moment, because of darkness and irresolution, doesn't recognize her own face.

J ay trims the tiller of the outboard motor and weaves his Boston whaler through the crowded marina, zigzagging in and out of the moorings but advancing steadily toward the casino ballroom and the navigation light at the end of the narrow man-made breakwater that extends from it like an apostrophe.

He wants to be on the harbor side of the building to better access

the concrete walkway that encircles it, but because of the fuel docks
and the harbor patrol headquarters he doesn't dare row closer than
the point of the jetty, so Jay secrets and secures his skiff in the shadows
among and scrambles his way back to the casino along the tumbled
curl of quarried quartz dividing Avalon Bay from the sea.

The harbor water is like dark glass.

Light skitters across it, nervous.

There's only one part of Jay's scheme that worries him:

Ginger doesn't know about it.

You wouldn't think that grade-school kids could do *The Pied Piper
of Hamelin* justice.

Watching from the deep shadows of the casino's vast hollows, Jay
imagines it was Public's mother's favorite fairy tale, back in the day;
how she might have loved the brutal justice of it, and passed this on to
her son, and the romance: all those kids who never come back—but,
now, here, as, in a spotlight, five children, stage-stiff, in furry rat suits
and those weird German shorts with suspenders, begin to sweetly
sing the penultimate song in a musical, Public wears the squared-off
expression of a man who might grudgingly admit the performance
was not as painful as he expected.

Auf wiedersehen
farewell
good-bye—

Upturned faces of the parents glow in the backwash of the stage
lights; the old actress, front row, mascara tears streaming down her
face. Behind them, Jane Doe slides through the twilight to where

Public stands, hands in pockets, his eyes ticking to the wings, to Ginger and Helen. Wary. Expectant.

The marshals' heads overlap, they exchange words.

Ginger turns with a start when Jay touches her on the shoulder. Almost eclipsed by shadows, he puts his hands up, defensive, afraid she's going to take a swing at him, that she knows some cop karate or something, but she just stares at him until he lets his hands come down on her shoulders lightly and walks her farther back into the gloaming; his pants reek of salt water, her body throws heat against his icy-cold skin.

"I can get us out of here," he blurts out, more agitated than he intends to be. "But it has to be right now."

Ginger seems unmoved. Her eyes follow his worried gaze, over her shoulder, to the dark smudges that are Public and Doe, motionless behind the audience. "What did you tell them?"

"Yes or no, Ginger." Jay has a timetable in his head, an ever-narrowing window of opportunity, and he stays stubborn. "It's pretty basic, you know? This door or that one."

Ginger asks it again. "What did you tell them?"

And Jay says, "I made up a life."

Ginger stares hard, as if trying to look into him, and the sudden ache of doubt that Jay feels in his heart is not an illusion. Her eyes are black, her mouth set hard.

"I made up a life, what do you say to that?" he tells her, then, not sure he wants to hear her answer.

But a small voice behind Ginger says, simply, "Yes."

Helen. The rope for the clouds wrapped around her hand, her posture and expression intent, no nonsense.

Ginger's slow turn. Her astonishment. Her disbelief.

Now Ginger's the one who can't speak.

Dropping to her knees, to Helen's level, eye to eye, Ginger's staggered look swerving to Jay, and back to Helen, who tells her gravely:

"Mommy, say yes."

Ginger reaches out and touches the corners of her daughter's lips with fingers made unsteady by all those emotions Jay has promised would rule. It's as if she can't begin to process everything she's thinking and feeling. Blinking back tears. Fracking a crooked smile.

Center stage, spotlit, a solitary child in a fat rat costume stands, alone, dwarfed by the cavernous casino darkness, blasted by a spotlight, singing her refrain when Helen's forsaken cardboard clouds drop and strike the floor end-up with a firecracker pop, and quiver for a moment indecisively. The audience gasps. The clouds gently tip and bow and flatten, and the little girl sings, high, softly, eyes closed, unsuspecting that her sky has fallen.

Auf wiedersehen . . .

When Doe and Public come bursting into the jumbled backstage area they will find, amid scattered props and children and stage parents and teachers vexing in baffled confusion, that the rope Helen was holding dangles in the darkness like a punctuation mark, limp, untended. *"Auf wiedersehen . . ."*

Nimble in the darkness, Helen scrambles out along the jetty rocks, but Ginger has the wrong shoes, mommy-watching-musical shoes, and she'd take them off, but wherever they're going, she says, she may need them, so she and Jay stumble after Helen like three-legged-race contestants to where the skiff rolls on gentle waves that lap Casino Point.

Helen tumbles in, excited, she can't stop talking: "It's just like Milo, except we have this boat instead of a car. Across the Sea of Knowledge to the Lands Beyond! Mommy, you're Tock," Helen explains, as Jay steadies the boat and Ginger clambers aboard, "and you"—Helen points at Jay, who has no idea what she's talking about—"Humbug, because you can't be King Azaz or the Magima—Magimathi—*Mathemagician*—and not Officer Shrift or Alec Bings, either . . ."

Jay shoulders the boat away from the rocks and then jackknifes himself up over the gunwale, getting his pants soaked again, barking his shins, the black, frigid water sloughing into the skiff as it lists wildly under his weight. Ginger, still dumbfounded, can't take her eyes off her chattering Helen, but her hand finds Jay's shoulder and stays, as if steadying herself on him against the turbulence of her upended world.

Or is she protecting him from it?

The sea heaves black and the lights of Long Beach wink insolently in eddies of thick air coursing above the sea, and light blinks from an opening casino side door and two figures emerge as the skiff clears the point and leaves their sight line, but there is still a drift of the music and the full cast singing its curtain call—

. . . *hello again, guten tag, hello, hello* . . .

Jay's design asks Public to presume that his fugitives are headed for the mainland. After gauging how long it will take to get helicopters up and over from San Pedro for the search and pursuit, Jay wants him to calculate that it might be smarter to wait for the skiff to cross the channel and pick it up after the insistent current pushes them south to the serpentine, less populated beaches of the Big Orange.

But that's not where they'll be. Even if Public decides to send up the air support, and some fast boats with high beams, he won't catch them. Because out on the open sea, beyond the reach of even the Descanso Beach surf lights now, Jay's skiff changes course, jets northwest at full throttle, hugging the jigsaw Catalina coastline, planing sawtooth rollers that crash against the blunt stone shores and rebound back, whisking the water foamy where flying fish fling themselves, argent apparitions, toward the moon and stars, much to Helen's delight.

The casino ballroom, quaint, golden, behind them, ringed with lights—a trophy somebody forgot—is slowly eclipsed by Lion Head Point and they are alone in the watery darkness, headed for Two Harbors.

"You're bait," Ginger says gravely, tenderly, and out of nowhere, as if she just figured out the last clue of a crossword. It jars and chills inexplicably. *What?*

"Fish don't eat people." Helen giggles and rolls her eyes, head cradled in her mother's lap.

But Ginger is looking only at Jay, fully eclipsed by the dark: he feels her gaze more than sees it. "What?"

"Bait. You know that, right?"

"No. I was bait before L.A. But this is . . ." He stares at her, lost again. "What are you talking about?"

"It's okay," she says after a moment, over the outboard's dull whine. A blade of moonlight traces one edge of her face, exposes one intent eye gleaming, black beneath the fence of her rowdy bangs, lips slightly parted: settled, serene: no one has ever looked at Jay the way Ginger is looking at him now.

"What?"

It's less a question than a confusion.

Ginger declines and shakes her head ever so slightly, turning so that he can't read her expression anymore, her fingers tangled in Helen's hair, and Jay, rudderless, riding the waves, wondering for the first time what new hell he's found.

| 30 |

FOAMING ROLLERS reel the empty husk of the Boston whaler, abandoned just shy of Perdition Cave, throwing it against the rocks and back again, and again, and again, while up on the steep incline of black sage and beard grass, in the shadow of West Summit, Jay and Ginger and Helen are moving as fast as they can.

They're due east of Two Harbors, the narrow strip of land separating the two shores of Catalina, perhaps two hundred yards wide. The bright cold blade of pale white from the Ship Rock lighthouse flickers across the fugitives and continues clockwise past them, and the night wind shoves the grass flat. Helen stumbles, but Jay catches her, and lifts her into his arms.

Scattered dim luster of houses and campgrounds limned around the two bays wink behind high scrawny manzanita and clumped stands of trees listing in the windy darkness as Jay leads them over the high ground, skirting the narrow isthmus and the orphaned weekender fishing trawlers and sailboats moored in the shallow water on the Pacific side, one of which the waitress Penny's husband cares for while its owners, according to Cody, "are chillin' in, like, Cyprus," which is how Jay knows it won't be quickly missed, and—yes, it's that simple—Jay is planning to borrow the boat and head out into the open Pacific where Public and Doe will never think to look for them.

He's learned from YouTube how to hot-wire an onboard engine. Or at least he hopes he has: there were several slightly conflicting demonstrations. With any luck, they can sail farther north, to Oxnard, Ventura, or Santa Maria, where the Feds shouldn't think to intercept them. And from there? Jay will improvise.

Ginger hasn't said anything since they landed. Sensing a change in her, a hardening, a vigilant rigidness, Jay can only hope it isn't buyer's remorse: a snowballing apprehension about what he's asked her to commit to—but there's no time for them to sort this out. Approaching the crest of the bluff, the wind seems to tremble and gain resonance, and suddenly a helicopter thunders up on island thermals and soars over them, searchlight sweeping the terrain, surreal.

"Down!" Jay barks. "Get down!"

Collapsing as one, the lump of Jay and Ginger and Helen waits, afraid to breathe, traced briefly by the edge of its twitching, probing light, and then left adrift in darkness as the chopper hurries north. They rise, run, summit, and—thunk, foom!—are caught short and stunned by a blind-dazzling of teal sparks when a Roman candle explodes above their heads to scattered cheers from below.

Thunk. Foom!

Another burst blooms crimson. Helen shudders and covers her head, Ginger shouts sharply down at a gathering of shadows, and a voice replies, "SORRY! We didn't know anyone would be up there . . ." And then asks, ". . . are you LOST?"

A campfire flares in the wind and spits sparks at the hillock's base, feathering with hellish light the youth church group and counselors gathered around it wreathed in an inky smoke. Thunk—the Roman candle—foom!—pitches another missile out, slitting the night sky, to explode golden, farther away, re-aimed.

The distant helicopter brooms the hills on the other side of Two Harbors.

Jay takes Helen's hand and starts moving again.

"WE HAVE PLENTY OF POPCORN . . . and cocoa." The woman's voice, contrite, followed by glittering entrails of a bottle rocket, the sharp bang of its report, and in the instant of its bright eruption the face of Sam Dunn stares up at Jay from among the church group, smiling, bookended by tweens with stars-and-stripes face paint staring skyward.

Jay falters, spooked. Looking back—

Ginger, disquieted, "What is it?"

—But now there's nothing but darkness where Jay saw Dunn. He wants it to be a phantasm: free-falling paranoia working his nerves.

"I don't know," he says.

Bait, he thinks. *Fuck.*

Toward the lowlands near the water, setting their legs stiff against the slope, slip-sliding down, they put the thrown spasms of fireworks behind them: the underbrush gets thicker: the soughing of sea on shore louder. Crashing through neck-high weeds, Jay scissors his arms out in front of himself to clear a path in his wake for Ginger and Helen, feeling their breathing and stumbling behind him, until without warning his feet lose contact with solid ground, it simply drops away, and Jay goes windmilling straight down into the fetid waist-deep water of a tidal swamp.

"Careful!" he shouts, too late, because Helen and Ginger tumble after him. He gropes for Helen first, but she comes up on her own, spitting, eyes stinging, blinking, wide, too surprised to cry. The brackish smell of salt and decay embraces them. Jay's lost all sense of direction, the weeds are too high, or the water too deep.

"Helen!?" Ginger sounds to be somewhere to his left.

"Over here," Jay calls out. "She's okay, she's okay, I've got her—"

"—Mommy?"

Shielded from the wind, an eerie quiet: the insistent lap of standing water disturbed, the hush of their breathing: a dire augur of ruin.

"So what's the plan?" Ginger's voice is fragile with fatigue and impatience. "I mean, this isn't exactly . . ." The rest is erased by the wind. A string of firecrackers pops, far away. "I mean, what the hell are we—"

"He doesn't have one." Dunn. Icy, grim, inevitable. "A plan." Jay draws Helen closer to him, and a blinding beam of light ignites the swamp; the grass goes translucent in its path. "He's a rat, running," Dunn says. "Isn't that right, Jay?" The light, Dunn's flashlight, darts off to pin Ginger, mired in a sinkhole fifty feet distant from Jay and Helen, and soaking wet.

"Mouse," Jay says.

"Plunging onward," Dunn adds.

Jay's eyes finally find him, on a far bank of the swamp, thirty yards away. Gun in one hand, and the flashlight in the other. Standing between Jay and their escape. The light swings back.

"What'd you tell the Feds?"

"Nothing they didn't know," Ginger says coldly.

"Ha." Dunn laughs. "They." He looks sidelong into the shadows where Ginger is. "You." Then, to Jay, asking again what he told Magonis: "The truth?"

Jay says, "Whose truth?" while stepping protectively in front of Helen.

"Yeah, yeah." Dunn kills his light, and Jay, momentarily night blind from its absence, has to use the splashing sounds he hears to calculate the pilot's movement, closing the distance between them, left to right. "I guess you've gone into business for yourself," Dunn says.

"Okay, sure. What about you?"

The search helicopter, skimming the slope of Howland Peak on the other side of the harbor, disappears behind a ridge, headed for the West End Light. If Jay can just keep Dunn talking—sure, then what? His mind screams: *What am I doing here? What have I done?*

"*Grudge of the Moon Lady.* 1980," Dunn's voice declaims. "Chin Bong Chin gets caught and held captive in a swamp by the Evil White Cat Spirit: Amy Yip in satin hot pants and a halter top—who wants to"—more staggering sloshing sounds—"shit," then silence, then, as if he never stopped talking, "—who wants to know Bong Chin's secret."

The swamp grass blazes again, revealing Vaughn, waist deep in the swamp water ten yards off Jay's right shoulder; Vaughn is sharply, almost comically, uplit by Dunn's flashlight, Nosferatu-ish, duct tape stretched across his mouth, arms bound behind him at the elbows and his eyes wide and scared.

"At first, of course, he stonewalls her."

Jay's pulse hammers in his throat. A reverb of church-group laughter strays through the swamp, disembodied. Another string of firecrackers goes off to a chorus of mock shrieks, and bottle rockets streak skyward to explode, their flash momentarily revealing Dunn again, arm outstretched, gun in his hand pointed at Vaughn's heart.

"So the Cat Spirit kills the best friend," Dunn says. "To get every-one's attention."

Jay shouts, "NO—"

The muzzle flash sears a ragged scar in the darkness between Dunn and Vaughn, and Vaughn jerks backward, coughs, and the night swallows them both.

Jay lunges across the water, leaving (he hopes) Helen to Ginger—lunges to where he (correctly) guesses Vaughn will fall, spun wildly by the bullet that just hit him. And sure enough, Vaughn sags into Jay's arms, a look of astonishment, nothing to say. "Oh, shit," Jay whispers, lost. "Oh, shit, Vaughnie. Oh, shit." It's Halloween night, it's his sister's doleful cry, it's the voices in the kitchen, his father's weight hitting the floor, the mermaid all over again, flowing, reeling, the mermaid, in onrushing water, roiling and flowing into his arms like this, like Vaughn, flesh and blood—

—into the liquid void.

Dunn's light rakes the swamp, its beam making reeds blush and blackwater ripplets shimmer, but it can't locate Jay or Vaughn, because Jay has moved them both.

"Hey, now," Dunn says.

He wags the beam back around and catches just a glimpse of Helen and Ginger crashing away through the thicket of the far bank. "Hey, now." He raises his gun under the flashlight's reveal, one on top of the other, intending to shoot them.

But Jay won't abide it, defying his terror, the water around him erupting and sheeting off as Jay rises out of it and crashes into Dunn, clawing the flashlight into the mire, where it sinks, throwing its sickly light through the turbid shallows.

A quickened disarray of arms and fists; bodies slur and Jay is already almost out of ideas. Momentarily back on his heels, Dunn throws up defensive elbows and forearms, letting Jay's inexpert blows roll off his shoulders while lashing out with his left and trying to re-grip and bring to bear the gun clutched awkwardly in his right.

Behind them, Vaughn surfaces, ungainly, upended, an ugly black-red shine slick across his side, face thrown skyward, sucking the humid air, unable to find his feet and probably drowning if he doesn't. Jay blinks the acid burn of salt mud from his eyes and hears a thrumming sound swelling transcendent like rage itself. He thinks it's in his head. He wants Vaughn to live, he wants Ginger and Helen to have run back to the church camp for help. He vomits swamp water and clutches desperately as Dunn spins and bucks, trying to shake him, and gain the advantage his training should make inevitable.

A warm gust of air hits them and blows Jay loose: the search

helicopter, dull rotor thrum visceral, seizes overhead, turning in circles, stabbing the swamp with the bright narrow shaft of its searchlight. Vague in the faint nimbus cast backward, leaning from the
open cockpit doorway, there is the suggestion of Jane Doe looking
down at them like Vaughn does at test subjects: alert, emotionless,
evaluating—

Bait, Jay remembers. *Ginger said I was. But*—

—salt grasses, cattails and reeds humbled sideways by angry turbulence, the down current upends Vaughn, from the shallow berm of
solid ground where he's found momentary purchase, and he disappears again under foaming water crusted with mosquito fern—

—Jay helpless as Dunn braces himself, priming the chamber of
his gun, glancing away distracted only for that instant when the helicopter's landing skid judders through his peripheral vision (Doe is flying that low), flinching his head and turning his shoulders, and when
he looks back for Jay? The soggy length of driftwood in Jay's hands
crushes Dunn across the ribs, spitting bark and water, continuing up
under Dunn's chin and leveling him.

The handgun disappears.

Jay wheels around to where he thinks Vaughn went under and
plunges his arms in the water, desperate to find his friend.

But another voice, not Dunn, not Doe, cuts through, above the
rotors' howl, "JAY!" It's Public, neatly bisected by the helicopter's cone
of light, half in, half out, holding a gun on Dunn, and Vaughn motionless at Public's feet, where he's dragged him to dry land. "WE'LL
TAKE IT FROM HERE!" he shouts.

Dunn looks to Jay, incensed, "You told them—me? Christ Al-
mighty. That was the best you could do? Oh, man—fuck—YOU
TOLD THEM YOU SAW *ME!*" Jay sloshes sideways, frantically groping now for Dunn's gun in the shallows, coming up with handfuls of
muck and fern.

"JAY!"

The chopper's tail twists, and the searchlight corkscrews with it, fluid. Freezing Jay in bright relief.

Dunn roars, "YOU FUCKING—LYING—SACK OF SHIT! You have no idea. Fuck. DO YOU EVEN KNOW WHAT THIS IS ABOUT!? DO YOU HAVE ANY—YOU AND YOUR FUCKING LAB-RAT FRIEND, DID YOU THINK YOU COULD JUST—" His face is flushed, his hair flayed by wind shear. "IF I WAS WORRIED ABOUT WHAT YOU SAW I WOULD HAVE KILLED YOU A LONG TIME AGO!" Dunn points at Public, his hand shaking. "HE'S THE ONE WHO'S FUCKING WORRIED, MAN! YOU *NEVER* SAW ME. He knows it. I WASN'T THERE!"

Jay's fingers curl around a blunt suggestion of steel, he straightens up with the gun, dripping wet, and points it shivering straight-armed uncertainly at the unarmed Dunn the way he's seen people do it in the movies. His finger fumbles for the trigger guard, wondering if there's a safety he has to flick. "Then why did you kill the stripper?"

Dunn's empty hands float out from his sides and he stares back at Jay with a careless look that says: *I don't know.* "Girls," he says, finally. "With all their . . ."

"And why," Jay asks, the nausea of exhaustion overtaking him, "did you just shoot my friend?"

Dunn is incurious, defensive, matter-of-fact. Almost apologetic. "Extortion—I thought you guys, the two of you, had the list and you were . . ." But it's as if saying it out loud, here, in front of Jay, causes Dunn to finally understand the absurdity of the statement, of all of his assumptions, and he just stops talking.

"No," Jay tells him. "You made up a story. So did they. So did I—"

—*A bladed reflection stares back at him (or he thinks it does), cropped, distorted (as it has to be), as if illusory (in distinct relief from the motionless moil of the strip bar), a face caught, for one impossible timeless instant in—*

"—But I don't know anything, really," Jay says. "Neither do you. Neither do they. You don't know." Jay's found the safety with his thumb, but has no idea whether he's sliding it on or off. "Nobody knows anything."

"Jay," Public says, closer, but Jay's afraid to look away from Dunn to see just how close, "step away and let us—"

"Jay?" Ginger interrupts sharply, "Put it down, Jay." In more high weeds and cattails, on the edge of the tidal basin, she has a gun, too—Jay looks to her and thinks, *Jesus, what movie am I in?* because her gun is aimed at Jay, unfaltering, two-handed, a real marshal. And like she means it. There are tears in her eyes. Mouthing the words, "Put the gun down," as Public shouts the exact same words at Jay from his position, his voice hedged toward impatience.

Bait, Jay remembers. And suddenly he knows that if he just had a little more time, if he could just think a little harder, longer, he will understand the change he's felt in her as they hurtled to this moment.

But he's still convinced she won't shoot him. So he pivots, back to his right, and aims his gun at Public, who's drifted down knee-deep into the swamp water among the Mexican rush. Close. Public's gun is aimed back at Jay. So. Stalemate.

"Shoot him," Dunn says to Jay, meaning Public.

Ginger's voice is calm. "Jay? No."

"SHOOT HIM!"

"Don't . . ."

Public begins, "A man got killed . . ."

Jay shakes his head. "A girl."

"All right . . ."

Dunn says, "He's gonna kill us both."

". . . a girl got killed, and you saw who pulled the trigger."

"Did I?"

The helicopter cyclones, twisting bright light bending.

"Shut UP!" Dunn screams at Public.

"—WELL," Public is shouting, too, over the din of the rotors, "SOMEBODY SAW SOMETHING."

Jay says, "I saw a girl die."

"Put the gun down," Ginger says to him, steel beneath silk, "put it down and walk away."

"HE'S ROGUE, MAN!" Dunn is drifting wide, dividing Jay's already divided attention. "I'M FBI, THIS GUY'S A BAD MARSHAL— we were ONTO HIM and—"

"—Jay?"

"THE DEAD MAN . . ." Public holds forth like he's giving a deposition, the Official Version of Something. ". . . WAS A FEDERAL WITNESS WHO CERTAIN COMPROMISED GOVERNMENT INDIVIDUALS WANTED SILENCED—"

"Derp derp derp," Dunn jeers.

Or is it just a new story Public is trying out?

"He's lying."

Jay looks at Ginger, her gun aimed right at him, and he frowns, resigned, confounded. *Which part of which life is this?* He lets his gun fall to his side.

"—YOU SAW THE SHOOTER—"

Jay smiles oddly. Time slows, pulsing with the helicopter's whorple-roar: Public, right, almost behind him now, moving in slow motion, and Dunn, left, different time plane, natural, equal and opposite, putting Jay between himself and—

"—Do you love me?" Ginger, immobile, asks in a whisper that Jay knows he can't possibly hear.

I don't even know her name.

"YOU SAW THE SHOOTING OF A DEPUTY U.S. MARSHAL BY A DISGRACED FEDERAL LAW ENFORCEMENT AGENT WHO WAS UNDER SUSPICION OF SELLING SECRETS . . ."

"LIES!" Dunn screams.

". . . And they murdered you to cover it up," Public concludes simply, with every intention of squeezing the trigger of his gun and killing Jay, but across the tidal swamp Ginger fires hers twice, first.

Golden Roman candle tracers slash the sky.

Laws of physics warp:

The first of Ginger's nine-millimeter slugs spins toward Public; chased by the sound of its discharge, the second rips through Jay's shoulder, berserking precisely the soft gap between humerus and scapula, and, though slowed by this leg of its adventure, is still humming along at nearly 1,100 feet per second when it punches into the chest and then heart of Sam Dunn, lifting him up off his feet, onto his back, mortally wounded, bleeding out.

Jay's body spasms when Ginger's bullet goes through him, and her other Dopplers past his ear, flashes silvery through the searchlight beam, to enter through an eye socket of the unfortunate skull of John Q. Public as he finally squeezes the trigger of his own gun, way too late.

Falling, Jay meets Public's disappointed gaze as life leaves him and his gun discharges harmlessly and Jay's sentience spirals in on itself, all a-shambles: *garbled voices, vibrant colors, swirl of black water, smell of Scotch, perfume, longing—frat boys clotted at the club's entrance—a flower girl's smile and the thump of blown speakers—*

—and Jay is front row, mesmerized by the gentle slur of pale naiad flesh across curving glass as a parade of suits passes, drawing his attention into the back reaches of the bar, behind the tank, where a wiry, restless seller at a table argues with a second man, a buyer, in jeans and a leather jacket, looming over him, this second man's face canted obscure, just turning away, like a door closing. Briefcase between them; the seller is closing it, nodding, putting it down beside his chair and leaving, on the table, a tiny flash drive which the buyer starts to cover with his hand as the shadows of the men in suits cross

the room of shadows, surrounding the seller's table; the buyer steps back like
he's making room for them, and starts to turn his face to the light.

Then chaos.

The room erupts.

Through a parting of the churning crowd, a glimpse of the seated seller
rising, intending to flee, but violently thrown back across the table by the im-
pact of a gunshot from a shooter farther back in the shadows—

—and this time everything goes very quiet—

—except for the dull pock as the bullet punctures the tank, the entire bar
in soundless motion, suits, girls, leather jacket, crowd surging scattering in
every direction and—

—half-risen, hand outstretched to the rupturing glass and the tank's
startled denizen, but to any witness or witnesses later asked, in fact staring
past her into the darkness behind her with something resembling recognition,
or cognizance, staring into that lightless back bar blackness where a gun spat
fire, staring at the exit door, staring, moonlight splashing in, a shadow pass-
ing through it, eclipsed when the door swings shut again. Staring.

The tank explodes. Water. Glass. Mermaid. Limp body tossed out at Jay
staggering shoulder-shot along the muddy banks of Two Harbors'
tidal swamp to the muddy berm where John Q. Public has sunk to his
knees as if penitent, and folds forward into the dark water.

Dead.

Dunn on his back in the grass. Hands fussing with his chest.
Gasping for air that will not save him.

Jay somehow keeps his feet, arm pressed tight against his side,
and, look of bewilderment, finds Ginger as she lowers her gun, slowly,
hands steady.

Bait. He thinks he says it aloud.

"Nobody saw anything," Ginger says.

Doe's helicopter circles like God's unsparing judgment overhead.

Dreamy: the tidal swamp rotates like a turntable in the magic trick of the searchlight's movement. The tumult of the helicopter rotor is so overwhelming it ceases to be noise and becomes one with Jay's shock. He angles his head back into the bright light and stares, dizzy, up, his face washed out and ghostly.

Doe, leaning out of the searchlight's halation, looking down at him.

Ginger, lifting Helen up out of the reeds.

The sparkling brittle sawtooth of wind-whipped water blasted white.

Jay surrenders to vertigo, and sinks, cross-legged, heavy.

Church campers break into the bright perimeter of light, stumbling across Vaughn's body first and crying out and kneeling to tend to him. One woman listening for a heartbeat, ripping the duct tape off, while another starts the chest compressions of CPR.

Time skips.

Someone drapes a blanket over Jay's shoulders and says things he can't hear.

Time skips.

A circle of men and children, heads bowed, praying. Doe's helicopter has been sucked into the night. Not even a distant sound of it remains. The swamp is filled with an exhilarating rush of wind through grass, soughing of surf, the low, fretful murmuring of the women working on Vaughn, and the mad ululation of crickets.

"There's no cell signal," one of the men from the church group cries out, and the CPR woman yells at him to run up the fucking hill until he finds one.

Jay wants to laugh, but lies back in the grass, played out. *Was it worth it? Yeah,* he tells himself. *But was it worth it?* No, he decides bitterly. Better not to have a life, than to have one and lose it. He feels light-headed. He feels dumb. Another fail.

Another fail.

Jay looks but can't find Ginger or Helen.

But, "Yes," he says, then, stubbornly, fiercely, into the wind, trying it out: "Yeah, it was worth it." He says it like he believes it. He can believe it. He's earned at least that.

A wave of shock nausea. His eyes close.

And the veil falls away—

—strip bar, that singular moment of the shooting, frozen in time, and Jay floats through it, unmoored. Glides past himself, past the half-fractured, near-bursting mermaid's tank and the pale, shocked underwater stripper with threads of blood beginning to leak from her chest.

As if illusory, in distinct relief from the motionless moil of the strip bar, a reflection stares back at him, distorted, caught for this timeless instant in the polished stainless steel of a structural support.

A woman. A grown girl.

Riot of hair pulled back, no makeup, straight-line mouth set hard.

It's Ginger.

She moves among the motionless, slides her spent gun back into the holster on her hip, palms the flash drive from the table, tucks it under her coat, and slips away. The back exit opens, splashing one hopeful measure of moonlight into the darkness as—

| 31 |

HE LOOKS UP.

There: the mazelike grid of cracks in the white plaster ceiling. Dull thrum of an old air conditioner. All that white noise, kicking on.

Cheerless light seeps down from the translucent windows, still no wall decorations, just the bed, containing Jay, the stainless-steel sideboard, and the one metal chair.

He remembers this part all too well; it's one of those glib pulp endings where the story circles back where it began and, for a moment, you wonder if the whole thing was a dream.

"How're you feeling?" Jane Doe is bedside. She's got her "HELLO My Name Is" sticker plastered to the lapel of her jacket but she's left the fill-in space blank. Jay turns his head in slow motion and the world crawls reluctantly with him.

Doe even says Public's line: "Sometimes that tranquilizer really kicks your ass," and waits, deadpan.

Jay smiles, languid in the anesthetic's wake, and lets his eyes stray back to the map of cracks in the ceiling. Déjà vu. Okay. Sure. Maybe he imagined the whole thing.

"Gee, where am I, I wonder?" he says drily.

"Witness protection. You're in witness protection, Jay." She sits down. She's flushed with color, like someone who's just come from running a 5K: playful, jacked with endorphins, oddly upbeat, after all that's happened.

"I remember," he says.

"What a shitstorm, huh? Empty out one can of worms," Doe quips, "and open up another."

"I'm in the program," Jay offers.

"Back. You're back in the program, yes."

"Vaughn?"

"Safe."

"Safe. Everybody's safe. That's how you roll."

Doe shrugs. "Don't give me shit about it, either."

Jay's wrist lifts away from the bedrail. At least he's not handcuffed, this time. But there's an IV shunt stuck in the vein in his arm, tubes snaking up to a clear bag on a tall stand. They have what they needed from him. He's not a captive. Just . . . what?

Doe hesitates, frowns. "Question? Something you want to ask me?"

"Dunn?"

"The man was not in a good place, morally or ethically."

"Undercover?"

Doe shakes her head. This is not something Jay should waste much time thinking through, she tells him. "It's not a black-and-white world," she adds. "We do bad things to get good results, we do good things that go horribly wrong. We're human, you know? Not perfect. We do the best we can."

"Why did you bring me back here?"

Doe doesn't answer right away. The skinny jeans and faded black Chuck Taylors make her look like somebody's Melrose Avenue hipster mom. Jay wonders if she's older than he thinks. "Dunn wasn't the shooter," she says.

"I know," Jay says. "But he was buying the list."

"Buying, trading, brokering. He was a middleman."

"And the end buyer?"

Doe smiles sardonically, says nothing. *Still out there,* is the unspoken answer.

"So you pretended to believe me, and I became the bait?"

Doe won't confirm or deny it.

"And the one guy who can isn't talking."

"Ever," Doe agrees. "RIP John Q. It's not optimal, but what can you do?" She tugs at the ends of her hair. Her nails are ragged again from where she's been biting them. Polish chipping off.

Jay has to ask, "Are you protecting me, or protecting yourselves from me?"

Doe looks at him candidly and tells him that he's free to leave, whenever he wants. It's not a bluff.

This is what he remembers:

A small girl he unlocked.

A duplicitous woman who unlocked him.

An invented island life.

Weight lifting from his heart.

"I need to use the bathroom." He doesn't, but has to say it.

Doe gives no knowing reaction, though; she's playing this awfully straight. She takes up and triggers the remote, and the whole bed changes shape, lifting him to another level of muzziness and pain. He discovers that his other arm is taped and strapped to his chest, immobilizing that side of him. And just as well: it feels like somebody has pounded a spike through his shoulder, impaling him on the mattress.

"You could, you know . . . bedpan."

"No," Jay says. He wants to ask about Ginger and Helen, but he's afraid of the answer.

"Okay. I'll send someone in to help you," Doe says. She stands and starts to walk out. Her shoes scuff tile. "Oh—" she adds, slowing, but not completely turning around, "you're gonna need to let us know if you want your family with you." And then she's gone.

Jay thinks, aloud, "Family?"

"Okay, well, I was watching?" Mouse squeak of sneakers and the rustle of a cotton jumper, and a small voice, coming from under the bed. "And they were filling you with all that intervenious water and stuff? And I thought maybe you'd puff up like a water balloon and pop . . ."

Jay shifts his body in stages, the stabbing pain coursing along his side from his neck to his hip; leans over the bedrail and looks down to where Helen is on her back, on the floor, just her head exposed, peeking up at him with the gravity of all her eight years.

". . . so I crawled under here, in case. Hello." She wriggles out. "And fell asleep." Helen stands up and looks at Jay soberly. And as his eyes rise to meet hers, he sees, behind her, in the open doorway to his empty hospital room, Ginger, hair in rebellion and still mascara-challenged, approximating the awkward posture of an eighth-grade girl at her first all-school dance.

"Well, not exactly asleep, though," Helen is saying. "Just sort of like with my eyes closed and resting?" She thinks about it. "But there were some dreams."

Ginger crosses from the doorway to the bed, all business, avoiding Jay's gaze. She lowers the bedrail for him to hold on to as he sits up and slides his legs off the edge.

"Marshal Doe said you needed some help."

"Helen was on the list," Jay says.

Ginger tugs at Helen's jumper, straightening it, as if she isn't listening.

"I'm talking about the list of names your husband was going to sell to Dunn."

Now she looks at him. Her eyes asking: *Where does this go?* And it's funny, because Jay is wondering the same thing. Helen is up on her feet, arms out, spinning. "Mommy said her old husband went away with a mermaid. She cried a lot."

Ginger allows that she did, but adds, pointedly, to Jay, "For the mermaid."

Jay reaches out, but Ginger leans away. Nothing is certain yet. Needing more from him.

Helen puts her hands over her face. "Go ahead. I'm not watching."

Common knowledge among behavioral biology fanboys like Vaughn, according to Vaughn: in a wide range of mammals, including monkeys, bears, cats, dogs, and, yes, mice, mothers are incredibly protective when their offspring are young and vulnerable. As part of this behavior, female mice will attack any threat against their offspring in what is variously called maternal aggression or maternal defense, depending on the researcher and the experiment.

Jay says, "It was you."

A mother mouse will even kill the intruder to her nest if she thinks her pups are in danger.

Ginger says nothing. Her eyes search his.

"They wanted me to remember you," he says.

Almost imperceptibly, Ginger nods. "Did you?"

Jay takes a moment before answering, mostly for show. The weight is gone. He remembers all that matters: his sister's viral giggles, his brother's sly wit, his father's sure hands, his mother's grace.

And the rest?

"I've never seen you before in my life," Jay says.

Ginger's smile is everything.

ACKNOWLEDGMENTS

I wish I could say I sat at the feet of famous scientists for all the mouse stuff, and spent a year on Catalina on a genius grant from some swanky foundation, living in a hut on the sea cliffs, writing with a pen made from California quail quill, but no, it just sprung out of my head, a jumble of experience, research, facts and fiction, that I wrestled to make sense of whenever I found the time; don't trust any of it but believe it all. Thanks are overdue to Scott Shepherd, my longtime friend and sometime coconspirator who has once again renovated and reinspired me. Benee Knauer deserves all the credit for pushing me to be a better, better, and better writer; also Victoria Sanders and Bernadette Baker-Baughman for their peerless guidance and support. David Rosenthal I thank for believing in me; Phoebe Pickering and everyone at Blue Rider Press for their hard work and collaboration. Julia Gibson and Aaron Lipstadt gave needed notes and encouragement on the earliest draft. Michael Convertino dug up more memory science than I knew what to do with, and my sister, Dr. Susan Pyne, helped me understand it. Susan Ruskin and Philip Seymour Hoffman saw in this story a movie that we nearly made and their thoughtful feedback as we pursued that dream had a subtle but profound impact on the novel.

And then there's Joan, who is my rock and my muse, and Katie and Joe, who make it all worthwhile.

© Kathryn Cashel Pyne

Daniel Pyne's two previous novels are *Twentynine Palms* and *A Hole in the Ground Owned by a Liar*. His screenwriting credits include the remake of *The Manchurian Candidate, Pacific Heights,* and *Fracture.* He made his directorial debut with the indie cult film *Where's Marlowe?* Pyne's list of television writing and showrunning credits is vast, and includes J. J. Abrams's *Alcatraz* and *Miami Vice.* He lives in Southern California.

CONNECT ONLINE

danielpyne.com

facebook.com/daniel-pyne-author-page